"I could have ~~the marriage annulled,~~
Lord Clayborne stated flatly.

Rebecca's startled eyes flew to his face, and her hand, holding the piece of toast, paused in mid-air. "Why?"

He ignored her interruption and proceeded sternly. "I have given the matter considerable thought and have decided not to. Not only would it be a great embarrassment to you and your family, but I would be made to look a fool, which I do not welcome. However, if a child is born prematurely, I may reconsider the matter."

Rebecca's head whirled as she tried to assimilate this speech. Her confusion turned to embarrassment, and finally to a white hot anger. Rising so abruptly that her chair tipped over, she gasped, "You cannot believe . . . You must know that I . . . Why, you insufferable toad!" and she ran from the room.

Clayborne was left seated in solitary splendor, considerably offended by this appellation. His pride severely wounded, he threw down his napkin, strode out to the stables and was not seen for the better part of the day.

His wife, however, had another method of venting her rage. She sat down and, with sharp, violent strokes upon her sketching paper, drew a cartoon of her husband . . . as a toad.

Novels by Laura Matthews

The Seventh Suitor
The Aim of a Lady
Lord Clayborne's Fancy

Published by
WARNER BOOKS

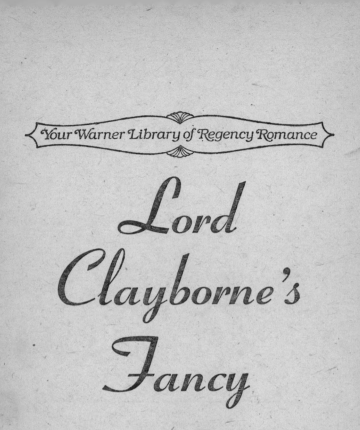

Your Warner Library of Regency Romance

Lord Clayborne's Fancy

by Laura Matthews

WARNER BOOKS

A Warner Communications Company

WARNER BOOKS EDITION

Copyright © 1980 by Elizabeth Rotter
All rights reserved.

Cover art by Walter Popp

Warner Books, Inc., 75 Rockefeller Plaza, New York, N.Y. 10019

A Warner Communications Company

Printed in the United States of America

First Printing: November, 1980

10 9 8 7 6 5 4 3 2 1

For Kris,
with thanks.

One

The head groom, recognizing her ladyship's scarcely concealed temper, proceeded to saddle the chestnut mare with the utmost expediency. "Fine day for a ride, my lady. Warm but with a touch of a breeze. And Firely eager to be off, as always. I could have one of the lads exercise her if you haven't the time to spare."

"I won't be above an hour, Hawkins," Lady Clayborne informed him as she allowed him to hand her up onto the mare. "Give my regards to your wife, if you will."

Gratified that she should remember his wife, and exasperated with his young mistress for going riding when her sister was expected at any moment, he told her retreating back that his wife would be pleased to be remembered, and (since she was already out of earshot), commented that some hostesses were at home to greet their guests. He slowly retraced his steps into the stables, exhorting the lads, "Look sharp now. We be expecting a traveling chaise in no short time, and I won't have it said that we was unprepared. You get lazy with the master away, and if there's one thing I won't have it's slipshod ways. That bridle belongs in the tackle room, and you'll have to do a sight better in polishing that brass, my lad. Step lively, now. If that chaise comes before you're finished, it'll be no beer for you this day."

"But, Mr. Hawkins, sir, Lady Clayborne said as how her sister weren't never on time above once in her life," the youngest boy protested.

"Never you mind. And you can be sure her ladyship

7

weren't speaking to the likes of you when she said such a thing, if indeed she did. Show some respect for your betters, boy!"

Unaware of the commotion left behind her, Lady Clayborne galloped across the meadow, reluctant to keep to any path, and sorely in need of a ride to soothe her ruffled sensibilities. She was not one, mind you, to regard the proprieties in a very strict sense, but it was the outside of enough that her husband should not have returned to welcome her sister. "I tell you, Firely," she addressed the unconcerned mare, "that he has been aware for no little time of Meg's coming. Where the *devil* has he gotten himself to now?"

Firely, not at all shocked by her mistress's tongue, realized that her rider was not overly concerned with checking her, and stretched her stride in anticipation of a very enjoyable gallop. Relishing the wind on those locks which had escaped her hat, Lady Clayborne gave silent thanks that his lordship's faith in her riding ability, at least, had led him to choose such a mount for her. The stables at her childhood home, Farthington Hall, consisting as they had largely of hunting mounts which the four sisters had, since earliest memory, been forbidden to ride on pain of instant death, had also housed such cattle as were needed for the various carriages, but little else of interest. Sir Rupert Farthington, who had as little interest in his family home as in his hopeful family, was wont to spend the greater part of the hunting season with his cronies in Leicestershire, and was not often seen at Far- thington Hall. Although Lady Farthington deprecated his absence, her daughters were at a loss to understand why, as she had little to do with him when he was there except keep him under her thumb. She exasperated him with her continual entertainments for the local gentry (while volu- bly deploring their lack of polish), and he was bored beyond bearing by the piddling stakes at whist.

As Lady Clayborne approached the home wood, she checked Firely to a more sedate pace and entered the wood on her favorite path, now sun-dappled and smelling of pine in the early morning heat. Her black locks were windswept from her gallop, but she looked enchanting in a red riding habit, decorated with gold braid à la Hussar. A slight young lady with a charming smile, she looked even younger than her twenty years, and if she were not precisely beautiful, she was certainly attractive. Perhaps her mouth was a trifle too wide, and her nose a bit too turned up, but she was not particularly concerned with these defects, never having been in the way of comparing herself with her sisters, or anyone else for that matter.

Lady Clayborne was aware that her sister Meg, who had shining red-brown hair and rosy cheeks, graceful height and a perfect figure, was considered quite the beauty. But even Meg did not compare with Mary, whose classical features and enormous green eyes would undoubtedly captivate the London beaux when she had her season next year. Lady Clayborne shuddered, however, to think what mischief her youngest sister might get up to in London, being not only the most beautiful but the most hoydenish of the Farthington girls. Where Trudy, the eldest, and married these two years past, had been the most compliant, and Meg very feminine and quiet, Mary was the most romantic. She was not romantic in the usual sense of dreaming of love and having beaux. (Indeed, she considered herself hardly used for not having been born a boy). She envisioned instead the joy of having an adventure. Any real adventure would do; that is, consorting with smugglers or highwaymen, for Mary was totally undisciplined, even to the point of being uninterested in all feminine accomplishments. She detested reading books, even the latest novels, unless they were full of the most improbable adventures, and she felt grossly put upon if she were exhorted to attend to any needlework. As for those other accomplishments which Miss Turnpeck, their governess, had tried to instill in her, Lady Clayborne had seldom heard such outrageous performances on the pianoforte, and Mary's watercolors might have been produced by a six-year old. Mary's saving grace was her natural elegance, for much as she wished to be a male, she was developing into a female of uncommon beauty who did not need to pay the least heed to the hours of instruction on curtsying and arranging a shawl; they came quite naturally to her.

Preoccupied with her thoughts, Lady Clayborne was startled when a voice said, "Rebecca, are we not expecting your sister Meg this morning?"

"Oh, it is you, Jason. I had given up hope of you," she replied somewhat tartly.

"But I assured you when last we spoke that I would be here when Meg arrived," Lord Clayborne answered gravely, his face a polite mask.

"Yes, but that was a month past and I feared you might have forgotten. Have you had a good trip?" she asked, more out of courtesy than in expectation of receiving any information from him. She had not been aware where his travels took him, except that they had to do with estate business. His estates in Yorkshire, inherited from an uncle some years past, of necessity involved long and wearying journeys, but his estates in Somerset and Dorset, inherited from his father, were closer and she did not think they could be very large, or require an extensive amount of his time or interest. He had, however, spoken little of them since their marriage some ten months ago, and she might be mistaken.

"It was satisfactory," he replied briefly, removing his hat to brush back the brown strands pushing forward onto his wide brow. He turned from regarding the path ahead to appraise her riding clothes. "That's an attractive outfit."

Making a hasty attempt to poke some of the curls up under her hat, she flushed slightly and said, "Thank you, my lord."

"Tell me how things go on at Gray Oaks. Have you kept busy?" Lord Clayborne asked, a hint of mockery in his voice.

Although she longed to say, "Little you care," she replied sourly, "It is a veritable whirl of activity here. Not long ago I drove to Chichester to purchase matching thread for my needlework."

Her husband laughed and remarked, "No doubt your sister's visit will serve to enliven your days."

Lady Clayborne studied the path before them, which led back to the stables, twiddled with her riding crop, and continued with some heat, "Congenial company is scarce here. Not that the servants are not considerate. Mrs. Lambert is an angel, but far too proper to engage in any real discussion with me." Mrs. Lambert, in spite of her running battle with the French cook and her relationship to almost everyone else on the household staff, ran the establishment with remarkable ease. She forever shouldered the burdens of the kitchen maid, who was her niece; listened patiently to the complaints of the upper housemaid, who was a second cousin; and bullied the head gardener, who was her brother. Lady Clayborne had witnessed her scolding affection for Lord Clayborne as well, and felt that Mrs. Lambert, though kindhearted and motherly, was not the person to whom she could unburden her heart. This was perhaps a wise decision since, as she had said to her husband, Mrs. Lambert withheld herself from her new mistress in a very proper manner.

"Mrs. Lambert has been at Gray Oaks since I was in leading strings," Lord Clayborne replied. "I hope you will not put up her back in any way. I fear she was alarmed when you redecorated the Green Saloon in blue and gold."

"She has assured me recently that she has come," Lady Clayborne mimicked the housekeeper's slow speech, "quite to like the room, though perhaps it would have been more in keeping, as your dear Mama did when she had the room redecorated twenty years ago, to have kept the color scheme in greens so there would be no confusion amongst any newer household employees as to which room was the Green Saloon." Lady Clayborne grinned and added, "Of course you understand, Jason, that she has instructed Griggs to refer to it as the Green Saloon, but he, never one to admit to her authority in the household, has come to call it the Blue Saloon. I had thought," she added anxiously, "that you were pleased with the change."

"And so I am. As you say, Mrs. Lambert has a strong sense of propriety but she has also a highly developed sense of what is fitting for Gray Oaks. You need not always be in agreement with her, for I would trust your good taste, but I beg that you will not offend her sense of what is proper to the mistress of Gray Oaks."

It was unnecessary, fortunately, for Lady Clayborne to respond to this instruction, as they were dismounting, to the obvious delight of Hawkins, who was another of Lord Clayborne's admirers. They were solemnly informed that the carriage from Farthington Hall had not as yet arrived, though it was momentarily expected. Lady Clayborne did not miss the impudent grins of the stable lads at this pronouncement, and though she was at a loss to account for them, she did not give it a second thought as she hastened into the house to change from her riding clothes, followed closely by her husband, who only delayed long enough to tell Hawkins that his valet would arrive presently with his carriage.

Lord Clayborne had just descended to the hall, and his wife was already seated in the Blue (or perhaps Green) Saloon, when they heard the sounds of arrival. Margaret Farthington alighted first from the carriage, with a sunny smile for her sister and brother-in-law. "Oh, Becka, I haven't seen you for ages!" She hugged Rebecca close, afterwards shyly offering her hand to Clayborne, who took it firmly. To Rebecca she whispered, "I have so much to tell you and I shall probably talk for the rest of the day, for Turnip has not ceased talking since we got in the carriage, and I am sure it must be my turn now."

The Farthington governess, Miss Turnpeck, was at that moment allowing Lord Clayborne to assist her from the carriage, murmuring, "Too kind, too good," all the while.

"I trust your journey has not been too tiring, Miss Turnpeck," his lordship remarked politely.

"Not at all! Most rewarding, I assure you. We made a stop at the Abbey Church in Romsey—a remarkable building. The moldings, and the original Norman triforium and clerestory of the choir, you would not credit! And Meg was so kind as to dally with me while I just took the merest peek at King John's Hunting Box. Imagine! The sense of history is overwhelming. And the ancient walls of Southampton! Do you know that the north and east sides were defended by a double moat? And you can ascend to the Rampart Walk. To think of the men who walked there ages ago! It gives one a thrill. Quite a pleasant thrill, you understand." Miss Turnpeck vigorously shook out her skirts. "There is a monument to our brave Lord Nelson on Portsdown. In the glory of Wellington's victory at Waterloo we must not lose sight of dear Lord Nelson!"

"No, certainly not," Lord Clayborne murmured.

"But you are familiar with all these sights, I have no doubt," Miss Turnpeck continued. "You had asked of our journey. And I do not hesitate to tell you that the Farthington carriage, although most certainly a superior vehicle, has seen better days. Well, of course, if that were not so, Lady Farthington would have use for it when in London. We are very lucky to have it at our disposal at the Hall and though it is not so well sprung as the more recent coaches, and the squabs are the tiniest bit the worse for wear, there were no problems. No broken traces or axles, no wheels came off, and not a horse cast a shoe. You understand that we used our own horses, and therefore made a rather slow journey. Possibly you are in the habit of hiring post horses yourself?"

Rebecca and Meg watched in amusement as Clayborne bemusedly agreed that he did.

"Yes, I would have expected that," the governess stated triumphantly with a sage nod of her head. "And you are doubtless familiar with posting houses all over the country, but I must confess that I have seldom traveled myself. We stayed last night at an unexceptionable inn where I assure you that the sheets were properly aired, as I am very particular, but not so fussy, I hope, as to take along my own sheets as I have heard of others doing. Our meal was not perhaps as tasty as we get at the Hall, but then we are fortunate at home. I should not complain, even if the fricassée was the least bit salty and the veal a bit overdone. Meg will tell you that the ragout disagreed with her, but I myself was not in the least discomforted by it."

Meg had no intention of telling anyone that the ragout had disagreed with her, of course, but by this time Rebecca was having difficulty maintaining a straight face and she urged her guests into the house. Although Lord Clayborne had received all Miss Turnpeck's information

13

with every appearance of great interest, his sincerity was placed in doubt by the brow he lifted to the two sisters. "I am sure," he ventured during a slight pause, "that Meg has found your companionship on the journey most welcome. You must wish, though, to go to your room to freshen up from your travels."

Miss Turnpeck, in a swirl of wraps despite the June heat, fluttered into the Tudor half-timbered residence which had been the home of the Barons Clayborne for several centuries. "What remarkable paneling! Such enormous beams! No, no, I could not think of resting until I have seen Meg situated. There is always a delightfully homey feeling about a Tudor building, do you not agree, Lord Clayborne?" she chirped, and barely waiting for an answer, rushed on, "Meg, dear, you must let me see you settled in your room. My, what a fine hall this is, and that huge fireplace. You could roast an ox! And, Meg, I have just been wondering, did you remember to bring your music for the pianoforte?"

Never stopping for a breath, but frequently pausing to gaze in wrapt wonder at the finely carved screens or the magnificent oak staircase, she passed like a whirlwind, shepherding Meg before her. With a despairing glance at her sister, Meg allowed herself to be driven inexorably onward. It was with some difficulty and fully a half hour later that the two young ladies shut the door behind Miss Turnpeck's retreating form, hearing her protest, "No, no, the maid shall show me my way. No need for you to bother."

"I had forgotten," Rebecca said mournfully, "how very talkative is your Miss Turnpeck."

"Had you? Well, I have not and I mean to have my turn now, if you please," she beseeched.

"Of course, goose. You have much to tell me of your London season, no doubt."

"Becka, it was above anything great! You didn't tell me there were so many balls, and suppers, and card parties and breakfasts, and operas, and the theatre. Mama and I were invited everywhere, and must have met hundreds of fashionable people. And my clothes, everything the first stare! Mama insisted I wait until we got to

London before she would consent to purchase so much as a fan for me, for she knew of the most expert modiste that I must go to. Well, you shall see from some of the things I have brought with me, but I did not think that you were so formal here in the country. It must be much as at Farthington Hall, so I have not brought the lot."

"Thank heaven," Rebecca murmured soulfully and grinned at her sister.

"Oh, you are quizzing me," Meg laughed. "But we did not go about town at all until the new clothes had arrived, and then I felt quite the thing. Do you know I had six new reticules and at least a dozen fans?"

"I cannot imagine how you managed with such a paltry few."

"I confess I found it difficult to use all of them. I had to take particular care to hide each one away after I used it so that the next would have a showing, for I was sure Mama would notice if I forgot any one. And some of them I did not like above half. But enough of that. I have so many messages to give you. Mama sent her best, and Papa, of course, before they left. They will be in Paris for a month or more and may stop to visit you when they return. Mary left a sen'night ago to visit Aunt Adeline in Bath because she is of an age with our cousin Sally, you know. Aunt Adeline did not invite me at all, but I had much rather come to you anyway."

"I hope Mary will enjoy herself. Was Mama pleased with your success in London?" Rebecca asked.

"Well, she would, of course, have been more pleased to find me married by now. After all, there is still Mary to bring out next year, and Mama feels a bit put about with me that she *might* have the both of us next season," Meg twinkled.

"But she may not? What is this, Meg? Are you planning to enter a nunnery?" her sister quizzed.

"Now, Becka, it is no such thing, you may be sure! There is nothing settled as yet, you understand, but dear Will Travers has been most particular in his attentions. He arrived in London soon after we did, you know, and oh, Becka, he seemed so different in town. His manners were so gentlemanlike, and his dress so distinguished.

Why, even poor Brummel would not have had the least objection to him."

"I find it difficult to picture him in other than buckskins. No, no, don't scold me. I am only funning. I shall have to meet this budding paragon. My own recollections are otherwise. Will joining us on our picnics and rides in the country. But then we have not seen him for some time now. Has he been up to Cambridge?"

"Yes, but he is down now and intends to devote his time to his estate. I thought at first Mama would not care for his attentions to me, but she has been most accommodating. I think she is in the way of finding him an eligible suitor."

"Does his mother approved of the connection?"

"Mrs. Travers came to town in early May for a spell and she was very gracious to me. I am thinking things are in a way to being settled. Certainly Will seems to think so," she added with a rosy blush.

"I am so happy for you." Rebecca kissed her sister's cheek and hugged her. "It sounds a splendid match to me."

"Will has not approached Papa yet, as he wished to sort out the estate affairs first. When his papa died last year he was still at Cambridge and he has yet to involve himself in the business matters attached," Meg said, knowing it was not necessary for her to explain to her sister that Mr. Travers, more interested in his books than in his estate, had no doubt left the estate business in rather a shambles, which it would take the inexperienced young man some time to right. "Of course, Mary will have it that I could not bring him up to scratch, but it is no such thing," Meg declared indignantly.

"Pay no attention to Mary. She was only teasing you, I'm sure."

Meg was inclined to be cross with Mary for not taking her romance seriously, but as she knew her youngest sister's propensity for outlandish behavior and an unruly tongue, she decided to dismiss the matter, knowing full well it would do her no good to dwell on it. "That reminds me," she exclaimed suddenly. "I met your friend Constance Exton in town and she asked especially to be remembered to you. She has gone with her family to Brighton for the summer and says she will write you in hopes that you will invite her to Gray Oaks for a few days so that she may have some peace."

Rebecca laughed. "Her mama is so insistent on pushing Constance at every marriageable man that Constance is quite in despair. I shall look forward to having her visit."

"I met your darling Captain Gray at Almack's and he never stopped talking of you. And I saw him in the park one day. He looks so handsome in his uniform—the 10th Hussars is it?—with his funny moustache and sideburns." Meg paused before she burst out, "And I saw Thomas a few days before I left home. He asked of you and sent his regards. His wife has just given him a son and both are well." Meg played with the fringe of her shawl and kept her eyes on her lap. "He seems to have settled down these last months."

"I imagine married life suits him, and I'm pleased they have a healthy boy. Now I must leave you to rest for a while. Join me in the Blue Saloon when you're ready." Rebecca got up abruptly, then hesitated at her sister's anxious look. Taking Meg's hand she said kindly, "You know, it is perfectly all right to talk of him. I no longer retain a *tendre* for Thomas and am happy to hear that all is well with him. Now, have a rest and we will talk more later."

Two

It was perfectly true, as Lady Clayborne had said, that she no longer retained a *tendre* for Thomas Burns. He was one of the few young men she had met at Farthington Hall and his obvious admiration of her had led to a puppylike devotion on her part. But she had soon found herself consoling *him* with the necessity of his marrying a young lady of fortune. The irony of it had not perhaps amused her at the time, for she had striven to be his friend at no small cost to herself. It had left her with a guardedness about giving away her heart again, though, and since she was not by nature inclined to light dalliance, her London season had not particularly recommended itself to her. She had enjoyed Captain Gray's amusing stories and lighthearted escort, but she though of him as a brother.

Lady Farthington, disturbed at seeing her second daughter leaning toward bookishness and not at all taken up with the season she was providing at such immoderate expense, eyed Clayborne enthusiastically. She was impressed with his handsome face and fine figure, to say nothing of his title and wealth. It never occurred to her that such a gentleman would tolerate, and even encourage, her daughter in her wandering pursuit of knowledge, but such seemed to be the case, for he escorted Rebecca to several lectures which her mother would have preferred to miss had her chaperonage not been necessary.

Not a particularly patient person nor a loving mother, Lady Farthington had bluntly pointed out to

Rebecca that she still had her two sisters to find eligible matches for, that Clayborne must be considered one of the few gentlemen who would permit her bookishness, and that it was unlikely that Rebecca would find such another suitor once she returned to the country. She intimated to her daughter that she did not intend, with such an ungrateful child, to repeat the experience of another London season, for her sister Meg was to be brought out the next year. While aware of the pressure brought to bear on her, Rebecca understood the reasonableness of her mother's arguments. She was not averse to Clayborne's suit, as she was fond of him and he was unfailingly kind to her, treating her as a person of excellent understanding; there were no other men of her acquaintance, including Thomas, who could regard a woman as being possessed of any real intelligence. The idea that she and Clayborne should admirably suit took possession of her mind, and since she was determined that her head should rule her heart in this matter, she accepted him.

Lady Farthington was in ecstasies. She was perfectly willing to ignore the rumor of Clayborne's involvement with Lady Hillston. Her daughter, never much interested in the *on dits*, would not likely have heard of this and she made no attempt to enlighten Rebecca. In fact, she had made little attempt to enlighten her daughter on any aspect of her contemplated married life. "Your husband will, of course, expect you to perform your wifely duties," Lady Farthington intoned, with a reminiscent shudder. "It is a wife's obligation to accommodate her husband whenever he wishes her, and not to question his behavior outside the home. You are to behave always with propriety and never give your husband cause for complaint. Clayborne will wish an heir as promptly as possible to ensure the succession. I wish you better luck than I had," her mother had commented with cold humor. Sir Rupert had never allowed her to forget that she had provided him with no son.

"Yes, Mama, I shall endeavor to please Lord Clayborne," Rebecca had replied optimistically. Confident in her ability to run a household, and how to conduct herself socially, she had sought no further information. For a country-bred young lady she was rather naive, having taken more interest in the library than the propagation of the estate animals. Miss Turnpeck had instilled in her four charges the sum total of her experience of marriage, which was of course nonexistent.

Rebecca's own wedding night, therefore, had been something of a surprise to her, and it had turned into a nightmare. Since the only kiss Rebecca had received from a man had been from Thomas, and that fleeting rather than passionate, she had had no experience of desire, and she was pleasantly indoctrinated. Clayborne had entered her bedchamber to find her nervously twisting a lock of her black hair about her finger, unable to meet his gaze.

"You look enchanting, my dear," he said gently as he climbed in beside her and took her cold hand in his. "Don't be alarmed. I shall take the greatest care of you. Only trust me, little one." Tenderly he had kissed her hand, and then her lips as she turned her face to him. With patience he had slowly won her confidence, and kindled her own desire, overcoming her natural embarrassment and fear. Consequently it was with no little astonishment that she found herself pulled very urgently out of bed after their marriage had been consummated, and made to stand shivering by the bed while he lit a candle. Clayborne jerked back the covers and pointed to the bed.

"Look at it!" he commanded harshly.

"But . . . I don't see anything," she quavered.

"Exactly!" he roared, and stomped unceremoniously from the room.

Rebecca, left frightened and confused, had no idea what was expected of her now. At length, after inspecting the bed for some time without enlightenment, she climbed back in, shivering and weeping, and eventually cried herself to sleep.

Afraid to face her husband, but even more determined to find some solution to the previous night's startling events, Rebecca descended warily to the breakfast parlor the next morning. Although she had felt sure Clayborne did not love her when she married him, and she had held him only in fond respect, the very harshness of his countenance and the coldness of his eyes when she met him put her on her guard. "Good morning, Jason."

He rose formally at her entrance and remained standing until Griggs had seated her, but he said nothing. The length of the breakfast table separated them, and she watched with trepidation as Clayborne indicated to the butler that they would serve themselves from the sideboard, and that Griggs would not be needed further. When he had left them alone, Clayborne asked coldly, "Do you wish eggs and kippers?"

"I will help myself, thank you." Unsteadily, she rose and poured herself a cup of coffee, spilling a few drops on the sideboard. The display of food was unnerving and she took only a piece of toast before reseating herself. There was nothing she could say to him without conceivably arousing his wrath again, for how was she to know what his fancy might find offensive? Whatever was he thinking of, worrying about a bed at such a time? Had she married a maniac? Silently, she nibbled at her toast, her gaze apparently caught by the fascinating design on her plate.

"I could have the marriage annulled," he stated flatly.

Rebecca's startled eyes flew to his face and her hand, holding the piece of toast, paused in midair. "Why?"

He ignored her interruption and proceeded sternly, "I have given the matter considerable thought and have decided not to. Not only would it be a great embarrassment to you and your family, but I would be made to look a fool, which I do not welcome. However, if a child is born prematurely I may reconsider the matter."

Rebecca's head whirled as she tried to assimilate this speech. Her confusion turned to embarrassment, and finally to a white-hot anger. Rising so abruptly that her chair tipped over, she gasped, "You cannot believe . . . You must know that I . . . Why, you insufferable toad!" and she ran from the room.

Clayborne was left seated in solitary splendor, considerably offended by this appellation, and convinced that, man of experience that he was, though he had never been with a virgin himself, he could not be wrong. His pride, severely wounded, permitted him to make no allowances for his wife's assumed deception. It did not matter that she was young or that she might have been deceived herself. He threw down his napkin, strode out to the stables and was not seen for the better part of the day.

This disappearance, of course, caused some comment in the household, as had the disclosure of the maid in charge of her lady's chamber. The general appearance was of a marriage not yet consummated, which elicited knowing nods and suggestive glances among the household staff, but caused no further comment. This state of affairs would probably have continued for some time had not Clayborne, the speculative glances finally having penetrated his consciousness, taken matters into his own hands. He waited in his connecting room one morning until he heard Rebecca leave hers and then, taking his penknife with him, he cautiously entered. Forced to skulk about his own house, he thought indignantly.

The room was deserted, and there was surprisingly little evidence of its occupation. No clothes, and few personal possessions, were scattered about the room. A locket lay on the bureau and he curiously flipped it open. There were miniatures, one of Rebecca and Trudy, the other of Meg and Mary, all smiling cheerfully. He snapped it shut, not willing to see that glowing look on Rebecca's face. It was not the expression she had worn the past few days, and it reminded him uneasily of the weeks in London when he was courting her. *Then* she had seemed full of vitality, possessed of every virtue. Now he knew better, and he was sickened by the deception.

Angrily, he returned the locket to the bureau top and turned to the bed. His wife was, or had become, a restless sleeper. The sheets were pulled out and the pillows were sadly crumpled; the counterpane hung at a precarious angle, mostly on the floor. "I hope she gets no sleep at all, plagued by her guilt," he murmured fiercely. Perhaps she had accepted him so that she might pass off someone else's child as his heir. He would not have it! With a ruthless gesture he cut his finger with the knife and allowed the blood to drip on the sheets, mesmerized by the spreading stain. The sound of movement in the hall recalled him and he quickly strode from the room, careful to close the door silently behind him. His finger continued to bleed for several minutes, even with a handkerchief pressed tightly against it. Fatalistically, he hoped it would leave a scar.

The task had irritated him, and the subtle air of satisfaction in the household which followed it merely roused in him an even greater anger toward his wife. Rebecca had no way of knowing what he had done. When she next returned to her room everything was in order and, though the staff seemed especially pleased with her, she only vaguely noticed, since Clayborne seemed less pleased than ever. He no longer joined her in the breakfast parlor, or for a midday meal, which he had done at first to alleviate any disagreeable rumors amongst the staff. Rebecca turned to the management of the household, but even here she was reminded of her husband's strange behavior.

Mrs. Lambert, pleased to have a woman about the house again, chatted comfortably with her new mistress as she discussed the various arrangements. "A blessing it is to have you here, my lady. Not that his lordship is not the soul of conscientiousness, but really one cannot expect him to take an interest in what we plan to preserve this autumn or whether the laundry maid is doing an adequate job. And he is as like as not to merely glance at the household accounts and assure me that they seem in perfect order. To be sure, I hope they are, but there is nothing like having the lady of the house, who is more knowledgeable on such matters, take them under scrutiny. Before poor Miss Caroline left to marry she ran the household smooth as one could wish."

"Lord Clayborne's sister?"

"Yes, poor lamb. She died giving birth to her first

child, and I have never even seen the boy. They live in Yorkshire, him and his father. I believe his lordship plans to take you there soon." Mrs. Lambert eyed Rebecca sympathetically. "You mustn't think his lordship unfairly preoccupied, my lady. There is much to see to about the estate before you leave. And him not used to having a wife around, don't you see."

"I understand perfectly," Rebecca replied woodenly, her eyes fixed on the stacks of linen she was inspecting. Having discovered that her husband, although perhaps not precisely deranged, had in some manner not entirely clear to her conceived the notion that she had not been a virgin on their wedding night, Rebecca had no intention of allowing Mrs. Lambert, or anyone else, to see her confusion. "If you will set aside any sheets that need mending, I will see to them."

After a morning spent over this drudgery, Rebecca decided to escape to the stables. For fear of running into her husband she had stayed close to the house, but her longing for a ride irresistibly drew her out. She had not previously inspected the stables at Gray Oaks, but had been introduced to Hawkins on her arrival the evening of her wedding day. Perhaps he would recommend a horse for her and she might explore the estate for an hour or two, without ever seeing her husband.

Her luck was out. The moment she stepped into the darkened interior of the building, she saw him conversing with his head groom, who deferentially tugged a forelock at sight of her. Clayborne turned slowly to face her, his countenance expressionless. "You have met Hawkins, Rebecca, but I do not believe you have seen the stables."

"No. I have been busy with household matters. This was my first opportunity for a ride and I had hoped that you or Hawkins might recommend a mount for me."

"Lawks, recommend a mount!" Hawkins chuckled. "And his lordship having gotten you the sweetest little mare ever I laid my eyes on!"

Clayborne abruptly gave the groom a task which would take him to the farthest stall and answered Rebecca's questioning look in a detached voice. "There were no horses here suitable for a lady, so I purchased one for you. Some weeks ago, you understand." Without another word he led her to the glossy chestnut mare.

Never before had she had a horse of her own, often not even an animal worthy of the name to ride. She ran her hands down the sleek sides and allowed the mare to nuzzle her shoulder. There was a lump in her throat when she whispered, "Oh, thank you, Jason. She's beautiful. May I ride her now?"

"Hawkins will saddle her for you. She has the name of Firely, but you must please yourself as to that. I will go with you to see that she is not too spirited for you to ride."

Her very real gratitude was shaken by this brutal handling of the situation. A week ago he would not have done more than beg her permission to accompany her, and watched with concern to see that she was indeed capable of managing the mare. Rebecca sternly repressed the desire to retort, and said meekly, "Very well."

When they were out on the lane he politely requested that she put Firely through her paces, much as he might have done with one of the stable lads, she thought angrily. But again she restrained her annoyance and did as he bid, though for some yards she felt rigid with the effort. Not for long could one resist the superb gait of the horse, however, and soon Rebecca had forgotten Clayborne's irritating presence and given herself over to the exquisite freedom of galloping across the meadows. She did not intentionally attempt to thwart or disobey him but was caught up in Firely's enthusiasm for a run. His own anger building now, Clayborne watched her take a fence with a thrill of fear. He would not acknowledge to himself that she had never looked more glorious, or that she handled the mare with expertise. All he could think of was that she should be sitting penitently in some chapel, damn her! How dare she enjoy herself when she had caused him such pain? He watched grimly, his riding crop tightly clenched in his hand, as she approached.

Her cheeks aglow with delight, Rebecca reined in beside him and exclaimed, "I have never, ever ridden such a horse! How can I ever thank you? She responds to the very lightest touch, and did you see her jump that fence? Like a feather floating over, blown by the softest breeze."

"You should not have jumped her until you knew her better," he responded coldly.

He could not more effectively have dampened her had he tossed a bucket of cold water over her head. Although her chin quivered slightly, she thrust it out determinedly. "It does not take long to learn such a horse's capabilities, Jason. She went for the fence without a pause. Had she shown the slightest hesitation I would not have pressed her."

"You didn't even bother to find out if she could jump something smaller first."

Undaunted by his glare, she bent to pat Firely's neck. "With a heart like hers? She would have been ashamed at anything more paltry." When the mare whinnied, Rebecca took it as agreement and laughed at her husband. "You see?"

Clayborne swung his horse around and said grimly, "See that you do not ride beyond the estate without an escort," before riding off, leaving her alone.

"Tyrant!" she murmured. "It would serve him right if I broke my neck. Without an escort, indeed. You may be sure, my pretty, that he has no intention of escorting me *anywhere*. I'm surprised he didn't sell you again, but he probably could think of no way to explain such an action to Hawkins."

Nonetheless, she kept to the estate for the first few days, and thereafter took a groom with her when she rode beyond its confines. There was no sense in exacerbating his anger, though she would dearly have loved to shock him. She dreamed of imprisoning him in the stables and jumping every fence in sight, bareback as she had as a child, and him impotent to do anything about it. Such visions gave her strength to face him when she had to.

Most days he was at home to dine, and before the servants he kept up an appearance of sociability with his wife. In detailing the trivia of the estate to her, he conveyed more information than he thought. Obviously he was concerned for his land and his tenants and his responsibilities weighed heavily on him. It had been otherwise with her father, and she tried to convey her appreciation.

"My father took little interest in his land, and has suffered from his carelessness. The Hall could be far more productive, as Gray Oaks appears to be," Rebecca offered one evening.

Clayborne waved the servants from the room and regarded her with steely eyes. "Your parents were obviously negligent with their daughters as well. I hold them very much to account."

"You are mistaken, sir," she replied through clenched teeth. "Negligent my parents may have been, but you have no one but yourself to account to for your ludicrous misconception. I fear for your reason, my lord."

"Go to your room!" Shocked at himself for blurting such a thing, he immediately retracted. "No, stay. I will not have my household upset by our disagreements. Finish your meal."

Rebecca, her appetite hardly stimulated by this atmosphere, toyed with her food. The enormous dining hall was so quiet that even the sounds of forks on plates seemed swallowed in the silence. She assumed a martyred air to cover her shame and anger, sighing pitifully as she pushed the remnants of her meal about her plate.

There were few attitudes that could have more infuriated her husband. Her injured, self-righteous bearing, given the circumstances, disgusted him. Had she no shame? She should be begging him on bended knee to forgive her! And, after a judicious amount of time, and sufficient repentance on her part, he would have been prepared to do so. But this! Adding insult to injury! There was obviously no hope for her, and his pride rebelled.

Since her husband made no further attempt to visit her suite, Rebecca soon adopted the habit of retiring to her room immediately after her meal, to draw or read sometimes, but usually to search her mind for a solution to this unbearably oppressive situation.

When this state of affairs had continued for several

weeks and Rebecca was looking rather peaked and thin, Clayborne announced at dinner one evening, "I leave in the morning for my estate in Yorkshire. I have no idea when I shall return."

"I am to remain at Gray Oaks, I presume," Rebecca said timidly.

"Certainly. Mrs. Lambert has been instructed to have a care for you and grant you any indulgence within reason."

"You are too good, my lord. Does this indulgence run to my refurbishing some of the rooms? Not the library or study, of course," she hastened to add.

"I cannot imagine why you should wish to do so."

"I plan a lengthy stay, my lord," she replied sweetly, her hands gripping the table edge for courage.

"I don't care what you do to the house. It makes no difference now," he retorted angrily.

"I am sure you will have no objection to any improvements I might make. I am thought to have exquisite taste," she taunted, desperate for some sign of interest from him.

"No doubt," he replied dampingly. "I shall mention the matter to Bridge." He refused to be drawn into any further conversation with her. It was painful for him to talk with her, to even see her in his home. When he had found, on their wedding night, that she was not a virgin, it had shattered him. He had invested the whole of his affection and trust in her, and she had deceived him.

For years he had considered himself gripped by a hopeless passion for Alexis Hannis. As a young man he had courted her assiduously for a year before she had chosen an older, richer and better-titled man. The blow had driven Clayborne to some excesses of behavior which he looked back on with regret. As Lady Hillston, however, Alexis had produced the required male heir and then had looked about her for amusement. When she had beckoned to Clayborne, he had come. He had despised himself for the weakness, and had seen as little of her as he could bear, but he had gone.

It had surprised him, therefore, to find that his meeting Rebecca had upset his equanimity. He was charmed by her youth and enthusiasm, her eclectic search for knowledge, her personal integrity. Compared with Alexis, Rebecca was a shining gem, pure and enchanting. After a mere few weeks of acquaintance, Clayborne had found to his amazement that he had fallen in love with Rebecca.

He did not tell her so. There was a reserve in her relations with him that warned him to proceed with caution. But he felt she was fond of him and he knew her mother would press for his suit, so he had asked her to marry him. She had not given her answer immediately, and he was glad that he had not told her that he loved her. It would have frightened her from him, to think that she could not reciprocate his affection.

Wish to God that he had told her, he thought angrily as he watched her across the length of the table. He would not be sitting with her now, this gem with its fatal flaw! The triteness of the sentiment made his hurt no less real, and it did nothing to assuage the pain that his wife acted the injured party. If she had told him before they wed, he supposed he would have accepted it. How could he not when he loved her? Surely such a confession would have been a sign of her remorse. But she had not admitted it then, and she would not admit it now. He took himself off from Gray Oaks filled with anger, confusion and hurt.

Three

Clayborne was gone the next morning before Rebecca awoke, and she wasted no time starting her project. Since Bridge, the estate manager, was by far the least amiable of the Gray Oaks staff, Rebecca had to marshal all her resources to approach him, but she was determined to spend her days doing something useful and refused to let him deter her.

Mrs. Lambert, once she recovered from the shock of finding that Clayborne had no intention of taking Rebecca with him to Yorkshire, did her best to ease her new mistress's loneliness by appearing to share her enthusiasm for the schemes Rebecca laid before her. A new bride should not be left at home, in Mrs. Lambert's humble opinion, and although she could not help but be horrified that the Green Saloon was to be done over in blue and gold, she did no more than unconsciously purse her lips when shown the new drapery and upholstery materials. She watched, perplexed, as Lady Clayborne threw herself wholeheartedly into the project, with excursions to Chichester, hours spent studying fabric samples and evenings doing needlework chair covers by the light of several candles. It was Mrs. Lambert who urged Rebecca to take time out for her rides on Firely, and who informed the butler, Griggs, who was inclined to sniff at all the activity in the lovely old house, that his new mistress knew what she was about. She even approached the estate manager in her zeal to vindicate Rebecca's projects.

"You may be sure, Mr. Bridge," she told him, "that Lady Clayborne is not spending a farthing above what is necessary. Why, she works the whole of each day on this undertaking. Never have I seen a more industrious young lady. And when her hands are not busy with a needle, she has her nose in a book in the library. Can't imagine what she sees in some of those old volumes—nasty, dusty things they be—but bless me if she doesn't forget her very meals with all her studies there."

Although Bridge might grunt at this evidence of Rebecca's activities, the young lady herself was in earnest. The books she pored over were any she could find—old medical texts, home remedy recipes, scientific journals—that might give her a clue to why her husband had thought her lacking virginity on her wedding night. In spite of her spate of redecorating, her paramount problem was never far from her mind and, although she learned a great deal from all her reading, she did not find what she was looking for. As she exhausted the resources of the Gray Oaks library, and the work neared completion in the three rooms she had chosen to refurbish, she found herself a prey to depressing thoughts which threatened to overwhelm her. There was no one to talk to, no one to whom she could confide her troubles . . . except Firely.

As Rebecca galloped across the fields on the patient little mare, she often spoke her thoughts, which were harmlessly carried away by the wind, while Firely's ears flickered back and forth at the sound. "Why can't I find out what it meant, that night in the bedroom? Is there some secret thing that should have happened? I cannot imagine anything more than I felt! Oh, why did Mama not tell me more? Why didn't I ask?" She drew in the mare on a hillock to survey the home farm and the stream which lay in the valley. "Everything looks so peaceful. I shall have to ride over to the farm soon and see how little Jennie goes on. Jason could at least have introduced me to someone my age. He has left me a virtual prisoner here, with no hope of reprieve. I trusted him, Firely. He was so kind and considerate before that night. No matter what Mama said, I would not have married him otherwise. And not even a letter from him! How does he think that looks to his precious household?"

She urged the mare forward once more, trying not to take her exasperation out on the horse. Instead, they pounded across the fields until Firely and Rebecca both were ready to rest, and Rebecca had achieved a more satisfactory frame of mind. "I shall be especially conciliating when he returns. Perhaps this long absence will have restored his equanimity. He will have thought better of his absurd notion, and even if he hasn't, well, I shall talk to him and he will understand." Through the rest of September and well into October she cherished this dream, clasping it like a talisman, as her only hope.

Rebecca was seated in the topiary, her favorite spot, and reading an entertaining novel when she heard footsteps approaching her along the path. The lingering smile on her face faded as she saw that Clayborne was wearing the scowl she had come to associate with him before he left. She did not speak as he approached her.

Surveying her critically, Clayborne commented, "You have put on some weight since I left." He had meant to add, in a sarcastic tone, of course, that he was glad she found it possible to enjoy her meals when spared his company, when the blaze of fury in her eyes shocked him into silence.

"I am not increasing, your lordship, as any maid in the house could no doubt inform you," she flared. "I see your journey has not dispelled your ridiculous obsession."

"Nor improved your disposition, ma'am. If you will excuse me." He sketched the travesty of a bow and left her, with breast heaving in agitation and anger, to glare after his retreating form. She could have wept with frustration to have all her plans upset at one blow. Why had she allowed herself to flash at him that way? Deep down she knew that it had been her fondest wish that when he saw her again there would be some sign of welcome from him, some tentative gesture of reconciliation. His scowl had unnerved her, and his words had brought back his cruel speech that morning long ago in the breakfast room. She had meant to meet him halfway, more than halfway, and she had failed. With a sigh, she closed the book in her lap and walked slowly back to the house.

The gown she chose to wear to dinner was one of the

most becoming, and cerainly the most modest, of the dresses she had purchased as her wedding clothes. Although she arrived at the Blue Saloon well before the dinner hour in hopes of encountering her husband there, he did not present himself until Griggs was about to announce the meal. Clayborne formally placed his wife's hand on his arm to lead her in, but did not speak until they were seated. While a footman ladled the *potage aux lantilles* into their bowls, Rebecca asked, "Did you find the Yorkshire estate in good order, Jason?"

"Yes. The harvesting went very well."

"And your brother-in-law and nephew, were they pleased to see you?"

"Yes. They sent their regards."

"Bridge seemed to find no difficulties here. I suppose you have spoken with him?"

"Yes, most of the afternoon."

"Mrs. Lambert told me that you are partial to sweetbreads with mushrooms," Rebecca suggested hopefully as she tasted the dish just served her.

"It was kind of her to remember."

A flush of annoyance crept into her cheeks, but she stoutly ignored this slighting of *her* having ordered the dish for him. "Your cook has introduced me to a number of new dishes. He makes a superb loaf of beef collops."

Clayborne offered no reply to this pleasantry and they sat in hostile silence for some time, attending to their meal with unusual concentration. Aware though he was of the beautiful new draperies and the delicate shade of the new paint, Clayborne could not bring himself to speak of them. Somehow it seemed a sacrilege that she had put her hand to his ancient, honored home. True, he had said that she might, and the results were certainly charming, but that *she* had done it . . .

Rebecca cleared her throat and said diffidently, "You have not commented as yet on the new decoration."

"Very admirable, I'm sure," he returned coldly. He thought perhaps he heard his wife, in a very soft voice, say "Toad," but he could not be sure and aside from giving her a stern look, he said nothing.

Matters did not improve and Rebecca was not surprised, and not displeased, when Clayborne left Gray Oaks again a week later, this time declaring that he was headed for Somerset and Dorset to settle some estate matters there. He did not return again until the week before Christmas.

In an excess of seasonal high spirits, Rebecca had made every effort to decorate the house in the most Christmasy manner possible. The housemaids giggled as they assisted the footmen in hanging boughs of evergreen and holly, with sprigs of mistletoe ever prominent.

"You'll have the girls good for nothing, my lady," Mrs. Lambert cautioned her. "'Tis the custom here that the young men may kiss a girl beneath the mistletoe so long as there is a berry left to pluck from the twig."

"Would you have me remove all the berries, then?" Rebecca asked, laughing down at her from a ladder. "No, no, that would never do. Any footman who is so enterprising as to pluck a berry each time he kisses a girl should be rewarded for the feat. These ceilings must be eighteen feet if they're an inch." She surveyed the Blue Saloon critically from her high vantage point. "Perhaps the bow is not centered perfectly on the mantle. Yes, that's just right. The house smells so delicious, and not just from the evergreen. What has M. Dussart in his ovens that makes me long for tea?"

Proud that she had declared a truce with the French cook for the duration of the holiday season, Mrs. Lambert beamed. "You'll not credit the assortment of Christmas biscuits and plum puddings that are daily mounting in the kitchens, Lady Clayborne. I've not seen the like since his lordship was a lad, and his sister in leading strings. We couldn't keep the two of them out from underfoot for love nor money."

As Griggs entered the room bearing a tray laden with samples of M. Dussart's work, he overheard these last comments and his eyes took on a faraway look. "Miss Caroline never left the kitchen without at least two gingerbread boys, and his lordship once spirited off an entire plum pudding, bless me if he didn't."

"And I've no doubt who helped him eat it," Mrs. Lambert retorted.

"That kind he was to share his booty with me, Mrs. Lambert, and me just an underfootman in those days." He straightened up with suspiciously misty eyes. "Poor Miss Caroline. How she would have loved to see her own little lad with his Christmas gingerbread boy!"

"Tut! Let's have no sadness for her ladyship," Mrs. Lambert protested, with a tender smile for Rebecca. "Lord Clayborne was a mischievous lad in those days, and no mistake. Why, I searched for days for the Christmas ornaments his Mama kept specially for the mantles, only to find he had hidden them away so we'd buy more from the peddler who called at that time of year. A ragged fellow he was, that peddler, and his lordship always had a soft heart for the needy. Won't he be proper pleased with the house all festivelike?"

"I hope so," Rebecca murmured fervently as she finished a buttery biscuit. "You should be having your tea, Mrs. Lambert. Don't let me keep you."

"Pooh. We have time enough to do the hall now." She gave an approving nod to the Blue/Green Saloon and marched from the room.

While Griggs bustled about unconsciously humming one of the Christmas carols Rebecca had been playing on the pianoforte the previous evening, and Mrs. Lambert ordered her underlings about in the quiet expectation that the lord of the manor would surely return for the holidays, Rebecca happily directed them all, feeling in charity with the whole world, even Clayborne. Her worthy sentiment was challenged immediately, as he chanced to arrive in the midst of this activity, with his perpetual scowl prominent.

"Welcome home, Jason. We are having the most wonderful time preparing for Christmas," she called cheerfully, her arms loaded with boughs. She paused in the act of setting them down, as she noticed that he was not alone.

"I have brought my uncle to spend the holidays with us," he explained stiffly. "Sir Henry Davert, this is my wife Rebecca."

The short, rosy-faced, elderly man beamed at her as he approached to take her hand. "A pleasure to meet you, my dear. I was in Egypt last spring and summer and regretted that I could not attend your wedding."

"In Egypt? Oh, I hope you will tell me all about it," Rebecca said. "I'm so very pleased Jason has brought you to spend the holidays. I shall have a room prepared immediately."

"We did not mean to inconvenience you, my dear," Sir Henry said. "But I was to have spent Christmas with a dear old friend of mine, but he died last week, and Jason convinced me only yesterday that I should come to Gray Oaks." As his expression flitted from cheer to gloom and back to cheer, Rebecca was at a loss to respond to this.

"I assured Uncle Henry that it would be no inconvenience at all," Clayborne asserted, regarding his wife steadily.

"Of course not. I'm delighted to have company." Rebecca might have said more, but she noticed the warning look in Clayborne's eyes and continued, "You must be wishing to refresh yourself from your journey. Mrs. Lambert will show you to a room."

When Sir Henry's chubby form had disappeared up the stairs, Clayborne drew his wife into the Blue Saloon and closed the door firmly. "I am sorry I could not give you warning of Uncle Henry's visit. As he said, it was only decided yesterday."

"It doesn't matter, Jason. Truly, I am glad to have him, as he seems a cheerful soul, and I imagine his friend's death has lowered his spirits somewhat. What was he doing in Egypt?"

"I'm sure he will be more than willing to tell you of that. I want to talk to you." He appeared to hesitate, pulled a snuff box from his pocket and flicked it open and closed with his left hand. Eventually he continued, "I would prefer that Uncle Henry not be aware of our . . . estrangement. He has been very kind to me, having been my guardian for several years after my father died. He is fond of me, and I do not wish to distress him." He raised his eyes from the snuff box to gaze at her for a long moment.

"You are asking me to act the role of a devoted wife?" she asked calmly.

"Exactly."

"Certainly I will do that for you. I only wish that you desired it in fact. I have given you no cause, believe me, to think what you do of me." At his impatient gesture, she said only, "Never mind. I must go and speak with Mrs. Lambert." She left him staring thoughtfully after her.

On the whole, considering the situation, it had been a happy holiday for her. Uncle Henry had been a wonderful conversationalist, full of digs in Egypt, pyramids and tombs, all of which had fascinated Rebecca. Clayborne, on a ride into the village of Herstley, had discovered that there was gossip about his strange marriage amongst the local gentry, and he had set out to crush it.

Drawing Rebecca into the library one day, he said abruptly, "You are to give a dinner party for some of our neighbors in two days time. I will give you a list of the names."

With as much dignity as her twenty years and five-foot-two height could command, Rebecca replied, "I am most willing to entertain our neighbors, Jason. I would remind you, however, that I am not, in spite of your odd notions, used to being ordered about like your housekeeper, though I am sure that you would show more consideration for Mrs. Lambert. There is no need for unseemly haste in preparing for such a party, unless you intend to depart immediately after Christmas. I would suggest a week from today would be sufficient notice to your household and your guests."

Aware of the reasonableness of her argument, Clayborne relented. "Of course you are right. There is talk in the village of our relationship and I merely wish to allay it as soon as possible."

"I can think of several better methods than a dinner party," she responded mildly, "but I am sure it will suffice for the present." She was not aware as she turned away of how his eyes traveled longingly over her body.

Her stubborn impenitence no longer had the power to subdue his desire for her. The warm greeting she had given him on his arrival, and the special trouble she had taken to entertain his Uncle Henry could not be ignored. His anger was tempered with gratitude; his confusion with a reluctant admiration for her precariously maintained dignity. Several times he had stood on the brink of tapping on her door, only to sternly remind himself of the last time he had visited her there. No, she was not like Alexis, but he had made a wretched mistake for the second time, all the same.

His physical attraction could be dealt with more easily at a distance, and he stubbornly departed again, this time for London. The hapless soldiers who had returned from Waterloo without prospects, some sick and handicapped, with nowhere to go, became his special interest. Since the government appeared to take no thought of them, Clayborne did. It provided him with an occupation he sorely needed. Although he made brief trips to Gray Oaks, they were unattended by any ability on his part to accept his lonely bride for what she was. He heard himself being distant and uncompromising with her, and he hated himself for it, but he could not overcome his disillusionment. A proud man did not accept an unrepentant woman as the mother of his offspring.

Four

Rebecca reviewed her disastrous marriage in the light of her sister's visit and hoped that her situation would not appear singular to Meg, for she had no wish to upset her sister, nor to have word of her estrangement reach her parents. She was determined to make use of Clayborne's rare presence at Gray Oaks to gain an understanding of his disgust of her and alleviate it if it were possible.

When Meg had rested from her journey and changed to a jonquil chemise frock with a cottage front, she arrived to find Rebecca seated in the saloon with a book on Egyptian archeology. She was rather astonished by this, in spite of her knowledge of Rebecca's propensity toward bookishness, and she commented on it.

"Jason's Uncle Henry visited us at Christmas and gave me several books on the subject. Quite fascinating, and I will be glad to lend you one of them if you wish," she teased her sister.

"Oh, no, thank you," Meg gasped in horror. "I am sure I would not understand a word of it. Mama still shudders when she recalls some of the lectures you forced her to attend during your season."

"Yes, and it was fortunate that Clayborne offered for me just when she had refused positively to attend another. Really, Meg, you need not look so aghast. They were most informative, I assure you, and I did not attend above half a dozen. Mama should not have put herself in such a fret, for Clayborne was not the least bit reluctant to escort me. I am sure he enjoyed them more than I did."

Finding this difficult to believe, but not wishing to pursue the subject, Meg took the opportunity to elucidate further on her stay in London. "I realize, of course, that Mama managed to obtain vouchers to Almack's for you and Trudy, but I had the greatest fear that she would find it impossilbe to get me admitted. She has not been on such good terms with Lady Cowper recently, I fear, because Papa accidentally ignored Lord Cowper at White's. You know Papa, Becka. Half the time he doesn't remember who people are. But the worry was all for naught; Lady Cowper was all graciousness. Will says she is the most popular of the patronesses. Oh, and it was everything I had dreamed of at Almack's. I was permitted almost from the start to waltz and—would you believe it?—Will is the most exquisite dancer."

"Of course I would believe it, love. He is certainly graceful in the saddle."

Meg was gratified by this encomium for her beloved and rattled on. "I had quite convinced myself that my season could not possibly be as exciting as yours, coming as it did after the thrill of our victory at Waterloo. You must have been in agony during the wait for news, but then the celebrations afterwards! The illuminations! The celebration balls! Well, I did not think London would be nearly so charming this year, but you would not credit all the excitement there was. What with Princess Charlotte marrying Prince Leopold—Will says the Regent kept her a virtual prisoner at Cranbourne Lodge for a year and a half when she refused to marry the Prince of Orange! How dastardly! The Prince is grossly fat. Did you see him?"

"Only in his carriage. He kept out of sight a great deal because of his unpopularity," Rebecca said.

"Yes, well, I should hope he would be unpopular for the way he treated her!"

Rebecca forebore to mention the multitude of other sins which rendered the Regent unpopular, and continued to attend to her sister's monologue.

"And then there was the fiasco at Almack's when

they tried to bring Lord Byron back to decent society. Mama positively insisted that we leave on the instant. Will says that Byron is England's greatest living poet, but of course he does not condone his personal behavior." Meg flushed at her very imperfect understanding of the situation. "So the next thing was that Byron left the country. And then, what should happen but Lady Caroline Lamb's *Glenarvon* was published. Will would not let me read it—that is, he did not positively say that I might not, but he told me it was not the sort of book from which I should benefit. But I heard all the *on dits* about it; nothing else was talked of, I promise you. They say Lady Caroline drew her characters from the very *haut ton*—not hesitating to malign her own husband and Lady Holland, who has always been kind to her. Will says it was a most disgraceful action and he is dreadfully sorry for William Lamb. Anyway, it was a very exciting season after all."

"I should think so," Rebecca murmured, amused at her sister's innocent enthusiasm about the peccadilloes of such prominent members of society.

"There were many evenings when we attended two or three balls in succession, with each hostess attempting to outdo the last. Will says he enjoys the breakfasts best, and I am inclined to agree with him, so long as they do not follow one of the late evenings. Will became acquainted with Lord Farley at Cambridge and had entrée everywhere. And I made a very dear friend of Althea Stonebridge—you will adore her, Becka. Will says she is just the sort of unexceptionable friend he would expect me to make. Lord and Lady Stonebridge were lovely to me, often including me in their parties for the theatre. Mama was delighted for the chance to rest, and Will was always invited, too, as my escort."

Meg noticed that her sister was growing a trifle restive with all these details of her season and she was abruptly reminded of her social graces. "Now tell me what you've been doing, Becka love. You have not said a word and I should hate to be like Turnip."

"A fate worse than death," Rebecca agreed with a laugh. "Let's see. When I came to Gray Oaks I found

Clayborne had bought me a superb little mare. You must see her, Meg, for she is the most beautiful stepper. But then you do not like horses so well, do you? Anyway, I ride most every day and for me it is heaven. I read a lot, sometimes in the topiary, which I shall show you later. The first few months I spent a great deal of time refurbishing three of the rooms. You shall tell me what you think of them. Clayborne was away on estate business for a while, so I had a free hand. Don't you think the draperies are handsome? I found the material in Chichester. I will have to take you there. It may be nothing compared to London for shops, but it is the most charming town."

"I'm sure Turnip must agree with you, for though we fairly flew through it this morning, she did not finish speaking of it until we reached your gate," Meg grumbled.

"She no doubt studied her guidebook for a week before you left, and entrusted it all to memory. Herstley in the closest village and since it will be in no guidebook I shall take you walking there. She will not care to accompany us, I hope. There are an inordinate number of elderly folk in the neighborhood, and in truth I don't believe I've met a soul under forty except for the tenants and their children."

"But how else have you whiled your time?" Meg asked curiously. "No cosy teas or morning calls?"

"Well . . . naturally there were some duty calls at first, and we gave the funniest dinner party at Christmas."

Meg was slightly shocked. "A funny dinner party? For the neighbors?"

"Yes, for Clayborne wanted the local gentry to meet me and his Uncle Henry. He has known all of them since childhood, of course, and put them all at ease. But the vicar, Mr. Rivers, who is extremely old and learned, practically fell asleep before the ladies withdrew. And the local squire, Sir John Denby, proceeded to instruct us all on his latest agricultural innovations in a voice so loud that my wine glass trembled. His wife, on the other hand, spoke in a barely audible whisper and her conversation consisted entirely of domestic matters, which she discussed in fatiguing detail, though of course I was not able to hear much of it. No, wait," Rebecca lifted an admonishing hand as her sister began to giggle.

"That's only the beginning. There were also the village gossips, the Misses Blackwell, who were able, in a very short period of time, to leave in shreds the reputation of anyone unlucky enough not to have been invited that night." Meg was now laughing unrestrainedly, and Rebecca, pretending to regard her sternly, said, "Now, Meg, I am sure this tale is most informative if you will but keep an open mind. For Miss Sarah fixed me with her beady eyes and kept nodding knowingly at me, but she was obviously impatient to get away so that she could discuss me with her sister. Miss Lucilla, on the other hand, would never quite meet your eye, even when she was speaking directly to you. Meg, you must attend, for you have not the full cast of characters yet," Rebecca urged, though Meg was now wiping her eyes on a tiny wisp of handkerchief, and clutching at her side, alternately.

"We also had with us Dr. Baker, the physician, descended from a very old and distinguished family. He is rather lean and serious-looking, and only entered the conversation if he wished to disagree, in the most scientific and eso—esoteric, I think it is, vocabulary that you can imagine. I could not understand every third word."

"They sound," Meg gasped between giggles, "like a most stimulating company."

"And indeed they were. For when we had adjourned to the Blue Saloon and I had played for them and the Misses Blackwell had sung the most amazing songs—religious, you understand—Sir John began in his booming voice to describe the use to which he was putting his south pasture. His wife, at the same time, mind you, was whispering about an unlit fire in the library grate the evening before, while Dr. Baker was disputing the wisdom of Sir John's choice of pasturage. Miss Sarah was staring right at the doctor and shaking her head in disagreement, while Miss Lucilla was looking somewhere over his left shoulder with a very vague expression on her face. Now,

Meg, I am sorry to have been so long in the setting of this scene, but I have reached the *dénouement*!" Rebecca proclaimed dramatically.

"I really do not think I can bear it, Becka," Meg gasped again.

"Of course you can, for it was highly instructive. You see, during all this shouting and mumbling, the vicar had been sleeping quite peacefully. I am sure," she admitted apologetically, "that it was my playing on the pianoforte which accomplished that. Nevertheless, when suddenly he awoke, he began reciting the twenty-third psalm, to the astonishment of everyone present. Most educational, I thought," Rebecca proclaimed, as she finally let herself join in her sister's whoops.

"Becka, there never was one like you to make the most of a sadly boring time. I can picture the whole, and I would have taken to my bed with the headache," she confessed.

"Well, perhaps it was not so bad, really. Uncle Henry has the most exquisite sense of humor and we had many a laugh over it afterwards. And I have drawn a character of each of them of which I am inordinately proud. I shall show them to you one day."

"Do you still do that? I remember the day Turnip found your drawing of her, and how we had to bear her Christian long suffering for weeks afterwards. And I have always kept the one you did of me, for though it is not perhaps flattering," she reproached her sister, still giggling, "it serves to damp any pretentions I might feel on occasion."

"I am sure it is a most unladylike hobby, but I thoroughly enjoy it. When in London I was inspired by Rowlandson's cartoons. I pride myself that I have developed a style of my own," Rebecca admitted. Their discussion was interrupted at this point by the arrival of Miss Turnpeck, who could be heard outside the saloon door assuring someone that she had had not the least difficulty in finding her way about the house and that she was sure the two young ladies were having the nicest coze, perhaps even having ordered tea by this time of the afternoon. Rebecca guiltily rang then, as the old governess entered.

Although the travelers had had luncheon trays in their rooms, she remembered Turnip's penchant for nibbling biscuits all through the day, which appeared to do her not the least bit of damage, as she was thin almost to gauntness.

"Such a delightful home you have, Rebecca," Miss Turnpeck twitted. "And the housekeeper—Mrs. Lambert is it?—so thoughtful of a guest. It was she herself, and not a maid at all, who took charge of settling me into my room. She tells me that her brother is the head gardener. I could see the most remarkable topiary from my window, and she says you read there frequently. May we have a walk in it some time?"

"Certainly. It is my favorite spot near the house. We shall walk there after tea if you wish," Rebecca offered.

"Nothing would give me more pleasure. So thoughtful of you. Meg dear, I am convinced that you will enjoy it immensely. Perhaps your room does not look out on it as mine does? Well, never mind, you shall see it soon. Oh, here is the tea tray. I find I am quite parched!" Miss Turnpeck exclaimed. Rebecca and Meg exchanged laughing glances, and Rebecca, her giggles of a few minutes before forgotten, assumed the role of lady of the house and poured for them as though she had done it often for the local gentry.

When Clayborne arrived to join them for tea, he politely inquired if the two ladies were now settled in. He was answered by Miss Turnpeck, at length, as he seated himself and accepted a cup of tea and some biscuits from Rebecca, forcing himself to return her hesitant smile.

"Miss Turnpeck has been commenting on the topiary and I plan that we will walk there in a bit, Jason. You might tell her how it was started," his wife suggested, remembering how this had been related to his Uncle Henry, who had never heard the story.

"There was a Lady Clayborne, perhaps a century and a half ago, who surrounded herself with all manner of exotic pets. Not just dogs and cats, but monkeys and a tiger or so," he explained in a lazy, exaggerated storytelling manner. "They even once had a giraffe and a camel, I am told, though I am not sure I credit that. It seems that the tiger broke loose one day and destroyed a large part of the animal population at Gray Oaks before he was captured. The then Lord Clayborne thereafter refused to have any other animals about except the hunting dogs and small cats, and his wife went into a decline, pining for her pets. In an effort to cheer his wife he instructed the gardener to train the growth into all kinds of animal shapes—some are quite fantastic—and it has been kept up to this day. You will see the giraffe and the camel she is supposed to have had."

"And did it cheer his wife?" Meg wanted to know.

"Well, perhaps it halted the decline," Clayborne admitted, "but I have heard that Lady Clayborne spent the better part of her days in the topiary talking to the animals and was at length considered mad!"

"Poor soul!" Miss Turnpeck cried with a delicate shudder. "I am sure there is nothing so comforting as having a little dog or cat about one. I have always had a cat, myself, even at Farthington Hall. They have been so good as to allow me to have one of my own, in my room. I would never have thought to bring it to the schoolroom, of course, but then the children always had all manner of puppies about until they would grow and be banished to the stables by Sir Rupert. I remember the mongrel you found, Rebecca. Such a scraggly thing he was! And you very nearly got run over for saving him from the wheels of that curricle. It was that young man—you remember him, don't you?—Thomas Burns. We saw him several times after that, and at your sister Trudy's wedding. Such a rackety fellow, dashing about Salisbury in that way. Why, he could have crushed you both! It does not bear thinking on," she moaned, which conclusion the sisters had reached some moments before, and shared a conspiratorial glance.

"But you know," Miss Turnpeck revived to say, "I do believe I have heard recently that the young man has settled down. Married shortly after Trudy, if I recall correctly, and they have a son now. Such a to-do as he made, blaming you for the whole. But then he was shaken by such a near accident, as he should have been," she said sternly. "And he did calm down after a bit; quite charmed him you did, naughty girl. Yes, and he came by only the next day, as I remember, to see how the poor dog was getting on, and you, too, of course."

By now Meg was looking distinctly uncomfortable and making faces at Rebecca, but her sister said only, "Really, Rags was a handsome dog once he was bathed and fed for a while. I missed him when he went away."

"I never did believe that he ran away," Miss Turnpeck declared stoutly. "I am sure I saw that young man near Farthington Hall on the day he disappeared."

"Now why would he have taken Rags?" Rebecca asked as casually as she could as she rose to suggest, "We should have our walk in the topiary now while it is still warm."

Clayborne observed this interchange with more interest than was apparent. He noticed Meg's discomfort and his wife's attempt to end the conversation, and he determined to find out more about this young man if he could.

"Will you join us for our walk, Jason?" Rebecca asked.

"No, thank you. I have business matters to attend to. Please excuse me." With a formal nod to his wife, and a smile for Miss Turnpeck and Meg, he walked thoughtfully to his study.

Miss Turnpeck managed to entertain her companions by recounting stories of the various cats she had owned as they wended their way through the topiary, exclaiming at the ingenious figures portrayed there. The topic of Thomas Burns was not revived.

But he was the subject of Clayborne's thoughts as he sat at his desk drumming his fingers on the chair arm. Clayborne was aware that Rebecca was not familiar with many men; it was her innocence that had first appealed to him when he met her. There had been Captain Gray, of course, but Rebecca had treated him much as a brother, amused but not intrigued by him. Her reaction, he felt sure, would have been far otherwise if she had loved him and had gone so far as to have an affair with him. From his own experience with Alexis, Clayborne was very familiar with the effects of such an infatuation.

The information he had gleaned at tea about Thomas Burns goaded his hurt and anger. Since there had been few young men in Rebecca's life, he felt a great desire to learn more of this one, and surely providence had provided a wealthy source of information in Miss Turnpeck. Fearful of what he might learn, Clayborne was yet determined to pursue the matter.

Five

Meg's visit settled into a pleasant routine. When the ladies breakfasted, Clayborne had already finished and left the house on estate business or fishing expeditions. Then Meg and Rebecca would take a stroll in the gardens or walk into the village to execute small commissions. Miss Turnpeck usually remained in the garden doing her needlework, and the sisters enjoyed the chance to be alone. After luncheon, from which Lord Clayborne also was usually absent, the ladies rested for a while and then Meg practiced on the pianoforte while Rebecca sketched and Miss Turnpeck read one of her innumerable guidebooks. Clayborne joined them for the evening meal, which was fairly early since they kept country hours, and then they would adjourn to the Blue Saloon where the sisters sang duets, or they all played cards and conversed. Rebecca, considering all this relaxing but hardly exciting, suggested a picnic for the following day and was seconded cheerfully by Meg.

"Could you accompany us, Jason?" Rebecca asked. "You must know several spots in the neighborhood."

"Oh, yes, please, Jason. We used to have the most delightful picnics when we were young, didn't we, Miss Turnpeck?" Meg asked.

When Clayborne hesitated, Rebecca felt annoyance rise within her. Had she not entertained his Uncle Henry? Had she not refurbished several rooms for him? Had she not overseen the house for months while he took himself elsewhere? Seeing the angry flush on his wife's cheeks, Clayborne hastened to **agree**, well aware that at Christmas his wife had played a role for him and he owed her no less, if certainly no more, than to do the same for her. "I know a delightful spot on the road toward Arundel. Will you arrange for the picnic hamper, Rebecca?"

"I will speak with M. Dussart first thing in the morning," Rebecca promised with a grateful smile.

"There is nothing quite so enjoyable as an al fresco entertainment, is there?" Miss Turnpeck asked cheerfully. "We often explored the neighborhood of Farthington Hall on our picnics. So many interesting historical sites to see! And on the road to Arundel, you say? Now there, I understand, is quite a magnificent structure. Not that we would be able to see it! Oh, no, I realize that we are far too distant for such a treat. Surely one of the most famous castles in the country, though, and I have read somewhere that they are contemplating extensive renovations. Or was that Warwick Castle? Well, it hardly signifies, does it? I myself have often thought that these large, old buildings must be exceedingly drafty, and just think what an army of servants one would need to care for such a place! And the fireplaces! I haven't the least doubt that nine out of ten of them smoke most execrably. And it is not pleasant—do you think?—to sit in a room where the fireplace smokes. One's clothes are tainted with the odor, and I am sure that the soot would discolor even the darkest of fabrics. You must not think, Lord Clayborne, that the fireplaces at Farthington Hall smoke. No, no, I have no experience of such a thing happening there, to be sure. The Hall is a comparatively modern building." As Miss Turnpeck paused for breath, Rebecca and Meg hastily pleaded tiredness and escaped to their rooms.

When Rebecca was in bed and reading the latest canto of Byron's *Childe Harold* by the light of her candle, there was a light tap on the interconnecting door between her room and Clayborne's. Considerably startled, she called, "Come in."

He wore a full-length dressing gown of red brocade with a long rolling collar which showed a black satin lining. Rebecca's eyes widened in wonder at its magnificence as he hesitantly approached her bed.

"I do not mean to disturb you, Rebecca. I came

merely to apologize for my reluctance to join your party tomorrow. I am aware that you were most kind to Uncle Henry and have every right to expect me to assist in entertaining your sister. In future I shall," he promised, and turned to leave.

"Stay a moment, Jason. Please sit down," she urged. "I wish to speak with you for a moment."

With a gesture of acquiescence, he pulled a chair near her bed. Although he was not scowling, his face was a mask she could not read. "As with your uncle, I would prefer that my sister and Miss Turnpeck regard ours as a normal marriage. However, you have not been at Gray Oaks above thrice since Christmas and I do not believe play-acting will solve anything." Rebecca did not allow herself to be distressed by the grim look developing on her husband's face. "Jason, I have read everything in your library that I could lay my hands on to try to understand what happened on our wedding night that so disillusioned you. There is nothing that will explain it to me, and I have no one I can ask but you. You will have to tell me."

"I have no desire to discuss the matter with you, ma'am."

"No? Then I shall be left in ignorance and avoided by you for the rest of my life, sir?"

He made a gesture of dismissal and rose to leave.

"Before you go, Jason, I wish you to understand one thing. I have no intention of allowing this farce to continue. I love Gray Oaks, but I am only twenty years old and I do not intend to be incarcerated here for the rest of my life in atonement for a crime I did not commit. No, stay." She spoke firmly as he made a move to go. "Either you make the effort to clear up this matter for me or I will return to Farthington Hall when Meg leaves. I do not care about the scandal it will cause for me, or even for you. I will not remain where I am treated as a leper."

It was possible, he thought, that even having been with a man she would not know how he could tell. So he told her, in a cool, emotionless voice. "When a woman is a virgin there is a thin barrier which must be penetrated for a man to enter her. The tearing of her maidenhead causes a slight amount of bleeding, and once torn it does not regenerate."

She stared up at him, her blue eyes enormous in their wonder and concern. "I see. Thank you for explaining. But . . ."

"You had no maidenhead."

"But Jason, that could not be. You must be mistaken!"

"It was *your* mistake, ma'am, to think that I would not be able to tell of your previous indiscretion." His face was set in the harsh lines with which she had become so familiar.

The injustice of his accusation, coming as it did upon his unnerving bluntness in describing virginity, shook her resolve to remain calm. "I had *never* been with a man before you! You must believe me!"

"I see no reason why I should, ma'am. Now, if you will excuse me." He was turning to leave when he noticed one large tear roll down her cheek, to be dashed away immediately. With an effort he forced himself to repress the stirring of compassion he experienced. He handed her a handkerchief and, feeling very self-righteous, was stomping back to his room when he heard her give a watery chuckle and say, "Well, at least now I know you aren't daft. I was worried about your fixation with the bed, you know." He slammed the door after himself.

The next day dawned hot and humid, giving Rebecca a slight headache and making her wish they were not going on the picnic. Her spirits were low after the discussion with her husband the previous evening and she felt that she had much to contemplate now, a matter which could hardly be aided by a picnic. Abandoning her bed reluctantly, she went in search of the cook to make arrangements for the food hamper and spent some time there, wishing the meal, at least, to be sumptuous, a sentiment with which the cook was in perfect agreement. When Clayborne was away from Gray Oaks, which recently was the majority of the time, Rebecca was in the habit of ordering far simpler meals, and the cook, with all his Gallic fervor, could indulge in an orgy of roasting, baking, grilling and such only when the master was in residence. Together they planned a menu which would have satisfied the appetites of a far larger party, but which pleased them both, and they parted in perfect charity.

Meg was in high good humor and looked charming in a pale blue muslin dress, trimmed with tiers of broad darker blue bands around the hem. She joined Rebecca in the breakfast parlor, exclaiming, "It is a perfect day for a picnic! Shall we take an open carriage? I think you can see the countryside so much better that way and you would not mind, would you, Miss Turnpeck?"

"Not a bit, my dear. I shall wrap myself about with plenty of warm shawls, and I shall bring along some extra ones for the two of you. I feel sure it will be the most delightful expedition," she enthused, quite rosy with the thought of it.

Rebecca mused that she would give a great deal to know exactly how many shawls dear Miss Turnpeck could call her own, but stifled her curiosity and chatted with her companions about the picnic, only excusing herself to discuss the matter of a carriage with Clayborne. She found him in his study, going over some papers with an abstracted air. Since she had never before sought him out for any reason during their marriage, he appeared a bit surprised when she entered to his summons.

"I wonder if you would arrange for an open carriage for the picnic, Jason, as Meg has desired it and Miss Turnpeck is agreeable."

"Certainly, if you all wish it. Do you feel well? You look a trifle downpin," he remarked, his intent brown eyes surveying her pallor.

"It's just the headache. I am sure it will go away when we are out in the air. I've arranged for the picnic hamper and we should all be ready in an hour, if that will be convenient."

"As you wish, but we could put the picnic off until another day if you are not feeling well."

"No, I shall be fine. Everyone is looking forward to it."

When the carriage was rolling along the country lanes, Rebecca did feel better, laughing with Meg and listening to Miss Turnbeck's monologues on the countryside. Clayborne chose a spot where a brook babbled by, with a view over the fields and forests. Meg and Rebecca wandered off arm in arm to discard their half boots and stockings and wade in the brook. The sound of their laughter and the sight of skipping stones brought an affectionate, indulgent smile to Miss Turnpeck's countenance.

"I remember the picnics we used to have at Farthington Hall when all four girls were there. So much giggling and getting into mischief as they did. I thought they would never grow up, but look at them now," she sighed, and though Clayborne did look at them, his expression was unreadable. Miss Turnpeck had set to helping the coachman lay out the food, and Clayborne, considering this an excellent opportunity, pursued his desire for more information.

"Yesterday when you were speaking of the stray dog Rebecca befriended," he began, "I think you mentioned a fellow with whom I have a slight acquaintance—Thomas Burns." He was trying to invent some physical description or pinpoint the area the fellow lived in, but it was unnecessary, as Miss Turnpeck seldom needed much encouragement to free her rambling tongue.

"Oh, do you know Mr. Burns? It turned out that he lived not so far from us, on the other side of Salisbury. Have you been to his family home? Wilsted Manor, I believe it is called." She did not allow Clayborne a chance to reply to this, so he merely smiled to encourage her. "Dressed like a dandy, he was, the day we met him. He wore those high shirt points so he could hardly turn his head. It's a wonder he didn't run over the both of them. We had been in Salisbury, you know, shopping for yardage for the girls' gowns for Trudy's wedding. Such a lovely wedding it was, with Trudy absolutely radiant and her young man so pale I was sure he would faint. They were married from the village church and I feel certain there were never so many people there before. And the wedding feast afterwards . . ." she exclaimed, ready to divulge all the details of it.

Clayborne did not wish her to be sidetracked yet, so he said quite untruthfully, "Most splendid it must have been. My wife has often spoken of it. And I believe Thomas," he unblinkingly used the young man's Christian name as if he were his oldest friend, "was there, too."

"Yes, and I was that surprised to see him. I didn't know that he was acquainted with Mr. Chalmers, Trudy's husband, you know, but they appear to have been close friends over the years. And I am surprised, as Mr. Chalmers is the most upright young man and I cannot for the life of me imagine his racketing about the countryside with Mr. Burns. Oh, excuse me, Lord Clayborne, if I am speaking of one of your close friends, too," she mumbled in embarrassment.

"No, no, a mere acquaintance. I have heard," he continued helpfully, and without the least remorse, "that he was quite ramshackle in those days."

"Yes, for Mary brought tales of him and teased Rebecca with them. Heaven knows where Mary would hear such gossip. I am sure she never kept her ears so wide open in the schoolroom," she sniffed. "Mary is the one for hanging about the stables and gossiping with the maids at the Bird in Hand, though I am sure that I do my best to have her act as a young lady should. I cannot imagine what it will be like if she is my only charge in the schoolroom next year. I shall be so distracted," she moaned piteously.

"Mary could certainly be a handful," Clayborne agreed. He flashed his most sympathetic smile at Miss Turnpeck and urged, "What was it Mary had learned about the young rascal?"

"Dear me, I am hard pressed to remember," she demurred, only to continue in full flow, "but he seems to have wagered and drunk a lot, in London and in the neighborhood. Mary told us of a curricle race he had with a friend of his where he drove another carriage into a ditch and did not stop to help for fear of losing the race. Such a wicked thing to do, and ladies in the carriage too,

57

no doubt. Young men these days are certainly outrageous—not you, my lord, of course I did not mean that." She became flustered again and dropped silent.

"Yes, Thomas was forever up to some mischief," Clayborne pronounced pontifically. "But I imagine such a scamp would seem fascinating to your four charges, off in the country at Farthington Hall."

"Well, you know how it is with these girls—any new face. But no, I think they were just given to funning about him amongst themselves, for though I saw him in the neighborhood several times, he came to the house but rarely. Though, as I said, I did see him the day the dog went missing, and I have always had my suspicions," she said nodding wisely, as she placed the last of the rhubarb tarts on the picnic rug.

"You think he took the dog? Why should he do that?" Clayborne asked curiously.

"Now there I cannot help you, for I cannot think of the least reason. But then, he seems to have done many things which don't bear scrutiny, so why not take the dog? Though I cannot believe that he would do it when he knew that Rebecca was so fond of Rags, for Mr. Burns seemed rather taken with Rebecca. But then he soon wed little Sybil Caruthers, whose grandfather made a fortune in India. Such a sweet girl she is, shy and quietlike, but ever so kind and thoughtful of others. She's a neighborhood girl too, you know, though my young ladies didn't see her so much, as she spent a great part of her early years with her grandfather. Only came back to Foxton when the old gentleman died. And imagine inheriting his entire fortune! It was the talk of the neighborhood for weeks, I assure you. But it did not affect her manner one bit, still the dearest girl." Miss Turnpeck gave Clayborne the impression that her life would have been a lot simpler if she had had the likes of Miss Caruthers to instruct in her schoolroom. "And now she is Mrs. Burns with a son. It does make one feel aged," she remarked coyly.

"But it is just these young people who keep you looking so youthful yourself, Miss Turnpeck," Clayborne responded gallantly.

Miss Turnpeck blushed happily, but disclaimed, "What a farradiddle, my lord. And there is Trudy about to set up her nursery, too, and who knows who next," she said slyly, blinking up at him.

"Indeed, who knows?" he responded calmly, if more coolly than she expected. "Shall we call the young ladies to luncheon? I fear there is a storm brewing," he remarked, indicating that the fleecy white clouds they had started their drive with were now becoming ominously gray, while the heat had become oppressive.

When Miss Turnpeck summoned the sisters, who were loath to leave their sport, Meg whispered, "Just like Turnip to spoil our fun."

"I have no doubt it was Jason's doing," Rebecca grumbled good-naturedly.

Overhearing this sally, Clayborne explained, "There is a storm brewing, Rebecca."

"I have no doubt of it, my lord," she responded saucily, and accepted his offer of assistance to seat her. She and Meg did justice to the extensive selection of cold meats, bread, fruit, wine and tarts while Miss Turnpeck kept up a rambling discourse on the vagaries of the weather, the destructiveness of storms, and somehow ended up complaining of the condition of the roads, a transition which her audience did not perhaps follow but whose obscurity was not commented upon.

With a glance at the sky, Clayborn rose first from the meal. "The storm is closer now. We should have everything packed away quickly."

To have the first excursion she had planned for her sister so abruptly brought to a halt was distressing for Rebecca. It might be days before she got the nerve to solicit his attendance at another such expedition, and she did not want Meg to be bored after her busy London season. The darkening clouds were still some distance away and she made a face at her husband and lingered, finishing her tart and wine. But she did not ignore the glare he sent her, and rose shortly to join the others in their preparations. "I had hoped we could gather some periwinkle and columbine," she said wistfully. "You see those clumps? Well, perhaps another day," she conceded, as she helped Miss Turnpeck pack the last of the food in the hamper.

They arrived at Gray Oaks just as the rain came, large drops spattering the dusty ground where the carriage stopped. The three women reached the house with muddied boots and hems, and repaired to their rooms to change, while the storm grew wilder outside. Fires were hastily lit in their rooms, as the day grew dark and chill after the earlier heat.

Rebecca huddled in a chair near her fire, while the wind lashed rain against the mullioned windowpanes and the thunder and lightning rocked the world outside. She assured herself, as she had many times before, that her fear of storms was irrational, but she had once been pinned under a lightning-struck limb and had not been found for an hour, soaked, chilled and in shock. Regardless of how she tried she could not seem to overcome the shivering which thunder and lightning precipitated in her. She was about to seek out Meg for comfort when the door from her husband's room opened and he stood there staring at her.

"I trust you will now wish to acknowledge the justice of our early return home," he said coldly.

"Please leave me alone, Jason," she murmured through chattering teeth.

"I am waiting."

"Well, wait somewhere else," she said with some asperity. She saw the muscle in his jaw tighten and said dutifully if exasperatedly, "Your pardon, sir. I fear I do not enjoy thunderstorms. I am grateful that we are safe at home and I regret delaying us."

"I accept your apology."

"Most kind of you, I am sure," she retorted. Thunder rolled outside and there was almost immediately a rending crack as lighting struck some nearby tree. She gasped and failed to conceal the shudder which shook her.

In a moment he was at her side, exclaiming, "I didn't realize you were afraid of storms. Why hadn't you said so?" But of course he already knew the answer, so he took her icy hands in his large warm ones and she felt immeasurably comforted.

There was a soft rap on the door, as Meg called softly, "Arc you there, Becka? I thought you would like company." Clayborne gently returned Rebecca's hands to her lap and opened the door to Meg.

"Oh, I'm sorry. I didn't know you were here, Jason. I won't stay," Meg mumbled, embarrassed.

"No, don't go. I am sure your sister will welcome your company, and I should see what damage has been caused by the lightning." He looked at Rebecca and asked gently, "You will be all right now?"

"Yes, thank you. I think the storm is beginning to pass," she replied. He bowed to the two of them and departed.

Meg pulled up a chair and chatted soothingly to her sister until the storm died away. Though Clayborne went outside to survey the damage, his mind kept returning to his wife. How many storms had she suffered through alone in her room while he had been away from Gray Oaks? How many times had she sat shivering with no one to comfort her? God, what a mess he was making of being a husband! He was overwhelmed by the now familiar feelings of sadness and despair, anger and hurt.

Six

That evening when the party was assembled in the large, trussed dining hall, Clayborne announced, "I have business in London which will take a few days."

"How splendid!" Meg exclaimed, assuming without hesitation that he intended to take the whole party. "And I have just been wishing that I might purchase a bonnet to match my new pink cambric lace gown. I am sure Chichester has very admirable shops, Rebecca, but Mama has taken me to the most marvelous shop in London and I am sure you will simply dote on Madame Piscaud's hats. The lavender one I have with the wide brim and small puffed crown we purchased there, and it is quite the thing, is it not? You have not been to town for some time, have you? I'll show you the steps of the quadrille, which Lady Jersey has introduced from France, in case we should go to a party. Would you like to go to London, Becka?"

"I have not been for a while," she replied cautiously with a questioning glance at her husband. When he nodded she continued more enthusiastically, "I should like it of all things."

"And you, Miss Turnpeck? Would such an expedition suit you?" Clayborne asked.

Miss Turnpeck was pink with delight. "It is many years, sir, since I have visited the metropolis. I wonder if we would have time to visit some of the sights? And I have a sister there who is a seamstress. I have not seen her these past ten years or so, but of course we write to one another regularly. I would be so pleased to see her again."

"Then it is settled," Clayborne pronounced. "Town may be light of company with so many gone to Brighton, but I daresay you will find enough to amuse yourselves. If you can be ready by the day after tomorrow, I shall send warning of our arrival to Clayborne House."

When Meg and Miss Turnpeck had headed for bed, Rebecca stayed behind for a moment to speak with her husband. She stood awkwardly at the door and could not meet his eyes. "I'm sorry if Meg forced your hand, Jason. She doesn't understand that you do not take me . . . that you usually travel alone," she concluded, flushed with embarrassment.

Clayborne crossed the room to her and took her hands firmly. "There is no need to apologize, Rebecca. I had intended to take all of you. You do wish to go, don't you?"

Rebecca raised her eyes to his uncertainly. "Very much," she admitted, "but I had not intended that Meg's visit should prove a burden to you. There was no need for you to include us."

"I wanted to. You have not stayed yet at Clayborne House and you are mistress of it." He dropped her hands, too conscious of their contact. His voice became more formal. "Shall I see you to your room?"

As she regarded his now withdrawn countenance, Rebecca sighed. "No, thank you, Jason. Good-night." She slipped silently from the room as he gazed after her, aware of the empty hands at his sides.

So it was that two days later the ladies found themselves shivering in the cold morning air as they ascended into the traveling carriage, having spent a day in between happily learning the quadrille's intricate steps, planning expeditions to Bond Street (and Westminster Abbey), to the theatre (and the Tower of London), and perhaps to Vauxhall Gardens (and St. Paul's, of course). Their comfort had been provided for with hot bricks and warm traveling rugs lined with fur, and each expressed her excitement in her own way. Since Miss Turnpeck's particular means was a rambling discourse on her chosen sights, the sisters felt no qualms at solicitously urging her to nap during the stage of their journey which followed a light luncheon. With a pillow at her head and resting easily against the comfortable squabs of the carriage, Miss Turnpeck was soon slumbering and snoring lightly.

"I'm sure I understand now how you felt on your journey from Farthington Hall," Rebecca remarked. "I feel certain it will be unnecessary for us to go to Westminster Abbey. We could not possibly learn more about the Cloisters or the Chapel of the Pyx, to say nothing of the Confessor's Chapel. How do you suppose she remembers all those dates?"

"No doubt she has been studying ever since Clayborne suggested the trip," Meg replied. "I saw her sneaking out of the library," she added, laughing, "and I do not doubt that she has it all written on her cuffs, and that is why she keeps shifting about so!" Then she giggled and said, "No, I have it. When she was a very young girl she was kidnapped by a band of bluestockings and forced to reside in a gloomy, haunted castle until she could recite the whole of English history without a mistake."

"And a knight in armor restored her to her rightful position as a governess when he fell under the spell of her snoring," Rebecca contributed.

"For her stepmother, you must know, was very wicked and would not tolerate having Turnip within her sight, reminding her, you see, of Sunday dinner."

The sisters' giggles left Miss Turnpeck undisturbed, and just when they had begun to further embellish their fairy tale, they were surprised to feel the carriage coming to a halt. Rebecca looked out the window to find they were on the open road, with no sign of a cottage, let alone a village. Much to her amazement, there was no sign of Clayborne, either.

"Why are we stopping here, Frantley?" she called to the coachman.

"My lord desired that the carriage await his return, my lady," he responded.

Rebecca cast her eyes heavenward in mock despair. "So much for our escort."

Puzzled, Meg frowned out at the deserted country-side. "We seem to be nowhere near any village, Becka. What do you suppose has happened?"

"I have not the faintest idea," Rebecca answered, "and his lordship does not seem to have found it necessary to explain his departure to us. Let's descend and stretch our legs. Turnip will doubtless continue her nap," she laughed, glancing at the dozing governess cradled happily in a corner, from which soft snores still emanated.

When the coachman had let the steps down and the sisters had tumbled into the warm sunshine, Rebecca once again questioned him. "In which direction did Lord Clayborne ride, Frantley?"

"His lordship took the path yonder," he said, indicating a narrow, overgrown trail to the right rear of the coach.

"Well, Meg, shall we explore it?" Rebecca asked with a twinkle, ignoring the coachman's reproving look.

Meg was easily led by her elder sister and her answering smile was suppressed. She replied demurely, "I cannot think Turnip would like it. I am sure she would exhort us on the dangers of a strange countryside and unknown country people, to say nothing of the wild animals which must obviously lurk in that wood yonder. Certainly we shall go."

"Now, miss," Rebecca informed her sister sternly as they set off, "you must remember that you are accompanied by a married woman and that every propriety must be observed, else you shall be left to your governess in future."

Blithely ignoring this homily, her sister asked, "Do you suppose Jason has some acquaintance in the neighborhood? I am sure I don't even know where we are."

"Nor I. But look, there are some people hurrying there, beyond the wood. I think," she said happily, "that we are about to have an adventure. How Mary would envy us."

"I have written Mary that we are to be in London," Meg replied, still rankling from Mary's roasting her about Will Travers. "I am sure she would rather be in London than Bath, but she was so sure that her holiday would be more entertaining than mine," she sniffed.

"Frankly, I can only imagine Mary getting into trouble in either place," Rebecca admitted, "for she is wild enough in the country."

"Yes, but do you know that Mama has the highest hopes for Mary's season next year? She seems to be entirely overlooking our sister's hoydenish nature, and sees only her beauty, which is considerable, I will admit," Meg allowed handsomely.

"I certainly do not envy Mama the chaperoning of her."

As they emerged from the wood they joined an odd assortment of dogs, children, a few chickens and perhaps twenty country people milling about, gazing in wrapt wonder at the most astonishing sight Rebecca had ever seen. There was an enormous red and yellow striped balloon, gently listing to one side, while the ropes holding the gondola were hopelessly entangled in a tree. Three men in the gondola were tossing ropes over the sides to the men on the ground below. The balloon, loudly emblazoned with the name *The Carberry*, was tilted at a perilous angle, and appeared ready to topple at any moment and eject its passengers to the ground below. Clayborne apparently had taken charge of the rescue operation and Rebecca murmured in tones of exasperation, "Just fancy his excluding us from such an exciting event."

"I saw a balloon ascent in London in the spring, but it was so crowded that I did not get so close as this," Meg said. "And Will was with me, so I did not pay perhaps quite the attention it deserved. Do you think they can get the men out without overturning the boat?"

"I fear not," Rebecca answered anxiously. But even as they watched, Clayborne was directing the men below to haul the ropes carefully on the right and the gondola slowly achieved a more level aspect. When this had been accomplished, the ropes were all held tightly and the gondola lodged firmly in the trees. The balloonists then gingerly, one at a time, descended, clinging to the ropes and dropping to the ground. When the last man, hampered by a useless left arm, had reached safety, a great cheer went up and there was much back-slapping and congratulations all about.

Rebecca urged Meg around the crowd as far away from Clayborne as possible, and the sisters made their way toward the two younger men, as the older one was speaking with Clayborne in a booming voice. "I am Josiah Carberry, owner of this magnificent balloon. Twenty-two trips I have made in it with nary a disaster." The crowd tittered at this, observing the lodged gondola and the shrivelling balloon. "We have had the misfortune of encountering some unexpected air currents, aggravated by a faulty valve, but the damage is negligible, I assure you," he proclaimed.

One of the balloonists, a tall, blond young man in the uniform of the 8th Light Dragoons grimaced ludicrously and commented, "No, indeed. For what is a broken arm in the interests of air travel?"

"You, young man, have nothing of which to complain. I forewarned you that ballooning is not an exact science. But you would have your way and join us for the ride." He forebore to mention that the captain had paid handsomely for the privilege, and turned to Clayborne to discuss the further liberation of his aircraft.

The young man grinned and, seeing Rebecca and Meg coming toward him, admitted to them, "I'm sure I shall never regret it, though my colonel may." He tried to shrug, but the movement gave such pain that he gasped.

"Here, I can make a sling for you with my shawl," Rebecca offered.

"Most kind of you, ma'am, but I could not allow you to dispose of such a delightful object," he protested gallantly.

"Not in the least, sir. You shall send it back when you're finished with it. Can you hold your arm just so? Does it ease the pain?" She was already fashioning a sling and proceeded to tie it securely at his shoulder.

"My thanks, ma'am. May I introduce myself? Captain Hardcastle, 8th Light Dragoons, your most obedient servant."

"Captain Hardcastle? Why, I have heard Captain

Gray speak of you. He said," she grinned, "that you are the most shocking loose-screw."

"Did he though? He's one to talk."

"I am Lady Clayborne. My husband, Lord Clayborne, is over there speaking with your Mr. Carberry. And this is my sister, Miss Farthington," she added as Meg and a plump, rosy faced woman finished attending to the other young man's wound. After making his bows to them, Captain Hardcastle introduced Mr. Carberry's assistant.

Clayborne, who had just noticed the sisters and abruptly excused himself to Mr. Carberry, was making his way determinedly through the crowd toward them. Rebecca forestalled any comment he might have made by introducing him to the two young men, and motioned Meg away as the balloon travelers sought to thank him for his assistance in their rescue.

Tugging at her sister's sleeve, Rebecca whispered, "I think Jason is not best pleased with our arrival here. We might do well to head back to the carriage before he can break away."

Meg, who had observed the frown on Clayborne's face as he approached their group, and who was accustomed to see him only as a suave and pleasant man, agreed with alacrity. They hurried off without a word to anyone and cast furtive glances behind them until they were out of sight, at which point they breathed sighs of relief and continued down the path toward the carriage, chatting excitedly about the balloon and its occupants. Clayborne, however, caught them up and dismounted before they reached their destination.

"I have made arrangements to send help from Guildford for the balloonists," he informed them. "Where is Miss Turnpeck?"

"She is, no doubt, still snoring in the carriage, as we left her," his wife answered, her chin defiantly lifted.

"Meg, please join her and see that she is not alarmed. Rebecca, I would have a word with you."

With a sympathetic glance at her sister, Meg scurried off. When she was out of earshot, Clayborne said exasperatedly, "I wish you had stayed with the carriage."

"We were cramped from the ride and curious where you had gone. Frantley told us which path you had taken, though it pained him, I could tell."

"I am sure he did not approve of your wandering off by yourselves."

"True, but then I did not ask him for his approval, nor did I require it," she said stiffly.

"And yet, had you stayed with the carriage you would have had his protection, and that of Miss Turnpeck. In leaving them you had none."

"We came to no harm, my lord."

"I realize that but I am responsible to your parents for Meg while she is with us."

"I am gratified that you feel such a responsibility for my sister, sir. I shall remember in future to consult you on her protection."

Clayborne regarded his wife with a puzzled frown which turned to chagrined enlightenment. "I was not saying that I do not feel responsible for you, Rebecca. You cannot believe that," he protested, his hand pushing distractedly through his brown hair. "I simply do not want to see *either* of you come to any harm, and it would have been safer, surely, to stay with the carriage."

"Yes, but then we should have missed all the fun. I think it rather paltry in you that you intended to exclude us from such a treat as seeing a balloon descent in the country," she retorted.

"My concern was with those in need of help. I am sorry that I did not inform you where I was going. Perhaps I should have done so, but frankly I did not think of it in the excitement."

Rebecca bit her lip in an effort to suppress her amusement at his confession. Then she was overcome not by the humor but the pathos of the situation and said sadly, regarding her feet fixedly, "It is so easy for you to forget me."

"I never forget that you are my wife," Clayborne returned, the muscle in his jaw tightening. "I have apologized for my abandonment of you, and I was sure you would understand my decision to help the balloonists."

"Of course I do. And I admit that I was not as sure that you would approve of our following you, but I did not do it intentionally to annoy you."

"No," he conceded, "I am sure it was merely your desire for a lark, and perhaps your irritation with me for leaving you behind. You seem to regard such instances as a challenge to you."

Rebecca lifted angry eyes to his. "Maybe I do. I have found no way to deal with you, Jason. Being humble and apologetic would not agree with me, you see, and I fear that is the only attitude you would willingly accept from me."

Clayborne experienced a feeling of unreality, standing in the afternoon sun in the middle of a journey discussing their marriage. Those angry blue eyes squinting in the brilliance were the same eyes that a year ago had been full of laughter and fun. Under the anger there was a sadness he could respond to, but he firmly reminded himself that it was her own fault. She had deceived him and she had no right to expect their marriage to be otherwise. "What I expect from you as my wife is an observance of the proprieties and a modicum of obedience to my wishes. I do not think that is asking too much of you."

"Perhaps not. But as we are on the subject, Jason, I might let you know that what I expect of you as my husband is companionship and a modicum of respect for myself. Obviously that is asking far too much of you, since I receive neither."

"As my wife I have endowed you with my name, my position, and my wealth. I consider those the only things you have any right to ask of me," Clayborne snapped in his annoyance.

"I realize that, my lord. And I constantly remind myself that, believing what you do, it is not an unreasonable attitude. Unkind and uncharitable, perhaps, but not unreasonable. My sister and Miss Turnpeck are waiting. Shall we proceed to London?" He did not answer, but

71

walked with her to the waiting carriage and handed her in, said a word to Miss Turnpeck, and returned to swing himself, disgruntled, onto his horse.

Miss Turnpeck was inclined to spend a lengthy time scolding the sisters for wandering about the countryside, though in all honesty she had not been aware of it, having slept until Meg returned to the carriage. Though Meg appeared suitably chastised, Rebecca chafed under the additional censure.

"Miss Turnpeck, I do not wish to appear disrespectful, but I am no longer in the schoolroom, and I will admit to no one but Lord Clayborne ringing a peal over me for my conduct. And it was no fault of Meg's, for I urged her to come with me, and would have gone alone had she not. It was my understanding that marriage would offer me the advantage of some freedom from chaperonage." She smiled ruefully at the subdued governess. "I lent the weight of my married state to our little expedition. Not that Clayborne approved, you understand. Far from it. But as he has already combed my hair over the matter, I really do not wish to discuss it further." As they left Guildford behind, having heard Clayborne arrange assistance for the balloonists, Rebecca said, "Now, let us talk about our plans for London."

Seven

Rebecca's stand with the governess greatly surprised her sister. Being a shy and obedient young lady herself, Meg could not imagine speaking so to her governess, but she was much impressed with Rebecca's calm self-possession. Nevertheless, Meg was startled by the change in her sister since the wedding. She found Rebecca, though in her usual healthy good looks, to be more subdued than was her wont. And yet, when Rebecca had told her stories and giggled with her, and skipped stones by the brook, Meg had recognized her sister's old high spirits.

Imps of mischief had danced in Rebecca's eyes when she showed Meg the sketches from the dinner party at Christmas. "These are the Misses Blackwell. I have only slightly exaggerated them, I promise you."

"But why would Jason invite two such formidable ladies for you to entertain? Surely there is more enjoyable company in the neighborhood."

"If so, I haven't met them," Rebecca murmured ruefully. She was not about to tell her sister that Clayborne had carefully chosen his guests for their influence in the neighborhood—for good or ill. When you are attempting to scotch rumors of marital discord, you are very particular about whom you invite. The drawings of Sir John and his wife were placed before Meg. "I understand they have any number of children, but I have not as yet met them."

"Oh? Well, you should make an effort to do so, Becka. They will think you inhospitable. I am surprised Jason has not suggested it."

Rebecca merely nodded and distracted her sister's attention with the drawings of the vicar and Dr. Baker. Inadvertently she had allowed two sketches of Clayborne to accompany these, but she hurriedly whisked them out of sight. Although Meg caught only a brief glimpse of them, her interest was aroused. Knowing full well that Rebecca had not intended her to see them, she said nothing, but her curiosity was too strong for her and she had actually sneaked into her sister's room, feeling many a pang of guilt, to scrutinize these drawings when Rebecca was out riding.

Since Meg was more than a little in awe of his lordship, she had been scandalized by the irreverent way in which her sister had pictured him, once as a toad king of the mountain with a totally forbidding expression, and once seated at a dining table, where his smoldering anger was portrayed as singeing the hair of the footman serving him, while Rebecca herself was a mouse seated far away at the other end of the table. Meg flushed with embarrassment and could not stifle the involuntary "Dear God!" which escaped her lips. There were, in addition, sketches of the servants at Gray Oaks, which were kindly, if amusing, and one of Clayborne gently exploring a horse for splinters, but Meg's eyes had again and again gone back to the first two sketches. She was afraid to think what they might mean and quickly bundled up the lot and returned them to their folder.

Meg was thoroughly perplexed by the sketches, and wished that she understood her sister's situation, but she did not really want Rebecca to confide in her, as she was sure she could not handle anything disagreeable. Since she had been a party to Rebecca's few clandestine meetings with Thomas Burns, she was not sure she believed her sister's protestations that there was no longer any emotion spent there. Rebecca had been sad when Thomas married and Meg's romantic nature led her to imagine that her sister harbored an undying, unrequited love. Perhaps she affected such a belief because her own intense attachment to Will did not enable her to suppose that her love for him would or could diminish regardless of circumstances. On the other hand Rebecca had seemed genuinely fond of Clayborne when they married, though it must be admitted she had not demonstrated a decided *tendre*. For the most part Meg remembered her sister's comments on Clayborne's kindness and intelligence, and Meg herself had been cognizant of these attributes when she had met him prior to the wedding. Now, however, she found him rather distant, and although he exerted himself to entertain them, several of his encounters with her sister which she had happened to observe were censorious. Meg lay awake their first night at Clayborne House pondering these problems, but as her thoughts quite naturally settled on Will, she dismissed her worries and fell asleep, content.

Miss Turnpeck, in her turn, first meditated on the kindly observance paid her by Lord Clayborne at dinner that evening, then became agitated when she remembered Rebecca's firm words to her in the carriage. Rebecca had never been shy and obedient as Meg and Trudy, nor was she so ramshackle as Mary, but she had been high-spirited and independent. Too independent by half, Miss Turnpeck thought, remembering the proud way in which Rebecca had spoken to her that day. Didn't wish to discuss it further, indeed! And yet Miss Turnpeck had been just the tiniest bit pleased, she had to admit grudgingly to herself, that Rebecca was becoming a self-possessed woman. In the past she had been confused by Rebecca's hoydenish ways, yet she of the four daughters had taken a real interest in her studies, surpassing Miss Turnpeck in her desire for knowledge. On numerous occasions Miss Turnpeck had surprised her, comfortably ensconced in the ancient and generally unused Farthington Hall library, perusing any of a number of books, familiarity with which the governess considered unnecessary for a young woman of her position. And some of them no doubt improper, though as Miss Turnpeck was not acquainted with them she could not be sure. Miss Turnpeck tucked her wispy gray hair under a plain nightcap and, noting the extreme comfort of her bed, was soon gently snoring.

Although Rebecca had been to Clayborne House with her mother and Clayborne during her betrothal, she had not spent a night in the house. It was an impressive Palladian residence situated in Berkeley Square and Rebecca found it rather intimidating after the less formal atmosphere of Gray Oaks. She had been considerably startled, on arriving at her suite of rooms, to discover that they had been refurbished. While a housemaid serving as her abigail helped her undress for the night she asked, "Do you know when these chambers were done over?"

"No, my lady. They was this way when I come here after Christmas," the young woman replied shyly.

"What is your name?" Rebecca asked kindly.

"Harpert, my lady."

"Do you like being at Clayborne house?"

"Oh, yes, it's ever so much nicer than my last situation. Such a fine house and his lordship ever so considerate. Once when I was dusting in the library Lord Clayborne come in and saw me looking at pictures of sailing ships in a book. My brother goes to sea and it made me feel good to look at them, you know. So his lordship says I can come to look at them when he's not about, so long as I don't get in trouble with the housekeeper. Now wasn't that nice of him?"

"Yes, indeed. And have you read more about the ships?"

"I can't read, you see, but I do look at the pictures now and again. I should like to know more about them, but the pictures is wonderful."

"Would you like to learn to read?"

"Oh, yes, milady, for you can never be a housekeeper 'less you can read. But there is no one to teach me," she said sadly.

"Perhaps we should surprise your brother when he returns," Rebecca suggested. "I shall spend a half hour a day with you and we shall see how you go on."

"You would do that? But why?" she asked skeptically.

"I believe that women must know a little something to get on. As you said, you could never be a housekeeper if you cannot read. Does your brother know how to read?"

"Yes. My uncle taught him when he was young. He can read anything," she proclaimed proudly.

Rebecca laughed. "And so shall you, Harpert, if you will work at it. Now tell me, when would be the best time for our lessons?"

"We're up early when his lordship is in residence, of course, and there is a bit of a break after breakfast is cleared, milady."

"Tomorrow when I have finished breakfast I shall meet you in the old schoolroom. I am sure there will be plenty of books there for us to use. You need only tell the housekeeper I have asked you to attend me."

"Thank you, milady."

When Harpert had seen her ladyship to bed and assured her that the staff had been pleased to hear that her ladyship was to accompany his lordship this time, she withdrew and left Rebecca to her thoughts. These were not exactly comforting, might in fact have been called mortifying, as Rebecca had not even been aware that Clayborne had been in residence in the house since their marriage. It had occurred to her at Christmas that he must have been in London to have met his Uncle Henry, but she had not pursued the thought, since she was engrossed in drawing some enjoyment from the holiday season. He had obviously been here since then, as Harpert had not even come to Clayborne House by Christmastime. How many times had he been here? How long did he stay? What did he do when he was in London? Rebecca felt angry frustration well up in her. She was in an intolerable position and she must make some decision soon as to her future.

In answer to the light tap on the connecting door between their rooms, she bade Clayborne come in. He entered carrying a candle, his maroon silk dressing gown glowing in the flickers of light, and his lank brown hair was slightly disarrayed.

"I will no doubt have left the house on business before you arise tomorrow," he said stiffly, "and I wished to consult you on arrangements for tomorrow evening."

"Please sit down, Jason. It makes me nervous having

you hover over me with a dripping candle." Rebecca smiled. "I wish to thank you for the changes in my rooms; they are delightful."

"I had them made at the time of our marriage as a surprise for you. I had intended then that we would spend more time here," he remarked reproachfully.

"It would appear," she said, remembering her grievance, "that you have spent no little time here yourself since then and I found it embarrassing to have been in ignorance of the fact."

"I saw no reason to tell you of my visits here."

"And I can see no reason why you should not have. Did you fear that I would beg to accompany you?" she asked bitterly.

"There was no question of that."

"Never mind," she sighed. "What was it you wished to discuss about tomorrow evening?"

Clayborne, relieved to drop the subject, ventured, "I thought you three ladies might enjoy going to the theatre. We could see *Hamlet* with Mr. Kemble at Covent Garden, or would you prefer the opera at Kings Theatre?"

"The play, if it is all the same to you. Miss Turnpeck has voiced her preference on more than one occasion, but frankly I am not sure that she has ever had much of an opportunity to attend either," she mused, adding without thinking, "I shall never become a governess. What a depressing life!"

Clayborne regarded her blankly, then with annoyance. "You forget yourself. You are not a penniless, aging spinster looking for employment. You are my wife."

"Certainly, Jason," she said calmly. "I was merely commenting on the plight of governesses."

Clayborne regarded her suspiciously, then rose to leave. "I shall arrange for Covent Garden." As an afterthought, he said more gently, "Good night, Rebecca."

"Good night, Jason," and enjoy your lonely, self-righteous bed, she thought with a sigh.

The next day passed in a whirl with a lesson for Harpert, shopping for slippers, bonnets, and the odd shawl or fan, interspersed with a side trip to St. Paul's for

Miss Turnpeck. When the most flattering gowns had been chosen, and their hair arranged in the latest Grecian style, the sisters presented themselves to Miss Turnpeck and Clayborne in the drawing room to be whisked off to the theatre. The play was a great success, but during the first intermission Rebecca was surprised to have several acquaintances from her London season visit their box.

Adrienne and Thomas Woods, a couple she and Clayborne had met continually the preceding year, welcomed her back to town with warm assurances that she had been missed. "I thought to see you here in the spring, Lady Clayborne," Mrs. Woods told her. "Your sister seemed to enjoy her season; we saw her at every other ball and breakfast. And I did notice Lord Clayborne on Bond Street one day, but I was not so close as to be able to ask him of you. Have you found the country so entertaining that you have given up on town?"

Although she knew that Mrs. Woods meant no harm with this quizzing, Rebecca felt uncomfortable and looked beseechingly to Clayborne for assistance. Unruffled, he laughed. "Rebecca finds more than enough to do at Gray Oaks. One would think she had waited all her life to decorate the Blue Saloon and have a mare of her own to ride. We are fortunate in having very sociable neighbors, too. Not that our country entertainments can compare with London," he said ruefully. "A picnic on the banks of a brook would not, I fear, appeal to all. And Chichester has never been noted for its elaborate assemblies, though they are better than many I have attended."

Meg regarded Clayborne with astonishment, for one would think from the way he spoke, though he did not precisely prevaricate, that he and his wife had led a life gay to dissipation in the countryside. With a shrug for her sister, Rebecca took her cue from him and elaborated on their life of wedded bliss. "Jason has been very indulgent, you see, Mrs. Woods, allowing me to do over several of the major rooms. I turned his household topsy-turvy, I fear, in my enthusiasm. His uncle visited at Christmas and that meant additional entertaining. What with one thing and another, there just didn't seem an opportunity to get to London this spring," she added, with an impish grin at her husband, "but Jason had to be here a while. It is lonely at Gray Oaks without him, of course, and he insisted that we come with him this time, but for the present I imagine I will spend the majority of my time there."

When Mrs. Woods proceeded to discuss Mr. Brummell's hasty departure from England, Rebecca stole a glance at her husband and found to her surprise that he was smiling almost amiably at her. Though she told herself that the smile was solely for the benefit of their visitors, she could not repress the lump which appeared in her throat and made her able to answer only in the most meager of sentences. How long it had been since he had shown her even the slightest sign of approval! She enjoyed the second act of the play even more than the first.

During the second intermission Captain Gray erupted into the box exclaiming, "Of all famous things, Lady Clayborne! I had no idea you were in town until I ran into Ted this afternoon," he said, airily waving to the man at his elbow, Captain Hardcastle. Recalling himself, he bowed to the other occupants of the box. "Ted has just been telling me how you came to his rescue when his balloon crashed."

"Had a mishap," Captain Hardcastle corrected. "Your servant, Lady Clayborne, and yours, Miss Farthington."

"How is your arm, Captain Hardcastle?" Rebecca asked, noticing that it was in a new sling.

"Broken in two places, I fear, but I have little pain. I'm glad of the opportunity to thank you again for your help, and yours, Lord Clayborne."

"Did you ever hear of anything so crackbrained?" Captain Gray scoffed. "Going for a balloon ride indeed!"

"I am persuaded you are only jealous that you didn't conceive the scheme first, Captain Gray," Rebecca quizzed him.

Captain Gray's moustache twitched as he tried to suppress a grin, but he admitted, "It would be famous sport, though I had rather not break an arm. Clumsy fellow," he mocked his friend.

"No such thing. It is all a matter of wind currents and valves, you know," Captain Hardcastle returned knowingly.

"I read somewhere that when they first tried ballooning in France they first sent up a cock, a sheep, and a duck to be sure it would be safe for a man to fly. When they reached the balloon after its descent they found the sheep grazing and the duck quite all right, but the cock had a slightly damaged wing. The injury to the cock caused a great deal of concern, and it was feared that men should not try this manner of travel, but this fear was laid to rest when several witnesses swore they saw the sheep kick the cock before ever the balloon ascended," Rebecca offered, and tried to look serious.

"Those Frenchies. What a bunch of chuckleheads," Captain Gray scorned.

Captain Hardcastle unconsciously straightened his cravat. "Lady Clayborne, if we might be permitted to call on you tomorrow, I would welcome the opportunity to restore your shawl to you."

"We should be delighted to see you, but we shall be out until teatime, having promised Miss Turnpeck most faithfully that we will take her to see Westminster Abbey tomorrow," Rebecca explained.

"Perhaps we might escort you?" Captain Gray suggested, with a glance at Clayborne.

"An excellent idea," Clayborne agreed. "I shall be occupied for the better part of the day, my dear."

"Shall you? What a pity, for I am sure it is just the sort of expedition you most treasure, darling," Rebecca replied sweetly, her eyes laughing at her husband. "Perhaps another day you shall take us to see the Elgin marbles . . ."

"No doubt." Though his reply was dry, the slight smile which hovered about his lips acknowledged her jest.

Meg did not know whether to be amused or distressed by this interchange, so she ignored it and very prettily accepted the captains' escort for the next day.

Eight

The party which set off for Westminster Abbey was in high spirits. Even Miss Turnpeck's pontifications on the Coronation Chair, the uniquely delicate fan vaulting of Henry VII's chapel and the Limoges enamel work on the Earl of Pembroke's tomb, could not damp the sisters' spirits. While Miss Turnpeck read every inscription on every tomb, with historical asides as to why Edward V was not buried there and Richard III was, Rebecca and Meg enjoyed a lively dalliance with the two captains. Miss Turnpeck was engrossed in her pleasure for a full three hours, and the four young people merely tagged along and created scandalous jokes which defamed the characters of those buried in the Abbey. When they returned to Clayborne House the two gentlemen gladly accepted the invitation to stay to tea.

It was a cozy, laughing group that Clayborne walked in on a while later. He greeted the guests with great affability and remarked, "I need not ask if the expedition was pleasant, for you all seem satisfied. Was the Abbey all you expected, Miss Turnpeck?"

"Dear me, yes. I only wish you could have been there too, Lord Clayborne. Such a sense of history! Such an elegant edifice! The Abbey dates from an eighth century Benedictine abbey converted to a Roman church by Edward in the eleventh century. And the kings and queens who are buried there, you would hardly credit!" she enthused.

"Miss Turnpeck was able to see every one of their

tombs, I assure you," Meg laughed. "We were there for hours. Such a pity you should miss all the fun."

"I regret it," he assured her with a sparkle in his eye. "And I devoting my time to tiresome business matters." Meg was inclined to revise her opinion of him again. He really was a charming man when he wasn't being stern and forbidding with her sister. Whatever could be the problem between them?

"By the by," Clayborne was saying to Rebecca, "I saw Lord Stonebridge at White's and he was kind enough to extend an invitation to their rout on Saturday if we should be free. I understand," he said, turning to the captains, "that you will be there."

"Yes, for he is Ted's brother's father-in-law," Captain Gray replied, adding for Miss Turnpeck's benefit, as she was looking confused, "Ted's older brother is the Earl of Northbank, you know, who married Theodora, Lord Stonebridge's eldest daughter, several years ago. They are in town on their way to Brighton now, and the Stonebridges are having the rout in their honor."

"Oh, Becka, then we shall see Althea, and she is my very dear friend. You will remember that I have spoken to you of her," Meg said.

"That is famous indeed. I shall enjoy a party very much after . . ." Rebecca realized where she was heading and, turning swiftly to her husband, asked, "Shall we still be in town, Jason?"

"I see no reason not to remain a few extra days. It will provide a rare treat for us," he commented laconically.

"If your stay in London is to be short, perhaps we should plan another expedition for Miss Turnpeck," Captain Hardcastle suggested. "No doubt she would enjoy an outing to Hampton Court with a turn through the maze."

His idea was greeted with enthusiasm by the ladies and indifference by Lord Clayborne, who had no intention of joining the party but was not averse to having entertainment provided for his female entourage. Miss Turnpeck launched into an account of Hampton Court and its history, and only when she paused for breath were the young people able to make arrangements for the following day and for the captains to take their leave. When Clayborne had retired to his study and Miss Turnpeck had dropped off into a noisy nap, Meg said, "I do believe Captain Gray is taken with you, Becka. And Captain Hardcastle, too, for the matter of that."

"Pooh. Nothing of the sort. All these soldiers are bored to tears with no action now that Napoleon is banished and you and I are safe companions for them with your talk of Will and Clayborne's presence. But I must say it is agreeable to have such handsome, attentive young men about, is it not?"

"Yes, for though I wish dear Will were in town, certainly the captains are the next best thing."

"We shall have to look out proper outfits for such an expedition, but I am minded to ask Jason if he has a drawing of the maze. It would be above anything to play a trick on them," Rebecca said with a grin.

"How splendid! Do go ask him now."

When Rebecca tapped on the study door, Clayborne's impatient voice bade her enter. "I apologize for the interruption, Jason, but Meg and I wondered if you might have a drawing of the maze."

The book he was reading was put down immediately and he said thoughtfully, "I am sure I have a guidebook somewhere about, and if I remember correctly there is a loose drawing of the maze in it." He rose and went to the bookshelves, where he searched for a few minutes, finally pulling out an old guidebook. As he opened it a slip of paper fell out and he retrieved it, saying wryly, "It's a bit old and dusty, but will no doubt serve your purpose."

"Well, we did perhaps have in mind to play a small prank on the captains."

"Just don't get yourself into mischief, Rebecca."

"Certainly not, my lord. I shall be most conscious of my position and act with the utmost propriety," with which she smirked and flounced out of the room.

Clayborne returned to his chair, annoyed with himself for setting up her back again. He was on the point of retrieving his book when a commotion in the hall drew him forth.

Rebecca stood in the hall looking amazed and anxious. "Good God, Mary! What are you doing here? Why are you not in Bath with Aunt Adeline?"

"Oh, Becka, I am so happy to find you here," her youngest sister cried as she flung herself into Rebecca's arms. "I left directly I had Meg's letter saying you were coming to London, but I did not know how long you would be here."

"Let's discuss this further in the drawing room," Clayborne suggested, making his bow to Mary and shepherding the sisters before him as he spoke. The butler, who maintained a stolidly blank countenance, was instructed to send in more tea and cakes and to arrange for rooms for Mary and her abigail, a young, frightened-looking miss who was trying to obliterate herself in a doorway of the hall.

When the door was closed behind them, and Meg discovered that her younger sister had arrived, there was a renewed outbreak of exclamations, tears, and general disorder. Miss Turnpeck awoke abruptly and gazed on her youngest charge with astonishment.

"Ladies, please be seated," Clayborne commanded in a long-suffering voice. "I am sure Mary will gratify us with an explanation of her sudden advent."

"Well, I will, of course. You see, I came on the stage with Grimms. My abigail, you know," she explained to Clayborne.

"I am delighted to hear that you did not come alone," he murmured ironically.

"But, Mary, *why* did you come?" Rebecca prompted.

"Oh, there was never anything so horrid! Aunt Adeline is stuffy and pious—always reading a Bible to us. Sally is a sneaking, mean-spirited, chicken heart!"

"Miss Mary, you must not speak so of your relations!" expostulated Miss Turnpeck. "It is most unbecoming in you."

"Fiddlesticks! It is no more than the truth. I had rather live in a dungeon than with them in Bath. Aunt Adeline is forever prosing on about her good works and her duty to God, to say nothing of mine, while Sally is flirting with every link boy in town. Disgusting!" Mary growled.

"Miss Mary!" Miss Turnpeck was so shocked that she dug frantically in her reticule for her vinaigrette, which she was sure must be there, as she was never without it.

"There was never anything so wretched. I could not bear to be with them," Mary proclaimed dramatically.

"No doubt," Clayborne said dryly. "Could you not have written to explain your situation?"

"No, I could not," she flared at him. "I would not stay there a minute longer. Sally kept sneaking into my room to catch me reading a novel just so she could tattle on me. A novel! I don't even like reading novels as a rule, but I was so bored that I descended even to that. And her mama would berate me and drag me off to church to be purged of my sin," she said disgustedly. "And then Sally would have it that I was trying to attract the attentions of the young man who lived next door to us, just because *she* was smitten with him. And I did no such thing—the silly-faced fop he was! I would never dream of encouraging such a one," she declared indignantly. "Why, he could not even drive a pair."

Rebecca let out a strangled chuckle, which was met with a reproving glance from Clayborne, so she schooled her face to a solemn look to match his own. "No doubt, my love, but it would have been wiser to write us."

"But you do not know the whole yet! Sally told her mama of this fop and her mama forbade me to go to the party." Mary obviously considered that this clinched the matter, and sat back with some satisfaction.

"And what party was this?" asked Clayborne.

"Well, you know, Aunt Adeline and Sally go nowhere and it is the greatest bore. We sat at home reading the Bible or went to church. We did not go to the Pump Room above twice during the time I was there. And there was to be a young people's party where we were to meet a gentleman who had been driving a mail coach as a lark, and I so wanted to hear all about it. Aunt Adeline had finally agreed that we should go, for she knew nothing of the mail coach driver, of course, and then Sally spoiled that, too, the spiteful little witch."

By now Miss Turnpeck was having a fit of the vapors and Meg and Rebecca were required to pay their attentions to her. Mary shed two large tears in self-pity, and Clayborne stood with his shoulders propped against the mantle, his arms folded, and viewed the scene with ill-concealed irony. "We will need to discuss the matter further, but for the present I suggest, Mary, that you be shown to a room where you can rest from your journey and try to compose yourself. Rebecca, will you please see to it?"

His wife, unable to tell from his tone of voice whether he was deeply annoyed or not, did as he suggested. "Now, Mary," she said, as she escorted her sister into a cheerful room toward the back of the house, "I hope you will calm yourself. You are much too young to go junketing about the countryside like that, and you have upset all of them." She shrugged vaguely in the direction of the drawing room. "But, there, I know you have been sorely distressed and I mean to see you come about. Clayborne will know what to do, you can be sure."

"But he was displeased, wasn't he, Becka?" Mary asked unhappily. "I had nowhere else to go, with Trudy in Suffolk and no one at home at Farthington Hall. I did not mean to make trouble for you," she cried penitently.

"No more have you. I am pleased to have you here and know that you are safe. Do not mind Jason. He gets into the crotchets sometimes, poor dear. He does tend to be a rather high stickler and I fear you have offended his sense of what is proper, but it will not stop him feeling responsible for you, and so he will do what is best," she assured her sister. "Now do lie down for a bit and I shall send a maid to you later. I'm sure your own Grimms will not be up to it yet. I fear you have frightened the poor girl out of her wits." She settled her sister on the bed, kissed her, and drew the covers over her. When the exhausted Mary had fallen asleep, Rebecca crept from the room.

As she had no desire to face either Miss Turnpeck's vapors or Clayborne's tongue, Rebecca repaired to her own room. But there was no evading his lordship, for soon there was a tap on the door and he entered, a worried frown on his brow.

"I *am* sorry for this trouble, Jason. Now you seem to have a full complement of underage Farthingtons, to say nothing of their aging governess."

"I realize it is no fault of yours that brings your sister here," he replied equably.

"What are we to do with her, Jason? We could send her home with Miss Turnpeck, but then Meg would probably have to go, too, and I do not wish to lose her company as yet. Can Mary stay here with us? I cannot imagine what I shall write to Mama. She will be excessively angry, but she will hardly bestir herself from Paris."

"I am willing to have her stay with us, Rebecca, but she is a regular hoyden and is like to be a burden to you. Can you manage her?"

"She is my sister," Rebecca replied stiffly.

"That is little to the case. You are young yourself to have charge of her, and Miss Turnpeck, I can see, will be useless," he remarked dryly.

Rebecca said softly, "I can manage."

"I hope you can. And, Rebecca," he said seriously, "you are to come to *me* with any problems." When she looked skeptical he continued, "Do not imagine that I am an ogre. You are not in the habit of trusting in me, but I am your husband and you should learn to accept my protection, for it will be freely given always, no matter what problems we may have."

An agony of desolation swept through Rebecca, who felt her loneliness sharply at that moment, but she replied evenly, "Thank you, Jason. I shall remember."

Clayborne regarded her sad, downturned face. Gently he lifted her chin and said softly, "Please trust me, Rebecca." He stood there hesitantly for a moment, but merely continued, "I shall write to your parents and your Aunt Adeline apprising them of the situation." Then he touched her cheek and quickly left her.

Wonderingly, she raised a hand to the spot where he had touched her cheek. It was a gesture he had occasionally used before their marriage, and in those days she had taken it as a sign of affection. Why had he done it now? Although he was unbending a bit in public, he continued formal in any private encounter. She sighed and shook her head. No doubt he felt some sympathy for her because of Mary's advent, and the problems it was likely to generate.

Dinner was less than enjoyable that evening, with Miss Turnpeck flushed and scolding, Mary pale and quiet. Clayborne put an end to the scolding by pointedly taking over the conversation himself. There was no hint of reproof in his manner as he directed his remarks kindly to each of the ladies in turn. But Meg continued to look upset and Rebecca could not keep her attention on what her husband was saying. Everyone was delighted to escape early to their rooms, and it was only then that Rebecca remembered the drawing of the maze.

In the chaos of Mary's arrival she must have put it down somewhere, for she could not find it in her reticule or anywhere in her room. She drew a wrapper on over her night dress, took up her candle and walked barefoot to the drawing room. The house was quiet, the servants having retired after the houseparty was settled for the night. In the drawing room Rebecca searched on the tables and under the chairs, finally locating the drawing crushed under a cushion. Plumping up the cushion, she sat down to study the sketch, and noted the delicate female hand with curlicues of embellishment. She was about to put it away when she noticed a line at the bottom which read, "Next time you shall surely find me, Jason." It was signed Alexis. Rebecca grinned, and wondered if he had indeed found her the next time. Only one woman of her acquaintance had the Christian name of Alexis, and that was Lady Hillston. Rebecca had met that dashing young matron during her season last year and she chuckled out loud to picture the straight-laced Clayborne with her.

"Up to some devilment, Rebecca?" Clayborne asked from the doorway, startling her.

"No. It is just this old maze drawing. I found the

note amusing," she laughed, her eyes dancing in the candlelight, as she held it out to him.

When Clayborne had read the note, which he had long since forgotten, he did not share her amusement. In fact, he made to put the drawing in his pocket, thought better of it, and handed it back to her without a word. His face was unreadable in the candlelight, and Rebecca said lightly, "I shall make a copy of it and return it to your study."

"That will not be necessary. Shall Mary go with you to Hampton Court?"

"Yes, if you are agreeable. I am sure it would cheer her, and you must have noticed that all the animadversions she has borne have quite depressed her spirits."

"If they have depressed her willfulness, we will be in luck. But I am not against her going. No doubt she will get in less trouble accompanying us than staying home."

"You come, too?" she asked, surprised.

"I think it would be wise. Would you rather I did not?" He watched her closely in the candlelight.

"No, I think I shall be rather relieved to have you with us," she admitted.

He nodded and said only, "I will see you to your room."

When the party had assembled for Hampton Court there was some discussion as to the driving arrangements. Finally it was decided that Captain Hardcastle, since he was unable to drive with his broken arm, would share the carriage with Meg and Miss Turnpeck, while Clayborne would take Mary and Captain Gray would take Rebecca, in their curricles. As Meg would be just as happy to be nowhere near a horse, this arrangement satisfied everyone, except perhaps Mary, who was still worried about Clayborne's reaction to her arrival.

"I am sorry to have caused you such inconvenience by arriving as I did," Mary ventured timidly as they drove off.

"There is no question of inconvenience, Mary. My concern was more for your safety and reputation, but let us not speak of that any more. I gather you are interested in driving. When we reach open road I have a mind to let you try these bays of mine if you wish to." He smiled down at her.

Mary's face was transfigured with joy. "You cannot mean it!"

"Why, have you never driven a pair before? I made sure you must have."

"And so I have, but never such prime ones as these. I may not be able to manage them," she confessed, "for I have only driven round Farthington Hall in the phaeton with an old pair, and the stable lad had to be much coaxed to allow that. I waited until the coachman had taken Miss Turnpeck and my sister into Salisbury, you know. They don't expect me to accompany them since I have no interest in all their sashes and bonnets," she explained scornfully.

"I see," he said seriously, repressing a smile. "Here, I shall show you how to hold the ribbons, and once I have the edge off them you shall have a try."

Knowing him to be an excellent whip, Mary paid close attention. Clayborne found her an apt pupil and a disarming child, and was much inclined to be more favorably disposed toward her, though he noted that she was more likely to be occupied by pastimes such as riding and driving than those amusements her sisters found enjoyable. She spoke of balls with loathing, and of the theatre as past enduring. It would be no easy matter to keep her busy and out of mischief in the city, he thought wryly.

Captain Gray, undoubtedly encouraged by the sight of Clayborne allowing Mary to handle the ribbons, offered to instruct Rebecca. Since she had never driven even one horse, a pair seemed overmuch, but she was willing to try. After she had nearly ditched them twice, which caused more laughter than alarm, the captain suggested that she desist for the day, and they drove along companionably to Hampton Court.

Upon their arrival Captain Hardcastle emerged from the carriage with a stunned expression on his face, and none of the curricle riders had the least doubt that Miss

92

Turnpeck had once again taken an opportunity to expound on the intricacies of history commonly associated with this famous landmark. After they had made a tour of the palace, Rebecca and Meg, with due gravity, challenged the captains to see who could reach the center of the maze first, and the four set off immediately, while Clayborne proceeded more leisurely with Mary and Miss Turnpeck. They could hear the laughter ahead of them, and calls back and forth for a while, but soon these were rather distant. Growing impatient with the pace kept by Miss Turnpeck, who was actually hurrying more than she thought strictly necessary, her wispy gray hair becoming disordered, Mary led the way, delighted with the blind alleys which caused them to retrace their steps. Clayborne, perhaps wishing to keep Miss Turnpeck out of breath, had set an ambitious pace, but took pity on her and slowed his steps. Soon Mary was out of sight, and when next they came upon her she was returning in the company of Captain Hardcastle.

"He's lost the lot of them," she giggled, throwing him a wicked look. "And I do not think we shall ever reach the center."

"Of course we shall. Take pity on a wounded soldier, ma'am. Come, we shall find it together. I'm certain that it must be very close now." Placing her hand ceremoniously on his uninjured arm, they strolled off together. Clayborne and Miss Turnpeck listened to her artless chatter (she recounted her driving lesson), and followed close behind. They could hear other voices now, and soon came upon the rest of their party.

"Pooh, it is nothing," Rebecca was saying, while Captain Gray and Meg hovered over her. "Do cease this fussing."

"Oh, Jason, Becka has twisted her ankle," Meg cried when she caught sight of him.

"I tell you it is fine. I shall be right as a trivet in no time. And we won!" Rebecca announced.

"I'm not surprised," Clayborne responded dryly. "Let me have a look at your ankle."

"I will not have any fuss," she whispered fiercely to him as he knelt beside her, taking the foot in his hand.

"There is little the matter with it, and I am sure I shall be able to walk in a moment."

"There is nothing broken, in any case," he announced after probing gently with his fingers. "What has put you in such a taking?"

"I do not wish to spoil our day," she said firmly, but her lip quivered as she looked reproachfully at the swelling ankle.

"You cannot walk on it," he stated rather than questioned. "Well, that will not spoil our day. I can carry you back to the carriage, and we can still have our meal at the Mitre in Twickenham as we had planned."

"Carry me!" she exclaimed, horrified. "No such thing. Just lend me your cane and I shall manage."

Clayborne laughed at her horrified expression and said, "All right. Try the cane first, though I would not pinch you if I carried you," he promised.

"More's the pity," she retorted saucily, as he assisted her to rise. When she attempted to put her weight on the ankle she gave a gasp of pain, but determinedly grasped the cane and attempted a few halting steps. Clayborne stood, hands on hips, regarding her mockingly.

"My dear, I am afraid you lose after all," he announced and scooped her up into his arms. He proceeded to lead the party out of the maze, guided by Meg, who shamefacedly produced the drawing to give them directions amidst cries of "Unfair!" from the captains.

Rebecca felt herself blushing, much to her chagrin, and announced to her husband, "I feel most undignified. Are you sure it is quite proper for you to carry me about this way?"

"It is expedient," he declared. "Now you must not expect me to talk to you for your weight is quite making me puff," he said, smiling down at her.

"Wretch! I shall pay you back for that."

"No doubt." Then he grew more serious, saying, "Rebecca, your sister Mary is a charming child, but we shall have to give some special thought to keeping her amused in town. I gather she has a deal more affection for horses than people, generally." He continued after a slight pause, "My sister was like that."

"Your sister? I have never heard you speak of her, though Mrs. Lambert has."

"She died several years ago in childbirth. Have I never mentioned her? I was very fond of Caroline. Her husband and son live near my Yorkshire estate, much retired. I think he has never quite got over her death."

"And your nephew? What is he like?"

Clayborne grinned. "I'm fond of the little tyke. He's four by now. I saw him last fall when I was at Easingwold. He wanted to know all about you." This brought a frown of recollection, and an end to their easy badinage. "You will be most comfortable in the carriage, I think," he observed as they approached their vehicles.

"Would you do something for me, Jason?" Rebecca asked, mischievously.

Clayborne deposited her gently against the squabs and looked doubtful. "What?"

"Would you take Miss Turnpeck up with you? Just to the inn, you know. I am sure she would be thrilled, and it is not so very far, after all," she pressed, demurely. As the others had reached the carriage by now, Rebecca called, "Miss Turnpeck, Jason thought you might enjoy a short turn in his curricle, just to the Mitre, you know."

Miss Turnpeck flushed with pleasure, and turned an adoring look on Clayborne. "You are so thoughtful, my lord. I should dearly love a ride in such a handsome vehicle."

"Vixen," he murmured to Rebecca, then climbed down from the carriage and gallantly handed Miss Turnpeck into the curricle. Captain Gray took up Mary and the party set off for the Mitre to partake of a much needed repast. With a chuckle Rebecca settled back in the carriage and glanced at Meg.

"Really, it is too bad of you, Becka," her sister protested, laughing. "I have never seen such an expression on Clayborne's face as when you called to Miss Turnpeck. Had he agreed?"

"Not exactly, but I am sure he was about to. Could he deny me such a small favor?"

"Small!" Captain Hardcastle exclaimed. "I have never in my life endured such a chatterbox as on the journey down. It was absolutely wicked of you, Lady Clayborne," he scolded gleefully.

"Do you suppose," Meg asked with great solemnity, "that he will teach her to drive his pair?"

"I regret that I didn't suggest it to him," Rebecca said, disappointed. "Meg, you should have done so. It would have made our day."

"Yes, but now he will be in a temper, Becka, and very displeased with you."

"No, I don't think so, for he is scrupulously fair by his own lights and I was only repaying him for a most ungracious comment on my person," Rebecca laughed.

So the three of them drove contentedly to the inn, where they joined the others for a gay meal of roasted leg of mutton, boiled ham, chicken, beans, boiled plum pudding, potatoes, gooseberry tarts and raspberries with cream. Clayborne was his most urbane, and gallant to Miss Turnpeck, though he insisted that she should ride in the carriage for their return, as it would be too chilly a drive for her in the curricle. He took Rebecca aside as they were departing and declared, "Most unhandsome of you, madam," but his eyes were smiling and he said, "She enlightened me on the history of Twickenham—did you know Pope lived there?—and I assure you nothing could be of less interest to me."

"Your just desserts, sir."

"How is your ankle now?"

"It is sore, but I can walk with the cane and I am sure it will be healed in a day or so. I shall dance at Lord Stonebridge's."

"I am delighted to hear it. Do not neglect to save a dance for me—the first waltz, perhaps?"

"Certainly. I shall be honored, my lord." She made to sweep him a curtsey, but she sighed with a jab of pain from the ankle. At a gleam in his eye, she knew he was threatening to carry her to the carriage once again, and said firmly, "No, no. I assure you I can walk now. Just give me your support and I shall be fine." They left thus companionably for the carriage and Meg heaved a sigh of relief as she watched them go. She found his lordship's temper rather erratic and was pleased that the pair seemed to be getting on better, even after Rebecca's joke on her husband. Though Meg herself had not the slightest desire to play a prank on Will, she was happy to see Rebecca cheerful again. In fact, Meg felt so in charity with Clayborne that she agreed to drive back with him, since Rebecca would need to rest her ankle in the carriage and Captain Gray had claimed Mary.

Aware tht Meg was not fond of horses or sporting vehicles, Clayborne kept to an unhurried pace and skillfully directed the conversation to topics of interest to her. She was totally unaware of the information he obtained from her regarding Rebecca's younger days, merely pleased that he should show such a marked interest in herself and her sister and life at Farthington Hall. Satisfied with their discussion, Clayborne assured himself that his growing tendency to subtly obtain information about his wife was not underhanded spying but necessary circumspection. If she would not tell him the truth, he had every right to find it out for himself. And when he confronted her with it . . . well, then perhaps she would admit her fault and they might come to some understanding at last. Carrying her to the carriage had been very unsettling.

Nine

Mary was chatting gaily with Captain Gray when they entered Clayborne House but she let out a gasp on sight of her Aunt Adeline and Cousin Sally. Her aunt glowered at her, and her cousin sniggered behind her mother's voluminous black bombazine gown. When she took in this sight, Rebecca halted at the doorway of the drawing room, turned swiftly to Captain Hardcastle and said softly, "I think we had best withdraw our invitation to tea for today. There is like to be a family . . . discussion just now." Her eyes were cast heavenward and she extended her hand in farewell.

"Certainly, Lady Clayborne. We should not be imposing further; you will need to rest your ankle." He tugged at Captain Gray's sleeve, gave him a speaking look which his friend immediately responded to, and they took themselves off, much to Meg and Clayborne's surprise, as they had just entered the house.

"Aunt Adeline is here," Rebecca informed her husband succinctly, while Meg's eyes widened in horror, and Miss Turnpeck, declaring that she was thoroughly exhausted, took herself off to her room.

Clayborne accepted this intelligence with equanimity and preceded his wife into the drawing room, where Mary and her relations were eyeing one another with silent hostility. "Ah, Mrs. Rotham and Miss Rotham, so nice to see you again," he remarked courteously with a bow. "Won't you be seated? Rebecca will ring for tea."

The ladies responded coolly to his reception, barely greeting Rebecca and Meg at all. But Rebecca seated herself, and they were forced to do likewise. Mrs. Rotham was working herself up to a denunciation of her late guest when Clayborne interceded smoothly. "I collect you could not have received my letter as yet. Mary arrived here safely yesterday afternoon and has kindly agreed to stay with us until Meg and Miss Turnpeck return to Farthington Hall. I am sure she will wish to take this opportunity to express her apologies for causing you any distress by her unexpected departure." He glanced lazily over at Mary, who had no such desire, but met his eyes steadily and murmured, still looking at him, "I am sorry if I caused you upset, Aunt." She then lowered her eyes and remained silent, while her aunt puffed and steamed.

"Well, I never! Ungrateful child! How dare you take off in such a wild, undisciplined manner? Causing your cousin and me such palpitations and fears, to say nothing of the inconvenience, discomfort and expense of a journey to London!" Mrs. Rotham had a great deal more to say, but Clayborne interrupted.

"Indeed, it was very wrong and unthinking of the child, but as you see she has come to no harm, and we are pleased to have her with us."

"I have come to take her back with me," Mrs. Rotham announced frigidly.

"That is kind of you, ma'am, but it will not be necessary. I have written to her parents to explain that she will be remaining with us and there is no need to put yourself out any further over the matter. Would you not like to be shown to a room to refresh yourselves from your journey? We do not dine for several hours yet and I feel sure you would welcome a rest," Clayborne concluded with his most charming smile.

Mrs. Rotham was not entirely pacified, but she had a great desire to see more of Clayborne House. Sally had left off her sniggering and was looking uncomfortable, while Mary continued to peruse the hands lying in her lap. The advent of the tea tray was greeted with relief. Rebecca said, "Meg, will you help me pour out? I am sure Aunt Adeline and Sally would welcome a cup of tea before they go to their rooms."

Meg, who found herself speechless in such circumstances, agreed to assist her sister. She smiled hesitantly at her aunt and cousin as she passed them their cups, and they unbent slightly. Encouraged, she offered, "We have had the most lovely day at Hampton Court, going through the palace and the maze. Have you been there?"

A lukewarm conversation ensued and Mrs. Rotham and Sally eventually departed for the rooms which had been prepared for them. Mary turned to Clayborne and said simply, "Thank you, Jason."

"I have to admit that it did not occur to me that they would follow you. Very resourceful, your aunt. Did you leave her a note saying you were coming here?"

"Well, yes, I had to say something. I could not just leave without a word. But now Sally will miss the party," Mary proclaimed, with an unsuccessful attempt to look penitent.

"You imp!" Rebecca exclaimed. "I do believe you are pleased about it."

"And so should you be, if you had had to live with that . . . that girl for a few weeks!"

"No doubt," Clayborne agreed dampingly. "I shall send them home in the traveling carriage tomorrow, but I hope you will all endeavor to make their stay . . . pleasant."

Grateful for her husband's handling of the situation, Rebecca replied with due gravity, "You may be sure, Jason, that we shall. I'll speak to the cook now."

"It might be wise," he suggested, "if you sent notes round to Captain Gray and Captain Hardcastle to see if they would join us for dinner and the evening. It's short notice, of course, but if they could come it would prove a useful distraction." He helped himself to a pinch of snuff and eyed her ruefully.

"Yes, I see what you mean, and we had no other plans for this evening. Poor Jason. It has become overwhelming, hasn't it?" Rebecca rose, forgetting her ankle, and winced slightly.

"On the other hand," Clayborne offered smoothly, "you may not be up to entertaining this evening. We have had a busy day and your ankle is still causing you some difficulty, I see."

"Pooh! I would not allow such a minor inconvenience to hamper me," she replied stoutly. "Meg will help me, won't you, dear?"

"Certainly, Becka," Meg responded promptly, rising to go to her sister. "The captains did not speak of any engagements this evening, so we may be in luck. Shall I see to some card tables being set out?"

"Do you suppose Aunt Adeline indulges in whist?" Rebecca mused.

Her sister giggled. "If not we can always get out the lottery tickets."

Mary, who had been sitting silent through this exchange, finally spoke. "Oh, she plays cards all right. And Sally cheats."

"Such admirable relations you have," Clayborne murmured as he replaced his snuff box.

Rebecca determined to ignore this comment. Instead she enlisted her youngest sister's help with the arrangements, and the ladies left Clayborne to ponder how he would entertain six ladies alone if the captains were unable to attend. He was not beset with this problem, however, as both accepted within the hour.

When the whole party had assembled for dinner, Rebecca felt reasonably satisfied with the gathering: Clayborne was being charming, the captains were in high spirits, Meg was attempting to draw out her cousin, and Mary, never one to sulk for long—and anxious to show Clayborne that she could behave—chatted with everyone indiscriminately. Mrs. Rotham and her daughter were flattered with the attention they received, impressed by Clayborne House and looked forward to their return journey in Clayborne's carriage with a mixture of awe and snobbery. Though Miss Turnpeck had persisted in proclaiming her fatigue, she had allowed that she might join them later in the evening, after she had enjoyed a tray in her room and rested a trifle longer.

Although the seating of necessity left Rebecca somewhat out of the general conversation, she watched the others with amusement.

Sally fluttered her eyelashes at Captain Hardcastle

and purred, "Oh, my dear sir, you were at Waterloo? You must be so very brave!"

The brave captain gallantly protested. "Not a bit, Miss Rotham. It is Captain Gray who performed great feats of courage."

But Captain Gray was ambitiously endeavoring to charm Mrs. Rotham, and did not respond to this attempt to divert him. "I have had the pleasure of being in Bath only thrice, ma'am, and not for many years. But the last time I was there I happened to arrive on a fast day, for the old king's health, I believe. After riding for hours, and calmly expecting to have a decent meal in Bath, for I had forgotten the fast day entirely, I arrived to find I could not get so much as a turnip."

"We are very strict in our observance, Captain Gray, and it does my heart good to hear that you found God-fearing innkeepers, so ready to disoblige a patron in spite of the profit they might have had."

Although it had not been Captain Gray's intent to warm the cockles of her heart with his discomfort, he decided that he now had her measure and proceeded to recall every Sunday service he had ever attended which might have some interest to her. Clayborne lifted a quizzical brow but followed Captain Gray's lead, and Rebecca caught snatches of his voice discussing the vicar's theories on Sunday school classes. Now and again he glanced at her, an unfathomable look in his eyes, and when she rose to lead the ladies from the room he gave her an encouraging smile. Strengthened, she was able to sit with her aunt and cousin talking of their activities in London, since so many of them had been worthy owing to Miss Turnpeck's presence.

Meg was induced to play the pianoforte when the men rejoined them, while her sisters sang and Sally was heard to say, "I am myself rather accomplished on the pianoforte, Captain Hardcastle, but I would never put myself forward in a group where my talents would outshine those of others. No, no, I shall not play this evening."

When they had all sat down to cards, with Mrs.

Rotham protesting that, "I take a hand now and then to be sociable," Clayborne noted that Sally did indeed cheat, and he grinned at Mary, who acknowledged this with a wide, conspiratorial wink. Needing just another nibble before bed, Miss Turnpeck joined them as the tea tray was brought in.

Mrs. Rotham was proclaiming, "I never have been much interested in London. Bath is so much more genteel and quiet."

Mary could not resist a grimace, but Clayborne replied easily, "In addition to which there are the waters and the baths. We can lay no claim to such health-inducing properties in London."

Delighted that her aunt seemed to have no desire to spend more time in London, and would no doubt happily climb into Clayborne's carriage in the morning, Rebecca encouraged her aunt to talk of Bath and her home.

"I should very much like to visit Bath one day," Miss Turnpeck contributed. "I have read so much about the crescents and the Pump Room. Mr. Wood created a most magnificent scheme, I understand. And the Abbey; I should dearly love to see the Abbey!"

"Indeed," Mrs. Rotham said coldly, eyeing Miss Turnpeck askance, as though the governess had wandered into the wrong room. Miss Turnpeck was thereby silenced so effectively that even Captain Hardcastle took pity on her and attempted to engage her in hearty conversation.

Ignoring this slight to herself, Mrs. Rotham announced grandly, "We must make an early start in the morning. Come, Sally, we should be getting to our rest."

"Oh, Mama, it is early yet. I wish to stay with the others." Her eyes traveled provocatively to Captain Hardcastle.

"Nonsense, child. Make your curtsey."

Sally sulked but her mother would brook no argument, so she simpered prettily for the captains and allowed herself to be led reluctantly from the room. There was a moment of silence when the door closed behind them, and then an audible sigh of relief.

Rebecca turned to Captain Gray. "I cannot tell you

how grateful we are that you could join us this evening."

He responded with his boyish grin. "Always pleased to be of service, Lady Clayborne. We should be off, if you have to speed your departing guests in the morning. I say, your ankle's all right now, is it?"

"Very well. I have no trouble walking on it, and the swelling is almost gone."

As he rose, Captain Hardcastle gave her his hand and made her promise a dance at the Stonebridge rout. Captain Gray, not to be outdone, made both Meg and Rebecca promise a dance, and the two young men departed to see a bit more of the night before they eventually sought their beds at first light.

The others started to drift toward their rooms, but Rebecca had a wordless signal from her husband to remain behind. "I can understand now why Mary escaped them," he confided with a grimace. "Will you have a glass of wine with me?"

Surprised, Rebecca nodded and seated herself on an oval-backed, serpentine-seated chair. Clayborne poured two glasses from the decanter brought in with the tea tray, and crossed the room to hand one to her. Not entirely at ease but attempting to appear so, he seated himself on a matching chair beside her while Rebecca sipped her wine and waited for him to speak. She noted that his brown eyes were soft and luminous in the glow of the candles. My God, he is going to try to seduce me, she thought, panicked.

"I think the evening went very well," he finally commented. "But I am thankful that your aunt has no desire to stay on here. It will be several days before the carriage is back in town to return us to Gray Oaks. You will not mind staying on, will you?" he asked softly.

"Of course not, Jason," she replied, a slight feeling of breathlessness overtaking her.

He smiled, a warm, tender smile, and took her free hand. Why is he doing this? she thought, even as his touch made her understand. "You look charming tonight, my dear," he murmured as he turned the hand palm upward and kissed it lingeringly.

Rebecca restrained a frightened impulse to withdraw her hand and found herself unable to meet his eyes. "Thank you, Jason."

He set his wine glass down, retained her hand, and with the other tentatively touched her cheek. To her annoyance, she felt herself blushing. He lightly brushed her brow, her eyelids, her lips, with his fingertips and she was no longer able to keep her eyes from his face. There was a tap at the door.

His right hand dropped from her face but he retained his hold on her hand. "Come in."

The butler, eyes firmly locked on the tea tray, asked, "Shall I clear, milord?"

"Yes, but leave the wine, and that will be all for the night."

The intrusion was brief. There was a dimming of the light in the room as the candles at the other end were extinguished. The rustle of the tea tray was quickly succeeded by the quiet closing of the door. Rebecca had not taken her eyes from her husband's face, nor he from hers. Her cheeks were enchantingly flushed.

Clayborne's hair had fallen across his forehead and his eyes were gentle. "Would you like more wine?"

"Yes, please, Jason."

He seemed reluctant to release her hand, but rose and brought the decanter over to refill her glass and his, setting it down on the semicircular side table with its kingwood veneer. Rebecca hesitantly lifted the glass and took a small sip as he reseated himself and pulled his chair closer to her own. She had placed her hand on the chair arm, and he repossessed it; his thumb gently stroked the back of it, his fingers warm on her palm. Ignoring his wine, Clayborne reached out to trace the shape of Rebecca's face, her upturned nose, the column of her long neck. In a trance she watched him remove the wine glass from her limp hand and set it down on the side table. He drew her to her feet and enfolded her in his arms, allowing her head to rest against his shoulder for a while before he lifted her chin so that her face was raised to his and slowly he lowered his head to kiss her forehead, her nose, her lips. At first Rebecca tried to think about what was happening, what the consequences would be. But after a moment her mind refused to function at all and she merely responded to the longing kisses she was receiving; gentle, passionate, lingering by turn, until she felt dizzy and clung to him helplessly.

Clayborne picked her up in his arms and strode with her to the door. He managed to open it without relinquishing his hold on her, while Rebecca nestled her head against his chest and refused to think. "Will your maid be waiting up for you?" he asked as they approached her suite.

"I told her not to, but I'm afraid she will."

"My man won't be. May I take you to my room?"

Rebecca could not see his face in the dark, and he could not see her nod, but he could feel it. There was a dim light from the fire in the room when they entered. She had never seen the room before, as her mother had shunned it on their tour of the house during the engagement. Clayborne sat down with her on his lap in a Hepplewhite winged chair and began to stroke her silky black hair. Releasing it from its combs, he allowed it to flow down her back, following it with his fingers. He began to unfasten her gown under the hair.

Rebecca clung to him, her arms about his waist. "Jason?"

"Yes, little one?"

"I'm . . . afraid."

The hands paused at her back and he studied her face in the flickering glow. "There is nothing to be afraid of," he said huskily. "I will not hurt you."

"Oh, Jason, I know that." Tears formed in her eyes and she blinked them away rapidly. "If you . . . if we . . . You are going to be so angry with yourself in the morning." When he did not speak, but merely regarded her intently, she removed her hands from about his waist and folded them in her lap. "You know you are."

"I don't care," he finally told her stubbornly, his hands again working at the fastenings.

With a sigh Rebecca replaced her arms around his waist and leaned her head against his chest. After a moment her gown was dexterously removed, and then her chemise. There was a sharp intake of breath from her husband and then his firm, warm hands were caressing her—her shoulders, her waist, her hips, her breasts. She lay quietly, shyly in his arms, a strange warmth starting to invade her body. His lips brushed her hair while he murmured soft, incoherent words. Then he lifted her and carried her to the bed.

Standing there above her, entranced, he began to loosen his cravat, his eyes roaming over her body. Why shouldn't he have her? She was his wife. And ever since he had held her, carried her, earlier in the day, the desire for her had grown until it overwhelmed him. She looked so vulnerable, the big eyes still overmoist, but softened with an awakening desire, trusting him. We could lead a normal, married life, he told himself firmly. But her voice haunted him—"you will be so angry with yourself in the morning." And he would be, he knew it. Angry that he had given in to his desire, that he had not kept her at the distance he intended.

Clayborne was now stripped to the waist, and he seated himself on the bed to remove his shoes. He reached over to run a finger along his wife's lips, and Rebecca recognized the moment of decision on his face as he leaned over to pick up the dressing gown his man had laid out for him. His voice came gently. "You are right, little one. Forgive me." Then he bundled her small frame into his long dressing gown and walked with her to the connecting door. "Rebecca?"

"I understand," she whispered sadly. "I'll go in alone, please, Jason."

He nodded, anguished, and watched her disappear silently through the door. Returning to where her clothes lay in a heap on the floor he began, slowly, to pick them up and smooth out the wrinkles. How was it that she could understand how he would feel in the morning? Why was it that she had stopped him for *his* peace of mind? If she was so sensitive to his feelings, why in God's name would she not admit that she had slept with another man? She need not even ask his forgiveness; he was ready to allow her to arrange that matter with her own conscience. But he could not live with the lie between them! Remembering their discussion on the road to town, he thought, I don't want you to be humble and apologetic, only honest with me, and somehow I will learn to live with the rest. Damn it, that's not asking so much, is it?

In her room Rebecca woke the dozing Harpert and sent her off. When the maid had left, she climbed into bed, still in the dressing gown. He had been so gentle with her, so . . . loving. Perhaps all men were like that when they tried to seduce their wives. No, she thought not. Men could have their wives whenever they wished, her mother had said, but Clayborne was not like that. If he wished to sleep with his wife, he would be kind. And for close to a year he had *not* chosen to sleep with his wife. Why now? Was his desire roused by their continually being together? And would it one day overcome his scruples? Rebecca *almost* hoped that it would. Somehow it indicated that his disgust for her had diminished. He was far too proud to sleep with her if he loathed her, she felt sure. And he had smiled at her sometimes these last few days. Was he softening in his attitude toward her? She hugged the dressing gown about her and fell asleep.

In the morning Rebecca and Clayborne stood side by side at the doorway to wave farewell to her aunt and cousin. They watched Mrs. Rotham settle herself smugly on the comfortable squabs and sigh, while Sally remembered the party she had missed in Bath the previous evening and glowered. Rebecca turned to him when the carriage was out of sight and smiled hesitantly. "Well, that is that. Meg and I have some shopping to do for the rout tomorrow. Mary doesn't want to come with us, so she will have to find something here to amuse herself."

Clayborne could think of little to say to her. The vision of her in his bedroom the night before seemed implanted on **his** mind. "Is your ankle satisfactory this morning?"

"Yes, it's fine. Can we pick up anything for you while we're out?"

"No, thank you. I cannot think of a thing."

Ten

While the sisters shopped, Meg, in her simple pleasure that things seemed to be going better with her sister's marriage, managed to convey most of the conversation she had had the previous day with Clayborne. Rebecca was amused and chagrined at once, for it immediately occurred to her that Clayborne was seeking information on a possible lover in her background. Trying to rattle any skeletons in my closet, she thought. Will he never come to believe me? Unhappily she thrust all thought of him from her and entered her sister's enthusiasm for a pair of white kid gloves with bows at the elbows.

Mary was not the least put out that she was too young to attend the rout, but since her sisters were busy with shopping and Miss Turnpeck had gone off to visit her own sister, she found herself with time on her hands. Clayborne felt sorry for her as she wandered aimlessly about the house and offered to take her to the park for a driving lesson. Overconfident in her enthusiasm, Mary nearly sideswiped a high-perch phaeton which pulled up directly, while its occupant imperiously beckoned to Clayborne. He excused himself to Mary, ordered the groom to stand at the horses' heads and strode over to the other vehicle.

The lady therein, dressed in the most elegant and revealing semi-mourning Mary had ever seen, did not trouble to lower her voice as she mocked, "Playing nursemaid, Jason?"

Clayborne bowed and took her hand, which he conveyed to his lips and let go. "My wife's sister, Mary

Farthington. She is in town with us for a few days." Although he lowered his voice, Mary, now very interested in the conversation, strained her admirable hearing to catch his next words. "Alexis, I have not seen you in months, not since Gerald died. How are you?"

"His family are smothering me. I cannot take a step without their being aware of it," she complained petulantly. "God, I could almost wish he had not died, if I am to suffer this much longer." She ignored his frown to continue, "But his mother is at last taking herself off tomorrow, and his sisters I can handle myself. I've never seen such a batch of teary-eyed dullards, with Gerald in his grave these six months past. Today is the first they have countenanced my driving in the park, and they would not hear of my doing so at the fashionable hour, of course!" Her voice softened. "I have missed you, Jason. When can we meet?"

Clayborne cast a hurried glance toward the curricle, but Mary was pointedly practicing with the whip. "Drive in the park tomorrow at the same time. I shall be here. I cannot stay longer now." With his voice raised to a normal level, he took his leave to return to Mary. His distraction was more than evident to her, however, as he completely forgot that they were in the middle of a driving lesson and took the reins and whip from her automatically to drive straight home.

Much disturbed by this incident, Mary nevertheless scorned talebearers and decided to make no mention of it. To be sure, Rebecca is better off not knowing, she thought sadly. And such a rival to have! *Far* too old to be wearing such revealing clothes. How dare she call me a child? I turned seventeen months ago and she would probably give her eye teeth to be my age again. Mary sniffed disdainfully as she went to her room to change for tea.

There were link boys to light the carriages on the gravel drive, a red carpet flowed up the entry stairs, and hundreds of dots of candlelight flickered in all the windows. Rebecca felt elegant in a white sarcenet tunic dress with a key design in scarlet, the robe crossing her bosom alluringly low, and Meg looked charming in a pale blue, long-sleeved jaconet gown, embroidered with tiny pink rosebuds and edged with lace ruffles. Clayborne had complimented them both with exquisite gallantry and Meg could tell that Rebecca was pleased.

The party was warmly greeted by Lord and Lady Stonebridge, and Meg and their daughter Althea fell into each other's arms as though they had not seen each other for a year, instead of a month. In the crowded salon they were immediately besieged by old and new friends, including the two captains. Reminding Rebecca of her promise of the first waltz, Clayborne strolled off to some acquaintances of his own and was soon lost from sight, not to be seen again until his dance approached.

"It is astonishing what an hour at such a function will reveal," Rebecca confided when they were effortlessly drifting along. "Here we have been in London some five or six days, and did you know I had not heard that Lady Doolittle has purchased a new phaeton, nor that Lord Carlisle has acquired his fourth wife? I feel sadly remiss and shall probably spend the better part of the evening catching up on the latest *on dits.*"

"I cannot see when you will find the time. You haven't missed a dance so far, I'm sure," Clayborne remarked lazily.

"Well, that's no problem. Most of my information has come from my partners. Not that they would gossip, you understand. Far be it from them. They have merely heard, and wonder if I have, that so-and-so has lost his fortune at the gaming tables and has had to sell his cattle to raise the wind for something or other." She giggled.

"Rebecca, how much champagne have you had?" he asked suspiciously.

"I do not recall, my lord. Should you like me to figure it out for you?" she asked pertly.

"Please do."

"Let me see. Captain Hardcastle brought me a glass just before the first set. But I did not finish it, you know, and it was gone when I returned. Mr. Trimble brought me a glass just after the quadrille. I did finish that, and a footman refilled it for me. When that was gone Captain

Gray felt sorry for me and lifted another from a passing footman. I should think that is all. No, wait. Just a moment ago Meg handed me a glass as she went off somewhere and I believe I drank it, too."

"My God," he exclaimed, appalled, "you must be half-sprung."

"I don't think so, sir. I feel marvelous."

"No doubt," he retorted dampingly.

"I seem to have no trouble waltzing," she informed him, peering owlishly up into his troubled face.

"Pride goeth before a fall," he declared pompously, but his eyes belied this sternness. "Come, I will find you a seat a bit away from all the racket and bring you a cup of coffee or tea, if I can find one."

"You know, I *am* feeling the least bit dizzy. Perhaps you are right," she admitted handsomely. He laughed and directed her to a seat in an adjoining room, where she gladly seated herself and wondered how her legs could have stopped taking orders from her. "I will be back directly I find you something less stimulating to drink than champagne," he said, and she nodded slowly, as she tried to focus on his departing figure.

When the dizziness began to pass, she realized that she was able to comprehend the dialogue between two dowagers on the other side of the doorway, who were obviously not aware of her presence.

"I tell you I saw her in the park with him this very day. And not at the fashionable hour. I had the coachman take us through the park, as my youngest girl was feeling ill from the heat and crowds in the silk warehouse, and I thought it would do her good, you know. Not that it did," she said with some asperity. "For we had to stop for her to be sick all the same. And there were Clayborne and Alexis having a very cozy *tête-à-tête*." She laughed and nudged her companion.

Rebecca tried to escape but her legs would not support her, and she sank back into the chair, wanting to cover her ears, but unable to force herself not to listen.

"Terribly ironic, I think. After hanging about her for five years like a whipped puppy, he finally married that young chit," the other dowager remarked, "and then

114

Hillston up and pops off within five months. Ridiculous to die of measles at his age. He couldn't have been more than thirty-five or so. Hillston's mama has kept Alexis tight to her side since then, but I hear the old dragon left for the North this morning."

"Did she indeed? Then no doubt Alexis will soon find her way back into society, for she is not one to hide her light under a bushel, so to speak." And the two ladies laughed and proceeded to discuss Brummel's flight from England.

Rebecca now felt very ill indeed. Her head throbbed and her stomach curdled, her cheeks were white and her mind refused to operate. In a daze she watched Clayborne approach her, balancing a plate and cup in the most natural manner. In slow motion she watched him set down his burden, take her hand and peer anxiously at her.

"You look very ill, Rebecca. Shall I send for the carriage?"

"It is early," she answered numbly. "Perhaps if I could lie down for a while." Her large eyes burned with unshed tears.

"It would be better to go home. Come, I shall help you up."

"Just see me to a room where I may rest for a while. I do not wish to go home yet."

Clayborne supported her to the hall where a maid led them to a retiring room and offered to bring her a cool cloth for her forehead. When Clayborne had her settled on the bed, the maid returned with the cloth, and he thanked and dismissed her before stroking back Rebecca's hair from her forehead to place the soothing cloth there.

"Leave me now. I shall return to the ballroom after a bit," she said dully.

"I shall stay with you for a while."

"Leave me *now*, Jason," she commanded quietly.

Clayborne eyed her speculatively, but obeyed. She lay numb in the silent room, refusing to allow the tears to come, her eyes locked unseeing on the French floral wallpaper opposite the bed. Some time later there was a light tap at the door but she did not answer. The door was pushed open slowly and Meg peered anxiously in.

"Jason said you were feeling poorly, Becka. Can I get you something?"

"I am better now. If you will assist me with my hair, I shall come straightaway. I fear I have sadly crumpled my dress."

"Oh, no, it will shake right out," Meg protested, wary of the remote look in her sister's eyes. "Are you sure you would not rather go home now? Do not stay because of me."

"I shall return to the party," Rebecca said firmly, rising from the bed and proceeding to the mirror. "I fear I had a bit too much champagne, but the dizziness has passed." She smiled at Meg's concerned look. "Really, Meg, I am the biggest goose. I even drank the glass you handed me."

When the sisters returned to the ballroom, Rebecca smiled and chatted with acquaintances but felt completely numb. She had not the slightest difficulty in maintaining this state through the entire evening. When Clayborne inquired after her health, she assured him that she was completely recovered. When Captain Gray, Lord Beavens, Captain Hardcastle and Sir Paul Barton requested dances, she conducted herself exactly as was expected of her. When Mr. Carson took her in to supper, she ate with good appetite. And when she was at length in her room at Clayborne House she instructed Harpert to bring her hot chocolate and breakfast in bed the next morning at eleven. Then she turned over and went immediately to sleep. She did not hear Clayborne enter to assure himself of her well-being nor feel his hand on her hair as he bid her sleep well.

In the morning she awoke with a slight headache and a general feeling of heaviness about her body, but she instructed Harpert to lay out her riding habit and to inform the groom that she would ride in half an hour. In addition Harpert was instructed to tell her sister Mary that she would be riding and would welcome her sister's companionship. Then she dismissed the maid and dressed herself, pulling the long black hair back and tying it with a red velvet ribbon. Mary promptly joined her in the entry hall and without a word to anyone they departed.

As they picked their way through traffic, Rebecca gave Mary a slight smile and said, "I shall now instruct you in the ways of the *ton,* my dear. You may ride or drive in the park at any time, but the fashionable people are there only after five. The outing is not for the exercise but for the purpose of seeing and being seen by others of the *ton.* And you must never on any account gallop your horse while you are there," she concluded as they entered Hyde Park. "It would be quite useless in any case, because the park is then so jammed with carriages, and people walking and on horseback, that it would be highly hazardous."

Mary remarked graciously, "I appreciate your coaching me, Becka, for I should never have known." The sisters shared a laughing glance, and set their horses to the gallop. There were few people about to remark on this, and neither sister at present cared in the least if they did. Their ride was long and strenuous and when at last they drew in to a walk, Rebecca's pale face had regained some color.

"Mary, did Clayborne take you driving yesterday?"

"No, it was the day before."

"And did he stop to talk with anyone that day? Perhaps a lady in mourning."

Mary keenly regarded her sister. "Yes, and Becka, I have never seen the likes of her outfit! I am sure that it was meant to be mourning but, dear God, it was barely decent!"

"Did you overhear their conversation, Mary?"

"Yes," she replied, staring straight ahead between her horse's ears.

"I am sorry to ask it of you, Mary, but I must know what they said."

Mary hesitated for only a moment and then repeated, practically word for word, the conversation she had overheard. She did not look at her sister once, nor did she make any comment on the scene she had witnessed.

"Thank you, Mary," Rebecca said softly. "It ascords well with something I myself inadvertently over-heard last night. I may need your help in this matter, and I know I need not ask for your discretion."

"You know I shall help you in any way I can, Becka. Clayborne has been very good to me, but you are my sister."

Rebecca reached over to pat her hand and smile encouragingly at her. Then the sisters rode back to Clayborne House without another word.

Since Mary was more comfortable with horses than people in town, she naturally gravitated to the Clayborne House stables and was soon on friendly terms with the coachman and grooms. Perhaps her family would not have approved of this association, but she found it enjoyable and came to no harm there. It was because of this inclination, however, that she was able to provide her sister with some interesting information.

"I think Clayborne does not join you for the card party this evening?" she asked Rebecca in the privacy of the latter's room.

"No, he has other plans, I believe."

"Frantley seems to think that he will be at Vauxhall Gardens tonight."

"I see. It may be necessary for me to cry off from the card party to stay home with you this evening, since you will be feeling mawkish, perhaps with the putrid sore throat." She smiled at Mary. "I feel sure Meg will not mind being accompanied by Turnip, and Turnip will enjoy it tremendously. I think you should be in bed, Mary, though there seems no need to call in the doctor. I shall be with you shortly."

For some time Rebecca sat in her room frowning with concentration. It was vexing at times such as these to be without a brother. She had no wish to flout convention or even safety to the point of attending the Gardens unescorted, but her mission precluded asking the escort of even one of the captains, devoted and obliging as they were. She had a hooded domino and a blond wig which would render her unidentifiable in the dusk, but she could not go alone. After pondering the matter for some time without reaching a satisfactory conclusion, she went to Mary's room.

"Grimms has already informed Turnip of my indisposition, and I have sustained a visit from her," Mary snorted. "I only just now rid myself of her by telling her that I was drowsy and needed some sleep."

"In a while I shall send word that you are not to be disturbed and that Turnip is to accompany Meg this evening. Mary, I cannot see how I am to manage it. I dare not ask one of the young men to accompany me, but I do not feel I can go alone."

"Well, of course I shall come with you."

"No, no. I could not allow that, and it would do no good. Two females together would be little better than one at Vauxhall. You have not perhaps met some schoolboy in London who could lend a deaf ear?"

"Nary a one, Becka. But I shall not allow you to go alone. Besides," she said frankly, "I am not willing to miss the adventure."

"I fear there will be little amusement in it for me."

"But you have been at Vauxhall before, and I have not. I have never seen the fireworks and I really should like to," she pleaded.

"Hmmm. I begin to see a possibility," Rebecca mused. "You are considerably taller than I but not so developed as yet. I wonder what discarded clothes we might find in the attic."

Mary's eyes rounded with wonder. "You would dress me as a man? Oh, I cannot thank you enough!"

"I should not do it. No, I will not do it," Rebecca said firmly.

"You would not be so cruel. I would be a perfect young man. Becka, I would be eternally grateful to you."

"It is not fair to you, Mary. What if we were discovered? Clayborne may be too preoccupied to notice, but there could be others of our acquaintance there."

"But Becka, I know practically no one in London. Only the captains, and if we should run into them I am sure they could be persuaded to keep our secret."

"Yes, I'm sure they could. Perhaps no harm would

come of it. It would depend entirely on how much you could really look like a man," her sister temporized.

"Then let's go immediately to the attic and see what we can find." Mary jumped up eagerly from her sick bed.

"Wait. We must think it through. How shall we get there without anyone knowing?"

"We shall take a hackney carriage, of course. With me to escort you no one will think a thing of it. It will not be difficult to slip out of the house," Mary assured her. "I do it all the time."

"You do? Where do you go?"

"Oh, just to the stables. But there is no harm in it."

"Clayborne would not like it," Rebecca warned her.

"Does that matter?"

"Yes," her sister sighed. "It matters to me. But it shall remain our secret."

"Then let's go to the attic. We're wasting time," Mary said impatiently.

In the attic Mary was first to come on a trunk of Clayborne's more youthful dress. She held up a waistcoat of the most shocking color and design and burst out laughing. "He must have looked the veriest quiz in this. Shall I wear it?"

"Certainly not. We are trying *not* to attract attention, you will remember."

Eventually they found a dark blue superfine dress coat with covered buttons which fit Mary to admiration, along with a plain waistcoat and a pair of buff-colored breeches. They added a pair of much darned white silk stockings and considerably scuffed black pumps. Their most treasured find, however, was a woman's wig of indeterminate age and color. Rebecca hastily departed to find a scissors and then set to the serious business of cropping the wig into a style à la Titus. Mary was remarkably pleased with the results, as she knew immediately that she would not be recognized either for herself or for a female. Adopting a haughty demeanor and wielding an imaginary eyeglass, she imitated Clayborne's most toplofty expression perfectly. Rebecca could not help laughing, and Mary exclaimed, "We shall carry it off to perfection!"

"So we shall. If you really wish to go, Mary, I mean to allow it, though I know I should not," she admitted sadly.

"Cheer up, Becka. There is not the least chance of my being recognized. You need only look to your own costume now, and lift me one of Clayborne's cravats—or maybe several of them. I shall need to get the hang of it. By Jupiter, I can hardly wait!"

Though she could not share her sister's enthusiasm, Rebecca was satisfied with the disguise. And as the hours passed with nothing to mar their plans she began to feel more confident. When Meg and Miss Turnpeck had taken just one more look-in on dear Mary, and assured Rebecca that there was no need for her to remain home, for the housekeeper was certainly competent, she dismissed them with a not entirely fictional headache of her own, and waved them off. She walked casually into Clayborne's room, the memory of her previous visit painfully close, and returned with three crisp white cravats over her arm. Although this had been a narrow escape, for Clayborne arrived just after her departure to dress for the evening, she was unshaken. When she had heard him leave the house, she proceeded to Mary's room and they put their plans into practice.

Eleven

Rebecca and Mary arrived at Vauxhall Gardens while there was still some daylight, but found that the ticket office could hardly be distinguished in the gathering gloom. Mary was appalled at the five shillings six pence she was forced to dispurse for each of them, but Rebecca urged her on to the semidark, narrow boarded walks leading to the gardens.

"Lord, Becka, they obviously intend to kill off the less hearty," Mary declared in a soft imitation of Clayborne's accents. "Why is it so badly lit, and everything painted so dark?"

"Just wait a moment and you will see," her sister replied as they rounded the last bend.

When they arrived at the gardens themselves, Mary exclaimed, "Fantastic! I had no idea it would be like this."

Tinted lamps shone everywhere, music was pervasive and thousands of elegantly clad people were strolling along by little temples with pillars and arches. A concert could be heard from the Rotunda with its huge bronze chandelier, but the young ladies avoided the area. They passed a specially constructed theatre where a tightrope dance was about to begin and wandered down numerous paths throughout the grounds—these often rather dark and obviously frequented by amorous couples.

When they did not find Clayborne and Lady Hillston, they drifted back toward the terrace where the reenactment of the Battle of Waterloo was taking place with its multitude of men and horses, gunpowder and shot. Mary could not resist staying until the French were banished in smoke and flames. She felt incredibly free in her breeches, strolling along totally unembarrassed. Aware of her sister's fascination, Rebecca pointed out the cascades of water, the tumblers, and the sword swallowers. Couples were seated in half-darkness in the decorated wooden arbors, and Mary gallantly offered to treat Rebecca to the refreshments, to be served on silver plate and waited on by men in scarlet livery, but her sister plucked at her sleeve and led her on toward the Dark Walk.

They passed the galleries opening onto the gardens, brilliantly lighted and raised some five feet above the ground, built in Italian style. The tables were decked with silver, and the sight and scent of flowers filled the air. Mary was intoxicated by the swirl of activity about them, but Rebecca pressed her on to the quieter areas, sure that she was more likely to find Clayborne in one of the sylvan grottoes than in a supper box.

"I see them, Mary," Rebecca finally whispered. "I wish to stay close behind them to hear their conversation, but we must be ready to bolt at any moment. On no account must Clayborne recognize us, so should there be any danger of it, I will fling my arms about you and you must appear to kiss me passionately."

Mary giggled and mimicked Clayborne. "My lady, it shall be my pleasure."

As Clayborne was approaching them, they turned aside for a moment before they began to follow. Lady Hillston was dressed much as Rebecca—and numerous other ladies, for that matter—in a domino which enveloped her, and whose hood made it difficult to recognize her. The hood, unfortunately, kept slipping back as she laughed up at Clayborne, and each time he would readjust it. "Always so proper," mocked Mary.

Rebecca felt the numbness invade her again and allowed Mary's arm to encircle her waist for support. This served the additional purpose of making them appear simply another enraptured couple who blended in with their surroundings. When they had drawn almost close enough to overhear, Rebecca hesitated momentarily, then went resolutely forward.

"Ah, Jason, I believe that was Lady Standand we just passed, and not with her husband, I'll be bound," Lady Hillston was saying. "And there are the fireworks. Quite remarkable. I should like to have such a display at Winthrop Manor one day. Could you procure such a thing for me?"

"I haven't the least idea. I could enquire if you wish," Clayborne answered.

(Mary gasped as a display of Roman candles, girandoles, and gillockes lit the night sky. She missed a bit of the ensuing conversation between her brother-in-law and his partner, but her sister was not distracted.)

"Do so. I have in mind to retire there next week, as Gerald's mother has gone off to visit her younger son in the north. You will join me at Winthrop Manor?"

"I cannot," he told her. "My wife and her sisters are here with me in town."

"Send them back to the country."

"I must go with them when they leave."

"Nonsense. You have often enough been away from that wretched country seat of yours."

"I have promised my wife that I will be available while her sisters are visiting."

"Then send them about their business. I dare say you have had them on your hands quite long enough." When Clayborne did not respond, she went on coaxingly, "It will be like old times, Jason, having you with me. Do not fear for gossip from the servants. I can handle that."

"I cannot come."

"You mean you will not come!" She stamped her foot angrily. "What do you fear? That naive little chit you married has not the least bit of worldly wisdom. She with her great blue eyes and trusting smile! I doubt she even knows of my existence."

"Does that annoy you, Alexis?" Clayborne asked smoothly.

"Of course not," she cried, and then continued in a softened, sensuous coaxing. "You were not so stiff-rumped in the fall."

125

"I should have been, God help me," he retorted.

"But you were not," she said with satisfaction. "You have not forgotten the night of the Standands' ball, or the picnic to St. Albans, I'll be bound."

"No, I have not forgtten. I tell you, Alexis, there will be no more such episodes."

"And what of tonight?" she asked, turning abruptly to face him, and causing Rebecca and Mary to halt quite unceremoniously in each other's arms. Lady Hillston reached out a small white hand to caress Clayborne's brow, cheek and lips. He did not respond in any way and her face clouded momentarily. Then she stood on tiptoe, pressed her body against his and kissed him. Gently he put her aside and said, "There will be no more, Alexis. I met you tonight so that I could say that, so that I could explain."

"I want no explanations! Of what use are they now? Six years ago they wagered at White's as to who would get me, you or Gerald. You were favored, but he had the better title and more money, and I married him. And I will do just that again. Yes, I will find another man with more than enough to offer me. What can you offer me? Nothing! You have become quite stodgy, Jason, you know that? You are not the fierce young man who offered me your undying love. And you are not the wild Corinthian dashing about the countryside changing inn signs and driving a stagecoach (Mary's attention was recaptured) when you were disappointed in my marrying. How I would laugh when I heard the stories of you kicking up such a storm! And poor old Gerald would look sick when I told him of my desire for you. Stupid man. He was such a chicken-heart, he dared not even answer me."

Her laugh rang out and caused other strollers to stare; Clayborne automatically pulled her hood forward again. She shook his hand off, threw back the hood and glared up at him. "I shall spend the next six months of mourning profitably, Jason. You should not be surprised to hear of my engagement next spring," she taunted him.

"I shall not care, Alexis," he replied calmly. "I will take you home now."

"Never! I am staying to enjoy myself. I have been caged for months with that old biddy and her long-toothed daughters and tonight I mean to kick up my heels, with or without you. Be on your way, Jason. I have no further use for you. I shall join Major Frome's party over there. Surely they will prove more lively company than you." Flushed with annoyance, she stalked away, leaving him looking pensively at the path at his feet for some time. Finally he shook himself visibly, sighed, and strolled off without a backward glance.

"What a witch!" Mary exclaimed involuntarily when Clayborne was out of sight.

"Please, Mary, we will not talk of it. Let us go home now," Rebecca said quietly.

But they were not to escape so easily from the gardens. As they were heading toward the exit, Mary gave a most ungentlemanly squeak. "Good God, Becka, there is papa's friend Mr. Cummings. He will surely recognize us!"

Rebecca halted in confusion. Mr. Cummings was a neighbor at Farthington Hall and had known both girls since they were born. Her abrupt halt had drawn his attention and she watched with fascinated horror as his puzzled expression changed to one of amazement when he assimilated her blond wig. His eyes darted to her breeched companion and the amazement disintegrated into incredulity. He stood there open-mouthed, unable to voice his surprise or disapproval.

It had by now, however, occurred to both Rebecca and Mary to ascertain who his companion was. With a sigh of unholy relief Rebecca found that the female with him was not Mrs. Cummings but an overdressed painted lady whom he would be unlikely to own, so she grasped Mary's arm tightly, nodded pleasantly to Mr. Cummings, and made to pass the couple. Loath to allow the matter to rest here, Mr. Cummings could see that no good would come of his speaking, now or later. He uncomfortably acknowledged Rebecca's nod and allowed the young ladies to pass, then took a handkerchief from his pocket, mopped his brow and muttered darkly and incoherently about what the world was coming to.

Mary choked on her laughter while her sister grinned and hurried them out of the gardens. "That was much too close for comfort," Rebecca whispered as they climbed into a boat. "And Clayborne may be home before us."

"I can get us in. There's nothing to worry about," Mary assured her, elegantly draping one leg over the other. When they arrived at Clayborne House she led Rebecca to the servants' quarters, produced a key, and they slipped in undetected. There was no sign of Clayborne when they reached their rooms, so Rebecca pressed her sister's hand, said, "Thank you, my love, you were magnificent," and presented herself to the curious but unquestioning Harpert to be readied for bed.

Mary was decidedly pleased with their adventure, more perhaps because it suggested further possibilities for getting up a lark than because of what they had learned, but there, too, she was pleased. It was obvious that Clayborne had been dismissed by that hellcat of his and now Rebecca need not suffer. Had she known it, Mary would have considered Rebecca's attitude incomprehensible, but her sister had not chosen to confide in her. So Mary spent the greater part of the next day in the stables blissfully unaware of the scene taking place indoors.

Alone in her room Rebecca was drawing a most satisfactory cartoon of Lady Hillston, dressed inaccurately in widow's weeds, but placed obligingly in Vauxhall where the lady herself was portrayed as the source of the fireworks. So intent was Rebecca on this occupation that she did not hear the door open, and she was not aware of Clayborne until she heard an oath behind her. She stifled her first instinct to hide the cartoon, knowing that it was far too late for that, and turned as calmly as she could to face him.

Clayborne's astonished eyes raked first her and then the cartoon, and, transferring the letter he carried to his left hand, he imperiously held out his right for it. Rebecca reluctantly parted with it, saying coolly, "You did not knock, my lord."

"Obviously," he replied curtly. "What is the meaning of this, Rebecca?" She could not make up her mind how to answer that so she said nothing. "I shall have an answer, and I shall have it now."

"Frankly, sir, I would rather not answer, now or ever. I should let it lie if I were you," she retorted with more courage than she felt.

"But you are not and I am waiting. I have all day," he said, disposing himself comfortably in a chair near her and never taking his eyes from her face.

"Well, let me see. That is a cartoon of Lady Hillston. I am in the habit of drawing cartoons, sir," she explained carefully, "as I find them most rewarding as an outlet for my spleen."

"Do you now?" he asked, almost curiously. "I should be honored to see more of them."

"But you shall not see any more of them. They are my own personal property, and I have no intention of exhibiting them to you."

"Let us return to this particular cartoon. How did you come to draw a cartoon of Lady Hillston at Vauxhall?"

"Ah . . . Because I saw her there."

"When?"

"Last night," Rebecca sighed.

"Let me understand this, ma'am. You were at Vauxhall last night. You surely did not go alone?"

"No."

"Who accompanied you?"

"It does not matter, my lord."

"But it does. Who accompanied you?"

Rebecca sighed again. "Mary."

Clayborne looked truly thunderstruck. "You are not telling me that you and Mary went to Vauxhall without a man to escort you?"

"Well, yes and no," Rebecca temporized.

"You either did or you did not. Do not fence with me, Rebecca. I will have the truth."

"Mary and I went alone, yes, but it appeared that there was a man in our party."

"Tell me the truth, Rebecca!" he roared.

"Quietly, please, Jason. There is no need to alarm

the household. Mary was dressed as a young man, and no one . . . questioned the masquerade in the least. She did an admirable imitation of you, and I believe is rather talented," Rebecca mused.

Clayborne raised his eyes heavenward and crushed the letter he held in his hands. "I cannot believe that you would pull such a prank. Mary perhaps, but not you."

"Really? Why, I do believe I am flattered, my lord," Rebecca murmured demurely.

For a moment it appeared that Clayborne would shake her, but he overcame the impulse and asked ominously, "And why, pray tell, did you go to Vauxhall? If it were some wild start of Mary's, surely you could have put an end to it."

"Please believe me that it was in no way Mary's idea. She is not in the least to blame for you cannot regard her considerable enjoyment once there to have been accountable for the scheme."

"Then I am to understand that you initiated the scheme. And I ask you again, ma'am, why did you go to Vauxhall?"

Rebecca hesitated, and decided that lying would not help the case, for surely Clayborne must know the reason, hound her for it as he might. "I went there," she said, moistening her lips nervously, "to see you and Lady Hillston."

"And why did you think to see me there with Lady Hillston?"

"Mary heard you were going to Vauxhall last night. Quite by accident, I assure you."

"But she did not hear that I was going there with Lady Hillston."

"True."

"Rebecca," he said with exasperation, "will you please simply tell me the whole?"

"I had rather not."

"I realize that, but I will have it, whether it pleases you or not."

"Very well. You see, when I was feeling unwell at the Stonebridges' rout the other night I reluctantly over-heard two women discussing you and Lady Hillston." She swallowed convulsively and continued, "I then asked Mary if she had seen you with anyone in the park, and against her will, mind you, she related what she knew."

"She overheard my conversation with Lady Hillston?" he asked incredulously.

"One of Mary's most endearing qualities is her keen hearing, my lord. She has a great deal of experience in eavesdropping. Perhaps you did not know."

"You might have mentioned it, but I had forgotten," he rejoined sardonically. "Please continue."

"Well, that is really about all. When she heard that you were going to Vauxhall we drew the obvious conclusion, and that is why we went."

"You went to spy on me?" he roared again.

"Hush! I should not call it precisely spying. You see, I did not wish to rely on hearsay, so I was determined to learn the truth for myself. I did," she admitted scrupulously, "encourage Mary to tell me what she had heard. She would never divulge such a thing on her own, you know, for she hates a tattle. But then she is my sister and did not refuse me."

"Admirable, no doubt."

"The fault, Jason, if there is one, is mine. You have no reason to be cross with Mary."

"We will leave that for the present. Were you successful in your endeavor?"

"You mean, did we overhear you and Lady Hillston?"

"Precisely. Overhear, eavesdrop, spy, what you will."

"Yes."

"And what did you hear?"

"Now, Jason, I really think it unnecessary to repeat that. I might just say that we came upon you when she was making plans for a visit to Winthrop Manor and we departed when she joined Major Frome's party." She stared sadly down at her hands, not sure why they were moving so restlessly in her lap, as she was willing them to be still. "I'm sorry if you were hurt, Jason. But I must confess that she did not seem worthy of your regard."

"You are impertinent. Nevertheless, it is true. She

has never been worthy of regard." He studied the cartoon carefully, as she watched anxiously, and finally he grinned. "You are very clever with a pen."

"Thank you."

"Tell me, Rebecca," he turned serious once more, "what had you intended to do if you learned of a continuing liaison?"

"You misunderstand, Jason. My intent was to discover for myself if what I suspected was true—that you married me with your affections engaged elsewhere," she said sadly.

Clayborne looked startled and then annoyed. "What difference could that possibly make now?" He had no intention of telling her the truth.

"It makes all the difference. You see, it means when you married me you knew that our marriage had very little chance for success. When you add to that the fact that you believe I did not come to you as a virgin, you get the shambles that our marriage has been for almost a year."

"You are trying to shift the blame to me," he said stiffly.

"If there is any blame, Jason, it *is* all yours. I have nothing with which to reproach myself. I'm sorry for you if you were hurt by Lady Hillston, and I'm sorry if you were hurt by me inadvertently, but I know the whole now and I must plan accordingly."

"Plan what?" he asked angrily.

"What to do for myself. I don't know for sure, but I will be thinking about it, and I will let you know when I make a decision."

"There is no necessity for any decision. You are my wife, and you shall act as my wife."

"No, Jason, I don't think so. But I will have to decide."

"Are you threatening to leave me?" he asked incredulously.

"If you wish to put it that way, I suppose I am."

"You cannot be serious! What would you do? Where would you go?"

"I tell you I have not decided. We will discuss the

matter further when I have had time to give it some more thought."

"We will discuss it now," he ordered.

"I think not, Jason," she replied calmly, and then could not help adding with due gravity, "I fear I am overwrought, my lord, and must rest for a while to recoup my strength."

"Stop your nonsense, Rebecca. You have never been overwrought in your life, and certainly not now, when you might have the grace to be!"

"You are unkind. Tell me, Jason, why did you come to my room in the first place?"

"Why? Oh, yes, I have had a letter from my brother-in-law asking if I will have my nephew George to Gray Oaks for a week while he's away on business. He's bringing George to London tomorrow and would rather we had him than the boy's grandmother, who is rather elderly. Would you be willing to have the lad?"

"It is thoughtful of you to consult me, and I would be happy to have him. I think it is time we returned to Gray Oaks."

"Obviously it is well past time. The carriage is back. I will have no more such pranks as you and Mary pulled last night. It is really beyond anything," he continued, working up to a nice pitch. "What if you had been recognized? You would not have been able to show your face in London."

"I cannot imagine a worse fate," Rebecca retorted. "In fact, we were recognized, but nothing will be heard from that quarter, I assure you. Mary made an admirable young man, and she knows almost no one in the city as yet. It was most unfortunate that we should have run into a neighbor, but he won't mention it." Her lips twitched. "I was perfectly safe in Mary's escort."

"Have you no respect for the proprieties, Rebecca?"

"Very little. Of what use are they to me? However, I shall attempt to respect them for your sake while I reside under your roof. I found it necessary this once to contravene them a bit, but I hope I shall have no further reason to do so."

"We will leave for Gray Oaks in the morning."

"Should we not wait for little George?"

"We will leave as soon as he arrives then," he retorted.

"He may be tired, poor tyke," she said solicitously.

"Oh, for God's sake, then we will leave the next day. You are enough to try the patience of a saint, Rebecca." Clayborne rose from his chair, a frown creasing his brow and his eyes dark with frustration. "And keep your sister out of the stables!"

"Unfair Jason. Your quarrel is with me."

Clayborne did not reply, but turned on his heels and stalked toward the door. Rebecca called after him, "I should like to keep the cartoon, Jason, if you do not mind."

"Well, I do mind!" he bellowed, but he retraced his steps, slapped it down on her writing table with a glare at her and stomped out of the room.

Twelve

After Clayborne's strategic withdrawal from his wife's room, he wandered about the house, deeply upset. Eventually he invaded the drawing room where Miss Turnpeck and Meg had just greeted a morning caller.

"So nice to see you again. What brings you to town?" Miss Turnpeck asked the visitor.

"A small commission for my wife. She will have it that a christening gown for the baby must come from London, and that I must be the one to choose it. Much I know about such things," the caller laughed.

"Oh, Lord Clayborne, here is someone you know," Miss Turnpeck greeted his arrival cheerfully.

Since Clayborne had never laid eyes on the young man before and the caller looked equally bewildered, Meg hastened to introduce them. "Jason, this is our friend Thomas Burns from near Salisbury. Thomas, this is Lord Clayborne. I have sent for Rebecca and Mary for we are all old friends."

Clayborne made his bow and studied the young man carefully while Meg engaged him in conversaion. Burns was shorter than he but very well formed; his clothes fit him to perfection, and he had a charming manner. His eyes were perpetually laughing, and his black hair kept escaping down his brow, to be brushed negligently back into place. He was relaying to the two ladies the local news in which they would be interested, particularly his encounter with Meg's Will a few days before. Meg hung on his words, and smiled and blushed alternately until Rebecca entered the room.

"Lady Clayborne, a pleasure," Burns greeted her with a bow, taking her hand and pressing it. "You are looking well." And indeed she was, as her color was still high from her confrontation with Clayborne.

"And you, Thomas. How are your wife and child?"

"Both very well. Sybil is regaining her strength very quickly and the little fellow is healthy, though he looks a bit red and wrinkled to me."

"I think they all do, you know. I'm pleased you came to call. What brings you to London?" she asked, and they drifted apart from the others while he again explained his commission. When they could not be overheard Rebecca asked, "And how is Rags?"

He chuckled. "Just the same as ever, always into mischief. Are you sorry you gave him to me? Do you wish to have him back?"

"Oh, no. He was always more interested in you than in me, ungrateful dog," she laughed. "I thought they were supposed to attach themselves to the one who fed them."

"Well, in that case it should have been your cook, not you. He is a frisky little fellow and I look forward to the day he and my Ned will be the best of companions," prophesied the proud father.

"You sound happy, Thomas, and I am so glad for you."

"Sybil is the dearest of women, Rebecca. Had I known her better before I married her, I should never have been such a gudgeon as to talk of her as I did. I hope you will forgive me."

"There is no need. I hoped only that you would make her happy," she replied simply.

"I believe I do," he confessed self-consciously. "And she is a treasure to me. You must see little Ned, too, for he is going to be a strapping fellow."

"Perhaps I will visit Farthington Hall in the next few months and then we could all call on you."

"Are you happy, Rebecca?" he asked kindly.

Rebecca was saved the necessity of answering this question, as Mary erupted into the room and burst immediately into speech. "Oh, Thomas, it's good to see you. I've been learning to drive a pair, and Jason says I shall make an excellent whip. Do you have your pair in town? May I drive them?"

"Hold on, young lady. So you have nagged someone into letting you drive at last," he said and threw Clayborne a look of commiseration. "I shall not be surprised next to see you perform at Astley's!"

"Now don't give the child any ideas," Clayborne remarked wryly. "She is by far too wild as is, forever getting into mischief." He fixed Mary with a stern eye and she realized at once that he knew of her Vauxhall adventure. She turned quickly to Rebecca, at whose slight nod she pulled a face.

With a shrug Mary turned back to Burns and soon had him immersed in a conversation on horses, which Clayborne eventually broke up to make the conversation more general. As Burns made his farewells, Mary began to edge toward the door, and just as she was about to slip out unchecked, Clayborne approached her and asked for a word with her in the study. Rebecca laughed at her comical look of dismay and joined the pair to say, "If it is concerning last night, Jason, I should like to be there, too."

Clayborne acquiesced with a gesture and followed the sisters, who went arm in arm. Before they reached the study, however, Miss Turnpeck had caught them up and she asked Clayborne with a puzzled frown, "I made sure you were acquainted with Mr. Burns, Lord Clayborne. Did we not speak of him one day at Gray Oaks?"

Looking mildly disconcerted, he replied, "I believe we did," before urging the sisters into the study, where he closed the door firmly against Miss Turnpeck's curious gaze. Rebecca could well imagine the import of this exchange, but she made no comment. Instead she turned to her sister to explain the present situation.

"I am sorry, Mary, that I have had to tell Jason the whole," Rebecca apologized, ignoring her husband's presence.

"The *whole*?" Mary asked incredulously.

"Yes, for he would have it. He happened to catch me drawing a cartoon of Lady Hillston and pressed me until the entire story was out."

"A cartoon? Oh, I must see it, for your cartoons are famous, Becka," Mary exclaimed enthusiastically.

"If you will pardon the interruption, ladies," Clayborne suggested impatiently, "I would be most appreciative if you both would sit down and attend to me. That's better. Now, Mary, I have spoken with Rebecca concerning last night's disgraceful episode and . . ."

At this point Mary burst into whoops, considerably startling her sister and irritating Clayborne to an intolerable point. "I fail to see anything amusing about it," he stormed.

"You wouldn't," she gasped out, and Rebecca, too, started to laugh.

"Neither of you have two serious thoughts to rub together!" he exclaimed in exasperation. "There is an unbecoming levity in both of you which I fail to appreciate."

"Too true," Rebecca retorted. "Were you a little less self-consequential and top-lofty you might find some pleasure in life."

"That is quite enough, Rebecca," he said coldly, his icy brown eyes striking her like a physical blow. "You are dismissed."

Mary gaped at this interchange between them, and shivered slightly as her sister rose, curtsied, and left the room, her face pale and set. Clayborne sat clenching a pen until it cracked, unaware of Mary's still presence for some minutes. When finally he turned to her she saw that his face too was drained and drawn, and that his eyes were neither angry nor cold any longer, but troubled and sad.

"I . . . I . . . am sorry if I was impertinent, Jason," she whispered. "You have been kind to me, much more so than I deserve."

"You remind me of my sister," he replied abstractedly, toying with the broken pen.

Mary would have liked to pursue this line, but did not think that Clayborne was in the mood for distractions. "I know we were wrong to go to Vauxhall and that I should not have dressed as a man," she hurried on. "I did not wish to upset you, but it was important to Rebec-

138

ca," she explained artlessly. "And I admit that I urged her to allow me to accompany her, for it seemed a grand adventure. As indeed it was. I shall not blame you if you send me home to Farthington Hall," she offered handsomely.

Clayborne managed the ghost of a smile and said, "We leave for Gray Oaks the day after tomorrow. My nephew will accompany us. You shall return to Farthington Hall when Meg does. For your own sake, Mary," he said tiredly, rubbing his brow with a weary motion, "try to find your pleasure at activities which will not ruin your reputation or endanger your safety. You may go now."

Stifling an impulse to comfort him as he sat dejectedly in the large ornate chair, Mary thanked him, and she, too, curtsied. After she had agreed to inform the servants that he would not be in for dinner, she left him alone and immediately sought out Rebecca, who was in her room staring vacantly out the window.

"He is very upset, Becka, but he did not come the ugly with me." And then with one of her unexpected youthful insights she asked, "It is not just Lady Hillston, is it?"

"No, Mary. It is not just Lady Hillston. We have a problem of our own which I cannot explain to you, but which seems to be unsolvable," Rebecca said sadly.

"He is such a good man, Becka. I am sure he would not mean to hurt you."

"No, he doesn't, but he is very proud. It is all a misunderstanding but it seems to have no remedy. Let us forget it. Did he speak to you about being in the stables?"

"No, not a word. He knows I go there?"

"Yes, he told me to keep you away from them, but I think it was only because he was angry with me. You shall have to decide for yourself whether you dare go there tomorrow, for the next day we return to Gray Oaks."

"He told me. I didn't know he had a nephew," Mary said curiously, and they drifted into a discussion of Clayborne's dead sister and the child who would visit them. "I shall help teach him to ride," Mary offered.

"That's kind of you, Mary. I'm sure Jason will appreciate your help."

Timidly Mary asked, "Could I see the cartoon of Lady Hillston, Becka?"

Her sister smiled and said, "You are incorrigible, Mary. I have put it away. Just a moment." She withdrew her drawing folder from the writing desk and submitted to Mary's request to see all the cartoons. Mary was delighted with them, as she did not share her sister Meg's disapproval of the irreverent nature of some of the drawings of Clayborne. "You've caught him at his worst and at his best, you know, Becka. Has he seen these?"

"Dear me, no," her sister sighed. "I fear I irritate him more than enough without that."

There was a tap at the door, and Meg entered to advise them that the captains were below requesting the pleasure of their company for a drive in the park. "Captain Hardcastle says he can take Becka and me with his groom driving, and Mary may go with Captain Gray. He has offered to let you practice your driving, Mary, as the park will not be crowded as yet." She awaited their assent and then hurried off to get a shawl.

In spite of the hot sun, a cooling breeze made the drive refreshing, and it was only marred by the sight of Lady Hillston, once again dressed in a very revealing mourning outfit and smiling coquettishly at a man old enough to be her father. The gentleman, stuffed into a fashionable coat with fobs and rings abounding on his person, gazed bemusedly at Lady Hillston and patted her hand proprietorially. Mary turned to wink at Rebecca, and in doing so lost control of the pair she was driving. Before Captain Gray could get the animals under control their confusion caused Lady Hillston's mare to bolt, leaving the old gentleman staring in bewilderment after her. Lady Hillston, hat askew and rumpled, was eventually rescued by a young Pink of the *ton,* to Mary's cries of "Bravo!" The widow, considerably disgruntled, ignored Mary and her party and rode off, with what dignity she could muster, her smiling groom in attendance.

Later Rebecca accused Mary jokingly, "I believe you did that on purpose, Mary."

"Well, no, but I would have if I could," she admitted frankly.

Clayborne was absent that evening, and the ladies spent a quiet time at home. Meg's friend Althea and her mother joined them for a few hours of music and conversation. When Rebecca mentioned that her nephew joined them the next day, Lady Stonebridge reminisced about his mother.

"Clayborne's sister, Caroline, was a beautiful girl. Totally uninterested in the *ton* and its entertainments, she seemed destined to be an old maid. Then she accompanied her brother on a trip to his Yorkshire estate and met Gregory Mott, who shared her taste for the country life, and they fell head over ears in love. They married at his estate in Yorkshire and I don't believe they ever came to London at all. So sad she should have died. I understand the poor fellow did not take it well at all. Clayborne spent most of the first year afterwards with him, until he began to cope again. How old is the boy now?"

"I believe he is four, and I look forward to meeting him," Rebecca replied.

Lady Stonebridge eyed her speculatively, started to say something, and then merely said, "I don't imagine he has ever been to London before. His father brings him, you say?"

"Yes, and we plan to go down to Gray Oaks when he comes. I'm sure he'll find a deal more to do there than in town."

And indeed she was glad, the next morning when she met young George Mott, that they were going to the country. He had brown curly locks and the most impish eyes she had ever seen. After exploring the house like a puppy, he begged Clayborne to take him to the stables. Clayborne, casting a meaningful look at Mary, informed his nephew that he wished to talk to his father for a while, but that Miss Mary would no doubt be glad to take him. Mary quickly replied that she would be pleased to oblige her brother-in-law and took George by his pudgy hand to escape joyfully from the house.

Rebecca was interested in her husband's brother-in-law. Mr. Mott was quiet and had polished manners, but he evinced a strong curiosity about her. His son bore an incredible likeness to him, but whereas the boy's eyes were gay, the father's were sad.

"I was sorry you could not accompany Jason when he visited us last fall, Lady Clayborne. We had thought to attend the wedding, but Jason said he would be bringing you with him to Yorkshire soon after, and so we excused ourselves. I'm afraid we don't go about much," he said apologetically.

Clayborne looked uncomfortable, but Rebecca paid no heed to him. She tried to draw Mr. Mott out about his estate and the life he and George led there. He explained that he had business to attend to for his mother which should not take above a week, two at the most, and he would come to Gray Oaks to take George back with him.

"Plan to stay with us a while," Rebecca urged. "I am sure Mrs. Lambert will not gladly give up little George once she has him about, and I would welcome the chance to get to know you better."

Mott agreed to consider it and soon went off with Clayborne to discuss some matters privately in the study. Clayborne returned alone a half hour later, excusing his brother-in-law, who had left, and handed Rebecca a letter. "Bridge sent this along from Gray Oaks for you. We shall leave early tomorrow, so be sure your sisters and Miss Turnpeck are ready." He walked over to the window and stood there for some time. When he did not say anything more, Rebecca took the opportunity to read her letter.

"My friend Constance Exton is writing me from Brighton, Jason. How her mother hounds that poor dear! May I invite her to stay at Gray Oaks for a while?"

"Certainly. Your friends are always welcome. It is your home, too," he said stiffly, not turning from the window.

"Then I shall write to her immediately and urge her to come as soon as she may. Will you frank it and have it posted today?"

"Yes." He turned finally to speak to her, his eyes

troubled, but she was already closing the door softly behind her. With a sigh he followed into the hall and ordered his horse brought round. There was really very little he could say to her in any case.

As she signed her letter to Constance Exton, Rebecca was summoned by Harpert to receive morning callers in the drawing room. She arrived there to find Miss Turnpeck, Meg and the two captains.

"We have just learned that you are to leave tomorrow for the country," Captain Gray announced. "You shall all be sorely missed in town."

"We have already extended our stay, and though we shall miss you, I must admit that I look forward to the peace of the country," Rebecca commented.

Captain Hardcastle urged, "Would you come for one last drive in the park? It's a bang-up day."

"Would you mind having my nephew and youngest sister accompany us?" Rebecca asked with a twinkle in her eye.

"Not at all," Captain Gray offered handsomely.

They set out in two carriages, Meg and Rebecca with Captain Gray, Mary and George with Captain Hardcastle. George was agog with the London scene, and kept up a steady stream of questions ranging from "Why is it so noisy here?" to "Do you suppose it would be fun to be a crossing sweeper?"

In the other carriage Captain Gray told his passengers that he was soon to leave London himself, as duty called, and he did not know when he would return.

"We've been most grateful for your escort while we've been here," Meg assured him.

"Yes," Rebecca concurred, "and I think Jason has appreciated your assistance with all these females as much as anyone."

"I could not wish a better husband for you, Lady Clayborne," Captain Gray said seriously. "I don't know if you are aware of some of the business which has brought your husband to town, but I have heard fellow officers speak of him admiringly. A lot of poor souls returned from Waterloo last year incapable of working, or dreadfully handicapped, and your husband has spent consider-

143

able time and effort, to say nothing of money, on finding them jobs and homes and medical assistance. It's an honor to know him."

"Thank you, Captain Gray," Rebecca responded automatically, though this information took her by surprise. He had never spoken of it to her, but she felt warmed by the knowledge of his concern for these unfortunate men. Though she had been aware of the respectful attitude of the captains toward her husband, she had not been able to account for it completely.

They continued their drive down Rotten Row, where they saw Clayborne himself on his favorite horse, so abstracted that he did not notice them for a moment. When he joined their party, however, he was cordial, assuring George that there would be plenty of riding in the country and, before he left them, thanking the captains for their kindnesses with the hope they would all meet again soon. Rebecca watched him until he was out of sight, sighed softly, and suggested that they should return to Clayborne House, as there was much to do in preparation for their departure.

Thirteen

"Will you take me fishing today, Uncle Jason?" George asked hopefully. "We could have our catch for lunch. Miss Mary says she cannot ride until the afternoon, and Miss Meg has some letters to write. And I would rather go fishing with you than anything else."

Clayborne rumpled the boy's hair and laughed. "Very well, we will go fishing if you will have Griggs see to our tackle." He watched fondly as the little boy gave a whoop of pleasure and discarded his napkin on the floor before vanishing from the breakfast room.

Left with all the ladies, Clayborne was reminded that yet another was to arrive soon. "I believe your friend Constance Exton comes today, Rebecca. Does she travel post, or shall I have the carriage meet her in Chichester?"

"Thank you, she comes post, probably at midday, if she gets an early start." Rebecca glanced around at all her companions—Meg, Mary, Miss Turnpeck—and felt a surge of guilt that she so looked forward to her friend's coming. But Constance was different—not family—and therefore someone she could confide in, at least in some small measure. Now she could begin to make her plans.

"Is there anything I can do to prepare for her visit, Becka?" Meg asked.

"No, love, I'm sure you've all been the greatest help just keeping little George happy. He must miss his father, but one would never know."

"He hasn't the time!" Mary laughed. "What with his riding lessons, and Meg always ready to play blind man's bluff or spillikins with him, and Miss Turnpeck ever

145

vigilant to instruct him in history. I doubt he has a free minute in the day." She turned, smiling to Clayborne. "He follows you about like a puppy, Jason. I had no idea small boys could think of so many questions to ask. Yesterday I heard him plaguing you with his curiosity about the carriages. Had you driven a gig when you were his age? Could he try it? Was the harness different for the gig and the curricle? Would your horses go in either of them? Did a carriage horse eat more than a hack? I wouldn't have had the patience to answer the half of his questions!"

"I'm sure I was just as inquisitive when I was a child, and I don't doubt that you were, too," he replied, amused. .

The contretemps between the two of them in London was long forgotten, Rebecca knew, and her husband treated Mary as he might his own sister. With Meg, too, he was relaxed if not so easy-going, and his thoughtfulness to Miss Turnpeck won the admiration of them all. Unfamiliar as he must be with the likes of the eccentric governess, he found no difficulty in dealing with her. It is only me, Rebecca thought despairingly. He cannot come to terms with me. "If you will excuse me, I should see that Constance's room has fresh flowers." She offered her husband a hesitant smile as he politely rose.

"I can bring George back early so that we will be here when your friend arrives."

"No, please don't spoil his fun. Constance will want to refresh from her journey before seeing everyone.... But thank you!"

Her friend arrived full of laughing apologies. "Do forgive me for accepting your invitation so precipitately, Rebecca. I could not bear another day in Brighton with Mother. For she *will* push me at every man in sight and I cannot tolerate it. She extols my nonexistent virtues until I am speechless with mortification. I wonder half the gentlemen in Brighton don't believe me mute!"

"I have an idea in mind, Constance, which I would discuss with you," Rebecca said, drawing her friend up to the room made ready for her. "I know you must be tired

146

from your journey and I should not pester you, but I have been so eager to speak with you that I cannot wait."

"Whatever is this? I am not in the least tired and beg you to tell me," Constance urged as she removed her large poke bonnet and dropped it on the bed. She shook out her long, blond hair and turned inquiring eyes on her friend.

Rebecca hesitated. "It is easy to tell you what I have in mind, but I fear I find it difficult to explain why. You are one-and-twenty now, are you not?"

"Last month." Constance eyed her curiously. "Is that to the point?"

"In a way, for I have in mind to set up my own establishment and I would have you join me," Rebecca blurted.

Constance's expression turned to one of incredulity. She grasped her friend's hand and asked sadly, "You wish to leave Clayborne, Rebecca? I cannot believe it. What's the matter?"

"Even to you, Constance, I cannot explain it," Rebecca replied, turning her head away. "We have been estranged practically from the day we wed and I cannot bear to be in his house any longer. I've saved my allowance for most of this last year; really there was little enough to spend it on," she admitted, "and I think I can afford to let a small cottage in the country somewhere. But I could not do it alone, for it would but add to Jason's distress and my parents would surely not countenance it. Besides, I should dearly love your company. I just wanted you to think about it. You don't need to answer me now, for you must consider many things. Your mother will not like it, and we would live secluded so that we would not be likely to meet many gentlemen for you. But we could read and I can draw. You would be able to practice your harpsichord to your heart's content. It should not be so dull a life," Rebecca finished with a twisted smile and a pathetic little laugh.

Constance's eyes filled with tears and she hugged Rebecca to her. "Poor dear, you are dreadfully unhappy, aren't you? I shall think about it, Rebecca, and we can talk more of it another time. Frankly, I have been considering such a scheme myself but never in my wildest thoughts did I think to have your companionship. Run along now so I can freshen up."

"It's good to have you here, Constance. Don't worry about me."

But Constance thought of little else for several days, though Rebecca did not introduce the topic again. Her friend's calm self-possession was impressive, but it seemed to have no influence with Clayborne. Although he was unfailingly gracious to Constance, as well as to Rebecca's sisters and Miss Turnpeck, with his wife he appeared stiff and withdrawn. How could a man who fenced with short wooden swords with his nephew, laughing in the summer sun at the child's antics, meet his wife in the hall not ten minutes later to offer only a formal nod, as though they were mere acquaintances passing in the street? Constance was horrified to find that Rebecca accepted this as a matter of course, going about her daily routine—the planning of meals, a reading lesson for Harpert, whom she had brought from London, the delivery of a basket of food to a sick tenant, a drive to take George to visit a neighbor's children—as though there were nothing amiss.

One afternoon when they were riding out alone she said, "I've been thinking about your proposal, Rebecca. I fear Clayborne wouldn't like it at all."

"Of course he won't, but it cannot be helped. He has taken me in aversion and I cannot tolerate being treated that way."

"And yet he's really not like that. He's good with everyone but you."

"I know. Don't think I haven't tried to change his mind, for I have. But I will not admit to a lie, and I doubt that it would help if I did," Rebecca murmured sadly. "There is nothing for it but to leave."

Constance studied her friend's dejected face. "Very well, Rebecca. If your circumstances don't alter in the next few weeks, I'll join you in your cottage. Where shall it be?"

"I've always wanted to see the Cotswolds. Perhaps

148

Chipping Norton or Moreton-in-Marsh. We could write to an estate agent there to see what's available. Shall I do that?"

"Yes. Find out what you can, and then we shall decide," her friend reluctantly agreed.

"Thank you, Constance. I know you cannot truly like the scheme, but I promise you it will be best for Clayborne and me to separate." Caught up with her own thoughts, she did not notice that they were silent on their return to Gray Oaks. They found Gregory Mott arrived, with plans to stay for a while, and his son ecstatically chatting of his new achievements.

"I've been riding a pony, Papa, and Miss Mary says I shall be a neck or nothing rider."

"I don't doubt it for a moment, George," his father laughed as he swung him up onto his shoulders and allowed the boy to convince him to come to the stables to see Bessie, his borrowed mount and "Quite the finest pony for miles around."

At dinner Mott thanked them all for their care of his son. "I believe you have kept him so busy that he's hardly had time to get into mischief."

"Well, not exactly," Mary giggled, "for one day I found him in the stables merrily cutting up a piece of harness leather to make a whip for himself."

"And once he took a pot of cream the cook had set out to use for dessert," Constance admitted. "He had found a stray kitten and wanted to feed it. You now have a pet to add to your household, I fear. George has been keeping it in his room and will not hear of its banishment to the stables."

"In other words, you've all been spoiling him shamelessly," his father suggested with a grin.

"I suppose we have, but somehow he doesn't ever seem the worse for it. He gives as well as takes, you know, and is considerate for such a young fellow," Constance replied.

"I have often thought so, but I feared it was my prejudice," he admitted. "You know, Miss Exton, it has just occurred to me that you might be related to Charles Exton, a friend of mine at Cambridge."

"My brother Charles was there some years ago. We are from Halesworth, in Suffolk," she added helpfully.

"Then it was your brother I knew. I hope you will pass on my kind regards to him, for I haven't seen him for five years or more."

"I shall be happy to do so," Constance replied.

"Have you other brothers or sisters, Constance?" Mary asked.

"No, Charles is the only one. He married some years ago and lives near Halesworth. Mama and I stay there frequently but mostly live at the house in London."

"What a pity, for you can never get a good gallop in London!" Mary declared virtuously, glancing at Rebecca.

"True, we shall have to keep a stable . . ." Constance began, looking at Rebecca, and as rapidly changed to, "My brother keeps a good stable, though, and it is lovely to ride near the shore there."

Clayborne did not miss this *faux pas* and it troubled him considerably, so much so that he came to Rebecca's room that night to speak with her. She was not surprised, although she would have preferred to have waited before she divulged her plans. Nevertheless, she had always found it impossible to lie to him when he regarded her with those penetrating brown eyes.

"Am I mistaken in thinking that you have some plan afoot to move away, Rebecca?" he asked grimly.

"No, you are not mistaken. I have asked Constance to let a cottage with me, and she feels it may be possible."

"I will not have it!" he declared hotly.

"You have nothing to say to it, Jason. Oh, pray, do not remind me that you are my husband. I am well aware of it, and equally aware that you do not act the role nor desire to. I'll go away and you'll be much happier for it. You do not own me, Jason," she reminded him gently.

He distractedly ran a hand through his carefully combed hair and paced about the room, lifting an object here and there only to replace it again. "You could stay at Gray Oaks and I would live on one of the other estates, if you wish to live apart from me."

"No, for Gray Oaks is your home and I will not deprive you of it. I do not wish to go to Farthington Hall, either, for I would simply be an embarrassment to my parents. Frankly, I doubt they would allow it. No, I must have an establishment of my own and be independent there."

"And why should I pay for an establishment of yours when I have a home to offer you right here?" he asked bitterly.

"I have not asked you to pay for it, and I do not intend to. My allowance will be sufficient, I assure you. I do not intend more than a modest cottage, you understand."

"And what of your stable?" he retorted.

"We have not discussed that. Constance was so struck by the idea that she spoke without thinking. Perhaps with her grandmother's inheritance she will even be able to keep a horse. I'm sure I don't know."

"And you? Shall you not miss your rides?"

"It is a sacrifice I am willing to make," she answered softly.

"I take it no sacrifice is too great to be away from me."

"Please don't distress yourself, Jason. Perhaps my allowance will even run to keeping a horse."

"And where is this cottage you are to let?"

"I have not as yet found one. And when I do I think I should prefer that you didn't know where it was."

"Why not?"

"Because it will be better if we break all ties. Perhaps you could yet get an annulment. You spoke of it once," she reminded him, paling at the memory of that scene.

"I was angry then."

"You are angry still. I would consider it, Jason, for though it would cause some talk, you would be able to remarry and have a family to inherit Gray Oaks."

"I will not consider it!"

"Please yourself. I shall not stand in your way."

Clayborne angrily clenched and unclenched his

hands. He finally blurted in desperation, "Was it this Thomas Burns? Only admit it, Rebecca, and I will never say another word!"

Rebecca's eyes blazed with an anger he had never seen there before. Her cheeks burned with color and her bosom heaved beneath the light night dress. "Leave my room this instant, Clayborne, and do not enter it again."

"Forgive me! I should not have asked you that, but I needed to know," he said, his eyes distraught and his face pale.

"Get out!"

With a helpless gesture he strode from the room. It was many hours before he slept that night, uselessly calling himself a clumsy, stupid idiot, amongst other choice names he had picked up in his rambunctious youth.

He arose early, totally unrefreshed and with shadows about his eyes. An early ride brought him no peace of mind, nor did the news that Rebecca planned an excursion to Chichester with Miss Exton. The party expanded to include George, who some days before had been promised the treat of seeing the toys in a shop there, and his father decided to join them as well. Meg and Mary had plans of their own, and Miss Turnpeck, though she did not admit it, was in the middle of a novel she did not wish to be parted from for even a few hours.

Rebecca began the journey cheerfully enough, though Constance did not miss the drawn look about her face. Soon, however, Rebecca became inattentive, preoccupied with the previous night's exchange with Clayborne, and it was left to Constance to maintain a conversation with Mott and answer George's questions. When they reached town Rebecca instructed the coachman to let them down at a shop in which George would be interested and excused herself on some private business. Mott watched perplexedly as she walked down the street, and Constance bustled George into the shop so that his father would follow. Soon intrigued by a set of wooden blocks on display, George was torn between them and a wooden soldier with arms that moved. While he was deciding Constance asked to see some ribbons and took an inordinate amount of time to choose between the yellow cross-grain and the lemon silk. Eventually Rebecca joined them; nothing was said of her mission while they ambled into shops and procured items from Mrs. Lambert's list. When they stopped for refreshment at the local inn, Constance again assumed the role of hostess, as Rebecca tended to look startled when someone addressed her. "George is becoming rather proficient at riding, Mr. Mott. Perhaps you will want to ride out with him and Mary this afternoon," Constance suggested.

"Would you, Papa? You will see that Bessie is quite a goer," George said proudly. "I have learned to make her go whichever way I want, and Miss Mary is teaching me to stop her without being hard on her mouth," he explained knowledgeably.

"I am eager to see your progress, George, but we shall have to ask Miss Mary if she's free."

"Oh, she shall be. She rides with me every afternoon for an hour or so."

"Would you accompany us, too?" Mott asked Rebecca and Constance.

Rebecca did not hear the question, so Constance smiled and said, "I would be pleased to, but I cannot answer for Rebecca, and I fear she is unaware of the invitation."

Mott laughed, his smile banishing the sadness from his eyes, as it did when he regarded his son. "We shall ask her again later."

Unaware of this exchange, Rebecca came out of her abstraction to suggest that they be on their way home, though she had barely touched her tea and biscuits. Mott and Constance shared a rueful grin, agreed and helped George to pack away his toys from the table. When they reached Gray Oaks, Rebecca asked Constance to join her in the small parlor.

"Whatever is the matter with you?" Constance asked exasperatedly. "Mr. Mott must have found you very uncivil, for you were completely unaware of all the stimulating conversation he provided us on the return journey."

"Did he? He seems quite a pleasant man, don't you think? I shall try to make amends for my inattention later on. I'm sorry."

"Where did you go this morning? Or am I not to know?" Constance quizzed her.

"No, that's why I brought you here. I have decided that the quickest way for us to obtain a cottage in the Cotswolds is to retain the estate agent in Chichester to look into the matter for us, and he has agreed to do so."

"Is there some hurry, Rebecca?" Constance asked unhappily.

"I have told Clayborne of our plans and I am sure it would be best to carry them out as soon as possible. The estate agent says it will be a matter of a week or so before he can get back to me, though. He'll go to Gloucester himself. It will cost a bit more, but it will be faster this way."

"It's my fault. I should have been more careful of my tongue at dinner."

"Do not blame yourself. He would have known sooner or later."

"Was he very angry, Rebecca?"

"I suppose so. It led to some hasty words I am sure he regrets. But they merely point to the impossibility of the situation." She twisted her hat in her hands. "Don't look so troubled, Constance. It will be better for both of us if I go. Now I must see Mrs. Lambert for a moment."

Constance remained in the small parlor for a while before joining Meg and Miss Turnpeck for a walk in the topiary. Rebecca, on her way to the housekeeper, was so absorbed in thought that she literally ran into Clayborne coming out of his study. He steadied her with a hand on her arm and stayed her when she made a move to pass him, firmly propelling her into the study. "I wish to apologize for my . . . rash words last evening. I beg you will disregard them," he asked anxiously.

"Of course. I do not wish to speak of it again. May I be excused?"

Clayborne regarded her bowed head for a moment,

before lifting her chin with his finger and forcing her to look at him. "I seem to cause you nothing but pain, Rebecca. Believe me, it is not my intention. You must do what will make you happy. I shall supplement your allowance so that you may live more comfortably and maintain Firely at your cottage." He stooped and gently kissed her brow.

Rebecca gulped back a sob, whispered, "Thank you, Jason," and fled the room.

Fourteen

Mary was delighted to show Mott her pupil's progress, and joined the riding party with alacrity. She engaged Mott in an intelligent conversation on both horses and the appropriate stages of learning to ride. Bouncing along on his fat pony, George exhibited his ability to make Bessie do everything but stop gracefully. While his father complimented him and suggested some pointers, Mary and Constance took the opportunity to race to an old oak; Mary won easily but assured her companion that she had a fine seat indeed for one who was not overmuch around horses.

"I was raised around them, you know, and Charles has a fine stable, though I could wish to be able to use it more often. Rebecca has been telling me that you're learning to drive a pair and are coming along well," Constance remarked.

"It's really bang-up fun. But if I were a man I should learn to drive four-in-hand and I would be a stagecoach driver," she proclaimed. "It's too bad to be a female for there are so many things I should like to do which I cannot. Did Rebecca tell you of our adventure in London?" Mary asked, her eyes sparkling.

"No," Constance laughed, "and you had better not either. If it was something I should know I am sure she would have told me!"

"Well, ask her just in case. I would never tell Meg, of course, but you're not poor-spirited as she is, always so proper and meek." When Mott and George joined them she rode ahead with Mott, laughing and at ease, telling him of her early experiences on horseback and the havoc she had wreaked at Farthington Hall. "For there was not a decent riding horse in the whole stable, since Papa had forbidden us the hunters. I did occasionally bribe a groom to let me ride one, though I was too young to handle them. I'm sure I could manage now, of course, but Papa has threatened any groom with dismissal who allows me on one of his hunters. It's too provoking."

Mott laughed and expressed his sympathy. "I'm sure you find Jason's stables much more interesting."

"Oh, yes, for Jason has a marvelous eye for horses. Have you seen Rebecca's Firely? Quite a prime goer she is, and Rebecca says I may ride her as often as I please. I had her out this morning while you were in Chichester. I don't understand how you can bear to be shut up in a carriage for such a ride!"

"It is trying indeed," he agreed with a grin. "I hear you've been learning to drive a pair. My wife Caroline was taught by her brother and she could drive to an inch. I understand Jason has been teaching you as well."

"Several times he has allowed me to drive that splendid pair of his, though I doubt I could do so when they were fresh," she admitted. "No doubt it will come to me in time, for he says I'm better already."

Mott smiled at her and assured her he did not doubt it. "Shall you be staying long at Gray Oaks?"

"As to that, I'm not sure. Meg is getting lonely for her Will and talks of going home in a week or so, but I had rather stay, you know. Turnip is a dreadful bore."

"Turnip?"

"Miss Turnpeck, our governess. She *will* prose on and on about my 'Wilful Ways' until I cannot bear to be in the same room with her. And although Meg does not say anything, she is forever looking shocked at me. You see, I do not do needlework or play an instrument or care if the linens are stored in a properly dry place. I cannot watercolor and learning stuffy old historical facts bores me. I can sing, though, and when we all sing together— Becka, Meg and I—it's rather fun."

"I hope we shall hear you sing one evening then," he urged, and turned in his saddle to question Constance.

"Do you sing, too? I've not enjoyed a musical evening for some time."

"We shall have to make up for that. I do sing and Meg is delightful on the pianoforte. Perhaps this evening we could have our own little concert, Mary."

"I wouldn't mind," she allowed. "You play the harpsichord, don't you, Constance?"

"Yes," she laughed, "but it did not seem necessary to bring it to Gray Oaks."

"I have a horn," George piped in. "And I have it with me. Can I play with you?"

"For a short while perhaps, George," his father granted, "if we have our concert directly after dinner. Then it will be your bedtime."

"Do you suppose Miss Mary sings like an angel, too?" George whispered to his father, quite loud enough for the others to hear.

"I have no doubt of it," Mott chuckled.

When Meg and Rebecca were advised of the proposed musical evening they set about selecting pieces which would be most enjoyable, and kindly vetoed Miss Turnpeck's suggestions, as they inclined to heavy, lengthy numbers. Mary made a discovery of her own from Clayborne, and went off to the attic on a dusty hunt, returning triumphantly with several footmen in tow who carried a beautiful if slightly dirty harpsichord. "His mother played it," she explained, "and I have found a toy drum for George as well, though perhaps I should not give it to him or we shall never hear the end of it!"

This concern notwithstanding, George was brought into the Blue Saloon and instructed in the proper use of the drum to accompany the ladies in their songs. While Constance tuned and requilled the harpsichord, George ran off to find his horn, which he returned tooting gleefully. He was rather cast down when the ladies advised him that it was not acceptable to play the drum and the horn at the same time, but he overcame his disappointment and trotted off to the nursery for his dinner, elated at the prospect of an evening with the adults.

After dinner the party assembled in the Blue Saloon in good spirits, and the entertainment proceeded. Little

George pounded out a pronounced beat on his drum while the ladies all sang some of Thomas Moore's recent verses. After accompanying them for another two songs, the boy was whisked off to bed, tired but happy as he assured them in a sleepy voice that Miss Mary did indeed sing like an angel.

In an effort to promote harmony between her host and hostess, Constance urged them to sing a duet, a gay little melody in which his baritone set off her soprano nicely. Even Mott agreed to sing with Mary and Constance, though he insisted he had not sung for years. The ladies chose the hauntingly beautiful "Robin Adair," which Clayborne remembered his sister Caroline had sung; he watched Mott for any sign of reluctance or withdrawal, but could see none. Mott joined in with evident enjoyment, perhaps even relief. After that Constance played a Scarlatti sonata so brilliantly they were left spellbound. There was a pause when she finished, then they broke into spontaneous applause, and she flushed happily.

"It's a lovely evening," Rebecca commented soon after. "Shall we all walk in the topiary before the tea tray is brought in? Mary and Constance have not heard its history, Jason. Perhaps you could tell them."

Clayborne escorted Mary and Constance, who were inclined to find the topiary's history amusing, and were good-naturedly chided for their lack of appreciation for so ancient a heritage. While Meg and Miss Turnpeck chatted of music and the merits of the pianoforte versus the harpsichord, Mott and Rebecca brought up the rear.

"You have all been so good to George and he seems to love you all dearly. He is convinced that Mary is an angel, you know," Mott said laughingly.

"She must seem one to him, for she is beautiful and interested in all the things he is. Jason says she reminds him of his sister Caroline."

"She is very like Caroline, in temperament as well as looks. I did not meet my wife so young as Mary is, though. When I met Caroline she was twenty and tired of the gaiety of London with its interminable parties. She wanted nothing more than to be in the country."

"Frankly, I don't know how my mother will cope with Mary in town next year, for she too does not find it amusing. She would rather be out riding or enthusiastically involved in some prank."

Clayborne joined them then and Mott wandered off to urge that Constance and Mary tell him how the history of the topiary could be so amusing. Rebecca could think of nothing to say to her husband, but walked calmly beside him a little away from the others.

"Rebecca, I have been thinking that we should have a small rout next week. Your sister Meg is anxious to return to Farthington Hall and it would be a nice conclusion to her visit. Perhaps we could invite her young man to spend a few days with us and then escort them back. It would ease Miss Turnpeck's mind, I am sure, for she does not relish the idea of the trip with Mary in her sole charge."

"What a splendid idea, Jason! Are there enough young people in the neighborhood this summer to justify our having musicians for dancing?"

"I believe so. Sir John has two sons and three daughters at home right now, and the Misses Blackwell have a nephew rusticating with them for a few weeks. You may not have met the Smithdons, but Bridge tells me they are all at home and they also have several sons and daughters. I'll help you with the guest list, and Mrs. Lambert will be delighted to have such festivity here again. I remember a party my mother gave. She died when I was fifteen, so I must have been even younger. There was a floor put in the courtyard and lanterns hung all about."

"Could we do that?" Rebecca asked eagerly.

"I imagine we could. Mrs. Lambert was here then and would doubtless remember more of the details. If you should like it, you have only to arrange for it."

"I think even Mary will enjoy it if it's out of doors," Rebecca mused. "I shall write to invite Will tomorrow."

"Good. I will urge Gregory to stay, too."

The next morning Rebecca broached the project to Mrs. Lambert, who was as enthusiastic as Clayborne had predicted. "I remember the party his lordship was telling you of, my lady. It was the talk of the countryside for months after! I'm sure the painted lanterns were put away carefully in the attic and we have only to look for them. Now the floor for the court, that's another matter. Probably long since been used for some other purpose, but Bridge shall have some carpenters in and have it ready in a trice. You would have extra plants about as well? No doubt my brother will help you all you want there. You speak to him this afternoon, my lady, and he shall have everything done proper, I promise."

"Can the kitchen handle the food, Mrs. Lambert, or shall I speak to the caterer in Chichester?"

"We have managed in our own kitchen for every party ever given here and I shan't see food brought in from outside now. That French cook is forever grousing as there's no call for his skills with such simple fare, and it will give him a thing or two to do with himself," Mrs. Lambert grunted. "Not that we won't need some help from the village girls, but that's as soon done as said. You just plan a menu with the cook, my lady, and Griggs and me'll see to it that everything is fine as ninepence. His lordship will no doubt see to the wines with Griggs. It shall be a happy day for us all to see such doings at Gray Oaks again."

Rummaging through the attic, the young ladies uncovered not only lanterns but streamers and poles, baskets which could be used to hang plants in and odd items they were sure could be put to use, such as the head from a suit of armor and several Egyptian vases. "From Uncle Henry, no doubt," Rebecca laughed.

After the invitations were sent, Meg waited anxiously until an acceptance came from Will which indicated his willingness to both attend the festivities and escort the Farthington Hall party home. Then she could not do enough, and gladly assumed any tasks assigned to Mary, who would rather ride out with George and his father than plan the details of such a function.

The old house again buzzed with activity. Constance and Rebecca devised a scheme for hanging the plants asymetrically around the courtyard, and supervised the carpenters both in the construction of the wooden floor and the placement of the streamer poles. The lanterns, which had been painted with flowers and rectangular designs, had faded somewhat, but Rebecca enjoyed restoring them with vivid watercolors of her own.

There were frequent trips to the village and into Chichester to purchase supplies and arrange for the musicians. Clayborne and Mott kept little George close to them on fishing trips and rides, but George was infected by the excitement and could often be found joyfully hammering on the dance floor or painting a lantern. Exhausted, but unwilling to admit it, he would allow Constance to regale him with tales of adventure until he fell asleep.

The day before the party Rebecca received a message from the estate agent in Chichester in which he informed her that he had found an adequate cottage for her in Chipping Campden which he had let per her instructions. He described it as a cottage of four small rooms on each of two floors, and said that the cost was well within the figure she had suggested. Although it suffered somewhat from deferred maintenance, he admitted, it was structurally sound and charming for a small property. If she would inform him when she intended to occupy it, he would send word ahead so that she would be expected. Rebecca sighed and sent a maid to ask Constance to join her in the small parlor.

"We have a cottage," Rebecca told her when she arrived. "We can occupy it at any time. Are you still of the same mind, Constance?"

"I . . . I believe so, Rebecca. Are you sure you wish to go?"

"I must. Do not feel sad, Constance. We shall have a very comfortable life there and you can join your mother in town when it pleases you. Jason has offered to increase my allowance so that I may stable Firely and we shall share her if you cannot afford a horse of your own."

"It isn't that. I can have a horse of my own, I'm sure. But Rebecca, Clayborne has seemed much kinder to you this last week. Do you not think perhaps you could mend matters between you?"

"I'm afraid not. I shall miss him, for even when he is stern and forbidding I . . . Well, never mind. Have you made any mention to your mother of the move?"

Constance giggled. "I have had the most amazing letter from her, which will be followed directly by all the possessions I had in Brighton. I am told I am a most ungrateful daughter with no respect for my elders and not the slightest regard for my duty to my aging parent. She cannot be above five and forty, Rebecca! She spoke of her lonely old age, as though she had not enjoyed my Aunt Ophelia's company for the last five years! I should expect a letter from my brother Charles any day now, I expect, but frankly I don't believe he will mind so very much. He has always felt sorry for me."

"My dear, you are a love to joke about it, for I am sure it must be a burden to you."

"Don't cast me in a martyr's role, Rebecca; it doesn't suit me. I'm delighted to be away from her. I feel more the thing just being at Gray Oaks."

"Then shall we plan to leave for Chipping Campden the day after Mary and Meg leave? I'll bring Harpert to keep house for us. She's a willing worker and a quick learner and though she has been a maid at Clayborne House and my abigail here, she assures me that she can cook and manage a cottage as well as the next one."

"We could manage for ourselves."

"I'm sure we could, but Jason would not like it, nor would your mother or brother. Besides, I've never spent any time in a kitchen, and I daresay you haven't, so we should probably starve to death."

"No doubt you're right, but I have always dearly wished to learn cookery," Constance retorted.

"No, really? Perhaps Harpert will teach us in exchange for lessons we could give her. I'm teaching her to read, and you could instruct her on the harpsichord or in watercolors if she were interested."

Constance's face fell. "My mother did not say she had sent my harpsichord, Rebecca. I am sure she did it on purpose."

"Oh, that is too bad of her! We shall see what we

can contrive," she promised. "Constance, I do not wish my sisters to know of this as yet. And Jason is not to know where we are going." When Constance had consented, Rebecca went off to seek out Clayborne, eventually finding him in the stables.

"Did you wish to speak with me, Rebecca?" he asked, coming out of the harness room.

"If you have a moment, Jason. It's a private matter."

He took her arm and led her from the stables, down an oak-shaded lane away from the house. "Is everything going forward to your satisfaction on the party?" he asked.

"Oh, yes. Everyone has done a wonderful job and all should be ready in good time. It is not that of which I wished to speak." She leaned over to pick up a stick from the path and twirl it back and forth in her hand. "I have let a cottage, Jason."

He had known it was coming but he felt as though he had been kicked in the stomach. A muscle twitched in his jaw. "Are you sure you wish to go away, Rebecca?"

It took a supreme effort to meet his steady gaze. No, of course she didn't want to leave him. Who could leave a man whose hair was forever falling onto his forehead that way, making you ache to smooth it back into place? But he doesn't want me to help him, she reminded herself sternly. "I must, Jason. Meg and Mary leave on Monday; Constance and I will go the next day. I will arrange with Mr. Darcy, the solicitor in Chichester, to direct my allowance and any correspondence of importance on to me . . . I have a favor to ask of you, Jason."

"Anything in my power."

"Constance's mother has sent all her things—and they should arrive any day—except her harpsichord, and Constance is sure she retained it from spite and will not be persuaded to part with it. Until the matter is straightened out, could we take your mother's? Constance will be blue-deviled without one, I fear."

"I've never heard anyone play as Constance does. Of course she may take it. Is that all you would ask?"

"I should like to take my abigail, Harpert. I brought her down from Clayborne House, you will remember, and she is agreeable to going with us."

"That is entirely for her to decide. Will you have no other help there?"

"No, I understand it is a small cottage."

"You haven't seen it?" Clayborne asked incredulously.

"It is some distance away. I have every faith in the estate agent. We have let it furnished and I imagine it is in need of some decorating, but we will enjoy that." She allowed the stick to drop from her hands onto the path. "I must ask that you say nothing to my sisters. I shall write them and my parents once I am settled, for I am sure it will be better to present them with an accomplished fact."

"I don't like it that I shall not know where you are, Rebecca. What if some emergency should arise?"

"You need only contact Mr. Darcy. I don't intend to inform my parents where I am, either, Jason, for I don't wish to have my father come charging in to try to transport me back to Farthington Hall. Of course I shall send you word of our safe arrival."

Torn by conflicting emotions, he simply gazed silently at her. It was foolish to pretend that it didn't matter to him that she was leaving. Nothing had ever mattered as much. But how could he keep her when he was destroying her happiness? Why would she not confess to him and be done with it? "Oh, Lord, Rebecca, couldn't you just go to Brighton for a spell?"

"That would solve nothing and would merely prolong the eventual departure. I'm sorry to cause you distress, Jason, but you will soon settle into a far more comfortable life and will not have to be forever leaving Gray Oaks to avoid me. I want to thank you for being so considerate to my sisters and Constance while they've been with us."

"I've enjoyed their visit, and it's made you happier. Perhaps we could have Mary live with us . . ." he began, but Rebecca was shaking her head. "No, I don't suppose we could. Will you allow me to send you to the cottage in the traveling carriage?"

"And have your coachman tell you and the whole county where we are? No, I thank you. We shall go post chaise and Mr. Darcy has agreed to hire a carter for our trunks, and now the harpsichord. Jason, if you knew where we were, you would be honor-bound to tell my parents when they asked you, and I cannot have that."

"I would not tell them."

"You would be in a very awkward situation."

"And do you not think I will be in an awkward situation as you are arranging it?" he asked, an edge to his voice.

Rebecca smiled sadly. "Now that is more like you, Jason. It is easier for me to go when you are angry with me."

"If you will stay, I will endeavor not to be angry with you."

A spot of color appeared on each of her cheeks and her eyes glittered with unshed tears. "Nonsense! It is eating away at you and you know it. I cannot convince you of the truth. We are making each other miserable and I am weary of this stupid life of pretenses. What you do with your life now is your business. I intend to make mine as pleasant as I am able in the circumstances!" Biting back a sob, she swung away from him and fled.

Stunned, Clayborne stood irresolute, then picked up a stone and hurled it with all his strength against a luckless tree some fifteen yards away. He stumped down the lane violently, muttering curses and throwing stones to punctuate each one. When he had vented his spleen he returned to the stables and rationally discussed with his head groom the merits of the gray he was proposing to purchase from Sir John.

Much as she wished to hide in her room to recover from her emotional outburst, Rebecca could not avoid the household matters which awaited her on her return to the house. Mrs. Lambert and the French cook were indulging in a loud argument and Rebecca had to spend time with each of them to regain peace. When she looked in on the progress of the lantern painting, she found George alone in the room, with red and yellow paint striped on his face, hands and clothes.

"I'm a Red Indian," he announced proudly.

She laughed until the tears, already too near the surface, threatened to flow, and then shook her head. "It won't do, George. Come, let's get you cleaned up."

He placed his hand trustingly in hers and looked up through his eyelashes. "Couldn't we show Miss Mary and Miss Exton first?"

"Only if we meet them on the way, young man. What would your uncle say if he saw you like that?"

"Oh, Uncle Jason wouldn't mind. He's a great gun."

Fifteen

In the bustle of Will's arrival and last minute preparations for the party, Rebecca saw Clayborne only briefly the whole of the next day until their guests began to arrive. Standing beside him for their last party, she smiled determinedly on each new arrival. Clayborne had never looked so elegant as he did in the velvet-trimmed coat of forest green broadcloth with buff-colored pantaloons. She nervously fluffed out the white ruffles at her cuffs and wondered anxiously if the violet-blue muslin gown with its sash of deeper violet had been the wrong choice. But her husband caught her eye with a nod of approval which sustained her through the ordeal of welcoming their neighbors. Really, one could not blame them for their obvious curiosity, what with Clayborne away from home for most of their marriage. Automatically she chatted with each in turn, directing one to the card tables and another to the courtyard. When she opened the dancing with her husband, she felt sure that the evening was going well.

"I believe it is even more charming here tonight than it was at my mother's party. And a youngster's memory is notoriously exaggerated," he commented.

"I admit I am pleased with it myself, and we are lucky to have such a fine night. You know, you might leave some of these extra plants about after the party for they do add to the courtyard considerably."

"Please, Rebecca, no mention tonight of your leaving."

"Of course not. Forgive me," she said contritely.

"Look, do not Mary and Mott make an attractive couple?"

"Yes, and it's good to see him enjoying himself. He has lived secluded for so long that I feared he would not join in our amusements." The movement of the dance separated them for a while, and when they returned to each other he asked, "Did you order some treats to be sent up to George?"

"Yes, and I have allowed that he may stay in Constance's room for a while, for it overlooks the courtyard. He will love the music and watching the dances, and he has been helpful in preparing for the party." She laughed, remembering his painted face.

When the dance ended, Rebecca joined the older women to talk for a while and assure herself that they were enjoying themselves. Some of them remembered the former Lady Clayborne's party in the courtyard and expressed their appreciation of its revival. Rebecca watched Constance whirl by to a waltz with Mott and Mary with Will, while Meg danced with one of Sir John's sons and Clayborne with one of his daughters, a pretty young lady with auburn ringlets who seemed to find him vastly amusing. Stifling an incipient melancholy, Rebecca slipped away to visit George.

She found him settled on the window seat in Constance's room, a cake in one hand and a glass of lemonade in the other, his kitten cavorting beside him. He greeted her with delight. "It's a famous party, Aunt Rebecca. I can hear the music ever so well and just look at Papa dancing. I've never seen him dance before!"

"Well, I hope he is having a good time. We shall miss you both when you leave. Do you look forward to going home?"

"Yes, for Papa has promised me a pony of my own, quite as nice a one as Bessie." He stifled an enormous yawn and asked, "Shall you come to visit us and see my pony?"

Rebecca hesitated before answering. "I am sure Jason will come one day soon, but I may not be able to."

"Why not?"

"Well, I have a project that could prevent it," she evaded.

"What kind of project?"

"I cannot tell you, for it is a secret right now."

"I see. Well, could Miss Mary or Miss Exton come to visit me?"

"Really, George, I don't know. Did you have an ice?" she asked in desperation.

"Yes, and they're famous. Could I have another?"

"I shall go and make sure one is sent up to you immediately," she promised, and gratefully escaped from the room, meeting Constance at the door. Once downstairs she directed that another ice be sent to George and rejoined the company on the terrace overlooking the courtyard.

Gregory Mott approached her with a smile. "I've been looking for you. Are you promised for the set that's forming?"

"No, and I have acted the hostess quite long enough."

"Then allow me the pleasure," he said, offering his arm.

"I've just been with George, who is stuffing himself with cakes and lemonade and ices, and having a wonderful time. He said he's never seen you dance before."

"I'd forgotten how enjoyable it is." His eyes became thoughtful. "I'd forgotten a lot of things until I came here. Perhaps I have denied George the society he needs. We've kept too much to ourselves, I fear, and it has been my fault." He gave a gesture of dismissal. "I shouldn't be discussing such weighty matters at your party, ma'am, but I did want you to know how much we've enjoyed ourselves while we've been here."

"We've loved having you."

There was no chance to rest after her set with Mott, for she was solicited by each of the young men and most of the older ones as well. Toward the end of the evening Clayborne claimed her for a waltz. "It's been impossible to get near you. Have you enjoyed yourself, Rebecca?"

"Enormously, Jason. And you?"

"Yes," he replied as he swung her around Mott and Constance. "I believe even Miss Turnpeck cannot complain, for she has won an enormous pile of shillings at the whist table!"

"No! A secret vice, I swear, for she was forever prosing at us that gambling is wicked." They laughed together, causing several of the watching matrons to nod wisely and predict that his lordship would not be from home so much in future.

When the last guest had departed and the ladies had wearily retired to their rooms, Mott urged Will to his bed and stayed Clayborne, suggesting a glass of brandy in the study. Though he was more than ready for his own bed, Clayborne acceded gracefully and dismissed Griggs, telling him not to wait up.

Clayborne seated himself comfortably, stretched out his legs and heaved a sigh. Mott did not reply to his languid comment on the success of the party, but paced about the room with a distressed countenance.

"You have spoken with Rebecca?" Clayborne asked at last.

"No, I heard of the plan from Miss Exton. I do not mean to pry, Jason, but I cannot understand how you can sanction such an undertaking."

"I am informed that I have nothing to say to it," he replied ruefully.

"Be serious! Rebecca is your wife, and a more attractive, charming woman you could not find."

"I am aware of it, Gregory."

"Then how can you let this happen?"

"It is a private matter I shall not disclose," Clayborne replied coldly.

"Of course not. Forgive me. But Jason, they are such babes. I do not doubt that they can manage for themselves in a cottage, but I shall not see them set out alone. Do you know where they go?"

"No, Rebecca will not tell me. I can contact her if necessary through a solicitor in Chichester."

"And you are satisfied with that?" Mott asked angrily.

"I have no choice. I cannot keep her here by force, Gregory."

"Perhaps you should," Mott retorted. "No, no, do not be angry with me. I shall convince Miss Exton that I am to escort them to their cottage, with a promise not to disclose our destination to you, of course. But it would ease your mind, would it not, Jason?"

"Certainly. Do what you can, Gregory. I have told Rebecca that she could stay here at Gray Oaks and I would not come here, but it will not do. There is no way to dissuade her from this madness."

"Really, Jason, I'm surprised at you! A man of your address and experience really should be better able to manage his bride," Mott said exasperatedly.

"Enough, Gregory. I have said it all to myself. She is a willful young lady and I am a stubborn, self-righteous man. Let's go to bed."

Mott was loath to drop the subject, but he realized there was really no more he could say. He managed to talk with Constance the next day and urge his escort on the two young ladies; and, though she knew that Rebecca would not be pleased, she was grateful and she knew Clayborne would be, so she accepted and presented Rebecca with the plan. "I shall feel much more comfortable with his escort, Rebecca, and anyway, I have already accepted."

"You will have him promise not to tell Clayborne our destination?" her friend asked.

"I have already. And he will have Firely tied behind his carriage, too, which I am not sure you could do with a post chaise. It is agreed then?"

"Certainly. You are good to put up with my cork-brained ways, Constance, for no one else would." Constance refrained from pointing out that Clayborne probably would, and went off to her room.

There were all of Miss Turnpeck's shawls to be retrieved from various locations in the house, and Meg's music to be sorted from Rebecca's own, while Mary could not resist one last ride on Firely, but the preparations for their departure were eventually completed, and there was a minimum of confusion in the morning as the household gathered around the carriage to see them off. In a final spate of rhetoric, Miss Turnpeck allowed Clayborne to assist her up the steps. "Too kind! No right to expect such distinction! A lovely home, perfectly lovely. *So* good of you to have us. I am sure Meg and Mary have thanked you, haven't you, girls? Yes, I was sure you had. No one could have been kinder . . ."

Meg cast a despairing glance at Rebecca, who grinned and said, "Just remember that Will is riding alongside, my love. Surely you can bear anything when he is with you." As Meg climbed into the carriage, Rebecca turned to Mary. "Do spare Turnip any trauma on the journey, my dear. I shall miss you."

Though little George was desolated to have Mary leave, he solemnly shook hands with her, and his father took the opportunity for a few extra words while helping her into the carriage. And then they were gone, the sound of hoofbeats slowly dying away in the morning heat. George immediately ran off to the stables but the four adults stood silent for some time. To break the awkwardness, and ever hopeful in leaving Clayborne with his wife, Mott urged Constance to ride with him, but Rebecca merely took the opportunity to settle some last-minute considerations.

"Gregory will take us to the cottage, Jason, as I suppose you know. It is thoughtful of him, and I am sure we will be much more comfortable with his escort. Should you like me to leave Mrs. Lambert with the impression that I am going to visit with Constance?"

"I am sure Mrs. Lambert is not so dull that your leaving with all your belongings, to say nothing of your horse, will escape her attention," he said coolly.

"You are right, of course. I had not thought of that."

"There are a lot of things you have not thought of," Clayborne retorted.

"I doubt it, Jason," she said softly.

"What will happen if Constance leaves to marry or go back to her mother?"

"I shall face that problem when it arises. But mind," she laughed, "I *have* thought of it."

"Will you call on me if you need help, Rebecca?"

"I cannot say. It would depend on the nature of the problem."

"I insist," he began hotly, then grinned sheepishly as she raised her eyebrows at him. "Very well, just know that I shall always assist you out of some scrape or finance some necessary luxury as I would if you lived with me. Promise me that much, Rebecca."

"I promise," she said solemnly, extending her hand for him to shake, which he did with due gravity, afterwards lifting it to his lips. Tentatively, they smiled at one another, her eyes wistful but with a determined hope for the future. She could not blame him for his belief, but she could not live with his constant anguish. In his eyes she read his regret for the past, and something more.

Clayborne steeled himself not to ask her to stay again. Letting her go was the only thing he could do for her to ensure some measure of peace in her life. Much as he wished he could forget her lie, his pride still rebelled at it, and even his reawakened love could not guarantee that he would not let her see his torture. If she left, there was no hope of reconciliation, and he had thought recently that perhaps she had, once or twice, looked on him more tenderly. That she . . . Well, he could not be right. She was leaving.

Rebecca forced herself to speak over the lump in her throat. "I must finish packing now. Would you see that they have Firely ready for the morning?"

The harpsichord was crated, their gowns packed, knickknacks carefully boxed, and by late afternoon their rooms already possessed a deserted air. Dinner was a subdued meal and conversation languished in the saloon afterwards. Rebecca leafed through some music that had just arrived from London and she accompanied Constance as they worked their way through it. No one spoke of what was on each of their minds. Eventually Mott and Clayborne were induced to join in the singing and the evening passed quickly, though they retired at an early hour.

Mott's traveling carriage and the carter's wagon were piled high the next morning with boxes, trunks and the harpsichord. Little George scampered about, reminding everyone that soon he would have a pony of his own, but secretly slipped off to bid Bessie good-bye. Knowing that prolonged partings would not help matters, Constance gently coaxed the party toward the carriage, leaving only Rebecca outside with Clayborne. He handed her a wrapped package and said gruffly, "It is a traveling artist's folder. I thought you might find some worthy subjects along the way." Then he stooped quickly and kissed her cheek.

"Thank you, Jason. I shall treasure it. Take care of yourself," and she allowed him to hand her into the carriage, where she sat back as Mott instructed the coachman to start.

Long after the carriage was out of sight, Clayborne stood staring off into the distance, and finally bestirred himself to return to his study. He found no peace there, nor anywhere in the house or stables. His entire staff were aware that Rebecca had left him, and much as he was dear to them, they had grown fond of their mistress, too, and blamed him for mismanaging things. It was the only day of his life when he swore at his valet.

In the traveling carriage Rebecca tried valiantly to regard this as an exciting adventure and discuss their future with Constance, but she soon gave up the effort and retired to her own thoughts. Harpert had been instructed to bring with her plenty of items to amuse George and she set herself to this task wholeheartedly. George's kitten curled up in Rebecca's lap and she stroked it absently. Mott and Constance talked quietly and at length, without anyone paying the least heed, only occasionally interrupted by a question from George.

It was a long and tiring journey for them all, with two nights spent on the road at comfortable if unfamiliar inns. When they arrived in Chipping Campden midmorning of the third day, Rebecca's spirits began to brighten somewhat. At the village inn they were met by a Mr. Quince, who accompanied them to the cottage, which had been aired and cleaned for their arrival. It was located a short distance from the village shops and was, like them, of the native stone of the area. Roses covered the exterior in a wild array, obviously unattended for some time, but charming nonetheless.

"It's beautiful!" Constance exclaimed with delight.

"Well, ma'am, I fear there is need for a great deal of decorating inside," Mr. Quince murmured.

No one paid him much heed as they hastened down from the carriage and into the charming little house. It was indeed as small as the estate agent had claimed it would be, and certainly had not seen any paint or wallpaper for half a century, but the young ladies were enchanted with it. Mott looked on skeptically, but George found it comfortable with its ragged carpets and scratched furniture.

Rebecca and Constance went from room to room, planning as they progressed, and Mott eventually commented dryly, "I can see you shall not be bored."

"Are you satisfied with it, Constance?" Rebecca asked.

"It could not be better . . . for our purposes, you understand," she explained to Mott as she laughed and picked up a broken stool in the kitchen.

"I understand perfectly," he grinned, "if your purpose is to spend the next year of your life restoring it to habitable condition."

"Tut!" Rebecca exclaimed. "It is not so bad as that. It shall be comfortable within the month, I promise you."

"Then you may expect me back in a month to observe the miracle," he retorted.

"Pay no heed to him, Constance. Let's see the bedrooms next." They climbed the short stairs to find the four small rooms off the hall. "You pick your room first and we shall have the coachman send in your trunk," Rebecca suggested.

Constance chose a room overlooking the village street, and Rebecca one facing on the rear yard with a stream at the farthest end and a tiny stable beside it.

Harpert also chose a room on the back side, and soon their trunks were being deposited hastily in their designated places. While Rebecca went off to scout out George, Constance assured Mott that they would do well in their new home.

"I cannot like to see you out of touch with your brother," he said with concern. "You will let him know immediately where you've located, will you not, Miss Exton?"

"I shall write him tomorrow, as soon as I find my writing paraphernalia," she chuckled. "You are good to have seen us here, Mr. Mott, and both Rebecca and I are grateful."

"I wish I could stay to see you settled in, but the journey is long for George and we should be on our way." He took her hand and said, "You will allow me to return in a month, Miss Exton?"

"It would give me great pleasure, Mr. Mott," she responded shyly.

"Gregory. And may I call you Constance?"

"If you please, Gregory." Their quiet moment was interrupted by a whooping George, who erupted into the room bearing an enormous outdated hat which he announced he had found in the attic.

"It would ever be like this," Mott sighed.

"I know."

Rebecca followed George in and shooed the males out of the cottage, thanking them profusely for their escort and asserting that they should not be delayed another moment on their long journey. Mott assured her he would write Clayborne of their successful journey and did not delay his departure longer.

The rest of the day was spent unpacking and shopping in the village for candles and food. Rebecca arranged for a village lad to come each day to care for Firely, and they made inquiries about a horse for Constance. Harpert prepared a simple but delicious meal for them and Rebecca and Constance sat down to plan for their new home in earnest.

"We can each do our own bedrooms. I shall purchase some material for Harpert and anything else she may need. She shall be in charge of the kitchen needs, and you and I can work together on the downstairs rooms," Rebecca suggested. "We need to keep the fourth room upstairs as a box room anyway." She grinned. "So much for Jane Austen's Robert Ferrars and his spacious cottages."

"I can hardly wait to begin. Mama did not allow me the least say in anything to do with the house in London and I am bursting with ideas."

"We shall not have a feather to fly with by the end of the week," Rebecca warned her.

"Speaking of feathers, the harpsichord will need to be requilled. I shall send to London for some condor feathers."

Rebecca lay in the unfamiliar bed that night wondering if she had done the right thing. She had come to want more than anything to settle matters with her husband, but she could not bear the anguish he lived with, inadvertently caused by her. To watch him suffer and not be able to reconcile himself was too painful for her. Perhaps the strong attachment for him which had grown in her these last weeks would diminish when she was away from him. And certainly he would be able to remake his life when he saw that she was sincere in her desire to give him the freedom to do so. The future stretched bleakly before her in spite of all the plans she had made for her new life.

Sixteen

It was almost a week before Clayborne received the awaited letter from Rebecca, in which she advised him of the safe journey and the condition of their new home, the pleasant countryside and the kindly neighbors. She spoke of the projects they planned to undertake and Mott's comments on the cottage. Her thanks for the artist's folder were again expressed and she had sketched a drawing of the cottage for him, with Constance in an apron waving from the window. She told him she had written her sisters and she enjoyed her rides on Firely. With the hope that he was well and that all flourished at Gray Oaks she signed it "Fondly, Rebecca." There was no indication that she would write again, and the letter had been forwarded by the Chichester solicitor.

Clayborne tried to read between the lines but eventually accepted the letter as it stood: Rebecca was happy and busy in her new situation and had no intention of involving him in her life henceforth. Since he had lived in anticipation that she might have regretted her decision, this letter merely cast him down further. He found it unbearable to remain in the country where the gossip was all of Rebecca's departure, and decided to escape to London where it was unlikely to be known as yet. He had no doubt that it would be known soon, but he could always go on to Yorkshire if things got too much for him in the city.

London did not prove to divert his black mood, for the balls were insipid, the card parties boring, and there were few outlets for his restless energy. He took to attending Jackson's Boxing Saloon daily and became proficient in the sport. Though he saw Lady Hillston flirting with anyone wealthy enough to be of interest, he made no move to approach her. Hours were spent in his library with a book open in his lap, but he stared vacantly into the empty grate. At White's he gambled, and because he did not care in the least, usually won. Occasionally he drove out to the races but could not remember which horse he had bet on.

When he had been in London for a week, he was surprised and a little uneasy to run into Sir Rupert Farthington. This was not particularly propitious, for when he asked, "How do you do, Sir Rupert?" that vague, short-sighted gentleman replied, "Very well indeed. And you, sir? Oh, yes, it is Clayborne. Married to one of my daughters, are you not?"

Rather taken aback, Clayborne replied, "Yes sir, your daughter Rebecca."

"Of course. Of course. Is she in town? I should visit her I suppose. And her mother will wish to know, of course."

"No, she is not in town," Clayborne declared exasperatedly. "I think you had best come home with me, Sir Rupert, for I have something to discuss with you."

Sir Rupert appeared very reluctant to accept this invitation, but Clayborne refused to allow him to join his cronies at White's until he had spoken with the negligent parent, offering him a choice vintage Madeira as inducement. When Sir Rupert was settled with glass in hand, Clayborne caught his attention by announcing, "Rebecca has left me to set up her own establishment."

The older man goggled at him and protested, "No such thing. You must be mistaken!"

"I assure you I am not," Clayborne replied patiently.

"Why should she do such a thing? M'wife assured me you were all the crack, well-breeched and nice spoken. Made Rebecca a ladyship, too. She's a good little puss. Wouldn't go causing any trouble."

"Sir Rupert, I tell you she has left Gray Oaks."

"Then perhaps she has gone to Farthington Hall," he suggested hopefully.

"She has not gone to Farthington Hall. She has let a cottage in the country with a young woman she met in London last year."

"Really? Where is this cottage?" Sir Rupert asked belligerently.

"I have no idea. She would not tell me and she assured me that she has no intention of telling you or her mother either."

"Whatever has come over the chit? I know what it is, you have frightened her. You young men, always rushing your fences! She's a shy chit, Rebecca, where it comes to men. Bookish, you know. You've made too many demands on the poor little thing," he said indignantly.

Goaded, Clayborne replied, "Quite the opposite, I assure you."

"Huh? What's this? So you are taking your pleasure elsewhere? You have hurt the poor young lady's feelings, no doubt. Women do not understand these things." He was full of reproach.

"Sir Rupert, I have no intention of trying to explain why Rebecca has left me. You shall learn that from her, if at all, which I doubt. I merely wished to apprise you of the situation and give you the name and direction of the solicitor in Chichester who will forward any mail to her." He turned to the desk and dipped a pen, scratching on crested paper for a moment before handing the sheet to his father-in-law. "I shall not detain you longer. I hope you will convey my respects to your wife."

Sir Rupert was ushered out of Clayborne House darkly muttering "Young sprig!" and Clayborne exasperatedly wondered if he was to expect a visit from Rebecca's mother. He was beginning to feel relieved on this score by the next day, when she was announced and he reluctantly had her shown into the library. Lady Farthington had not been informed of her daughter's waywardness until two hours before, owing to Sir Rupert's absentmindedness. She had been shocked and appalled, coming directly to Clayborne House on finishing her lengthy toilette.

Lady Farthington entered the room with handkerchief to eyes as to indicate her great distress. She would not actually shed tears, for she feared it was bad for the complexion and knew that it reddened the eyes, and she was justly proud of her large blue eyes. Regarding Clayborne with a tremulous, wistful smile perhaps appropriate to a younger woman but not suitable to her age or the flintiness in her eyes, she began her attack.

"I understand, Lord Clayborne, that Rebecca has set up an establishment of her own somewhere in the country."

"That is true."

"With whom is she sharing this cottage?" Lady Farthington queried, wrinkling her nose distastefully.

"Constance Exton. I believe you are acquainted with Miss Exton."

"To be sure. Just such another as Rebecca herself, bookish and uninterested in society. Plays the harpsichord rather well, though, as I recall. But her mother is a harridan."

"Just so," Clayborne said.

"What is the cause of this escapade, Clayborne? Is it known of yet in London?"

"As to the cause, you shall have to inquire of Rebecca herself. I do not believe word has reached town of it as yet."

"And what do you intend to do when it does? You will be a laughingstock and I shall have to retire to the countryside! I shall not be able to present my beautiful Mary in the spring!"

"It will be no more than a nine-days' wonder, Lady Farthington. I am sure Mary will not suffer from it at all. She is quite beyond worrying about such things, I feel sure," he mused, remembering her part in the episode at Vauxhall.

"I shall be the judge of that," Lady Farthington snapped. "What do you intend doing about the situation?"

"There is nothing I *can* do, ma'am. Rebecca has an allowance sufficient to maintain herself in this cottage and she shall do just as pleases her."

"I make no doubt it has something to do with Lady Hillston," Lady Farthington proclaimed. "Rebecca is so unsophisticated that I did not speak with her about it before the wedding. You were probably indiscreet." When Clayborne did not reply, she demanded, "Did she learn of you and Lady Hillston? I knew there would be trouble when I heard he died last December," she cried with annoyance.

"Again, Lady Farthington, I must refer you to your daughter."

"Oh, that ungrateful girl! She will ruin the whole family."

"Her present situation is not immoral, merely unconventional. I assure you that the blame is far more likely to be placed on me."

"And I am sure you deserve it!" she retorted hotly.

Again he did not answer her, and she stood glaring at him, impatiently tapping her foot. "What do you suggest I do?" she asked at length.

"No doubt you will wish to write her, but it will only put her hackles up if you berate her and insist that she return to you or to me. You would do best, perhaps, to indicate your support of her as your daughter."

"Nonsense! You would do better to stop her allowance and force her to come back."

Clayborne studied her coldly. "I cannot and shall not stop her allowance. It is part of the settlement and is hers alone. Furthermore, it would merely drive her to earn her own living in some manner, which I assure you you would not like. I daresay she could go for a governess or publish her cartoons—she is devishly clever with them. Would you feel more comfortable with that?" Clayborne asked softly.

"You are insolent, young man. It is no wonder she left you." Lady Farthington sniffed and walked from the room with all the dignity she possessed. Clayborne sighed as the door slammed behind her, in no way distressed that he had managed to upset both of Rebecca's parents, but singularly unhappy that she had grown up with such a lack of fondness from these self-interested and unfeeling people. He remembered his own parents with real affection, and though he had lost them both before he turned eighteen, he and his sister had been the delight of the late-married couple. Even his Uncle Henry, who was seldom in England now but had managed to spend a good deal of time with him and Caroline when they were orphaned, never left Clayborne with the least doubt that he was held in the highest regard.

At Farthington Hall Meg and Mary had received Rebecca's letter about a week after they left Gray Oaks and mutually agreed to keep the news from Miss Turnpeck. Meg was upset and kept murmuring that she had known something was wrong, wringing her hands and asking her sister what they should do.

"Nothing, of course, goose. Rebecca is able to manage for herself. She has Constance with her, and even Firely," Mary stated, as though that clinched the matter.

"But Mary, it will cause a scandal. It will be the talk of the *ton*."

"And what business is it of theirs?" Mary wanted to know.

"It does not matter to the gossips if it is their business or not," Meg cried despairingly. "They will say the unkindest things of Rebecca and Clayborne!"

"Well, and what they say cannot make the slightest difference to either of them," Mary pointed out.

"But it will upset Mama dreadfully, and she might be so shamed that she will not bring you out next spring," Meg retorted coldly.

"Bravo, then, I say. I have not the slightest desire to sit around stuffy ballrooms and receive ridiculous compliments from doddering old men. Perhaps I will join Rebecca myself. I shall write this minute and suggest it to her," Mary flung back at her sister, and glided out of the room to find her writing equipment.

Rebecca received this letter with a great deal of amusement, and told Constance that they had started a new style. "Perhaps we should found a home for way-ward young ladies. We could let a much larger house and have more servants, you know."

"How can you even think of such a thing when we are only beginning to make this place presentable," Constance grumbled good-naturedly. "I would welcome a ride. Has the saddle come for Thomasina yet?"

"No, but that need not trouble you. I used to ride bareback when I was a girl and I have a skirt which will do nicely. Do not look so amazed, Constance. You have no idea how much more comfortable it is than riding sidesaddle. You shall have Firely's saddle and we can ride up into the hills and have our luncheon there."

The young ladies left the blue draperies partially hemmed and went to change while Harpert prepared a basket of food for them. They avoided the village, as Constance could not feel that its inhabitants would be properly impressed with Rebecca's manner of riding. The villagers had accepted them calmly, and if they had not taken them to heart as yet, they were kind and helpful. Rebecca introduced herself as Mrs. Clayborne, and Harpert was warned to watch her tongue, from which the "ladyships" flowed too freely. The rolling green hills with their rushing streams invited exploration, and now that Constance had acquired a mare of her own they were pleased to leave the cottage work behind and taste the freedom of the summer day.

"It feels good to be on our own," Rebecca sighed when they topped a hill and gazed down on the charming stone village. "Here we have no one to be forever prosing on and on about the proprieties. And if the villagers should not care for our style of living it really need not concern us unduly, for it harms no one but ourselves."

"I am sure they find us most virtuous," Constance laughed. "Did Clayborne do that? Prose on about the proprieties, I mean?"

"Yes, sometimes. But it was only his way of venting his spleen. He does not draw cartoons, you know!"

"Most of us cannot," Constance retorted. "When I am especially angry I kick something."

"No, really? Perhaps I have never seen you angry," her friend grinned, "but I have no doubt that I shall drive you to a temper eventually."

"Do you miss Jason?" Constance asked abruptly.

"Yes," Rebecca replied simply. She sat looking past Firely's ears into the distance. "But I am rather happy here and I feel sure Jason will do better without me. It's like removing a thorn from your foot. It is painful to draw it out and sore for a while, but soon you are walking again and have forgotten all about it," she said sadly.

Constance took leave to differ with this philosophical idea, but she did not voice her disagreement. She was aware that her friend had been too engrossed in her own problems to notice Constance's own developing fondness for Gregory Mott. It amused her that Rebecca thought Mott was interested in Mary because she was so like his dear Caroline. But Constance had no intention of destroying Rebecca's illusions at this point, though she found herself frequently lost in daydreams and had some reason to believe that her regard was returned. She worked diligently to have the cottage looking attractive and comfortable, for although Rebecca believed that Mott was only teasing about returning in a month, Constance placed great reliance on his promise.

When they had settled in a picnic spot and were happily discussing the continuing renovation of the cottage, they were startled by a horse galloping close by them. It was immediately apparent that the young girl bestride the gleaming bay had lost control of him, for the reins hung loose and flapping against his sides. Rebecca immediately flung herself onto Firely and dug her heels into the mare, giving chase to the fast-vanishing bay. Firely caught her urgency and lengthened her stride until she began closing the distance as the other horse tired. Once alongside Rebecca grasped the loose reins and spoke gently to the lathered horse. Gradually he slowed his pace, with Firely matching his stride, and eventually Rebecca was able to bring him to a halt, shuddering and prancing. She turned to the girl, who was white with fear and had scratches about her face and arms where the branches had whipped against her.

"Are you all right? Here, let me help you down," Rebecca said kindly. She dismounted quickly and, commanding Firely to stand, aided the girl, who must have been no more than fourteen, to alight. Her legs would not support her and Rebecca steadied her to a seat on a fallen log close by. By this time Constance had arrived and tethered the bay to a sapling before approaching the others. Rebecca held the child in her arms and stroked her hair comfortingly, assuring her that all was well now.

"I . . . I am so gr—grateful," the girl whispered. "I th—thought I should be k—killed," she explained and tears oozed out of her gray eyes and rolled unheeded down her cheeks.

"Well, aside from a fright and some scratches, you are perfectly fine," Rebecca replied bracingly. "What happened?"

"He was startled by a rabbit and I could not bring him under control and he tore through the bushes and I lost hold of the reins and I do not know what Uncle Lawton will say!"

Constance mopped up the tears with her handkerchief and assured the girl that the horse appeared uninjured, so Uncle Lawton was unlikely to say anything.

"Now there you are wrong!" a masculine voice roared at them. "I shall have a great deal to say about it, Elvira."

Rebecca started up and eyed the newcomer coldly. "Please do not say it now," she urged. "Can you not see that the child is overset?"

He eyed her insolently from head to foot and then pointedly ignored her and turned to the girl. "Be home in half an hour to receive your punishment," he growled, then wheeled his horse, grasped the bay's reins from the sapling and rode off leading the second horse.

The terror in the girl's eyes startled Rebecca. As soon as he was gone the child began to shake uncontrollably and her tears flowed again, coursing down the ashen cheeks. Rebecca once more cradled the girl in her arms, rocking her softly and saying, "It will be all right. You shall see. Come now, try to get hold of yourself, my dear.

Constance and I shall see you home, never fear. You shall ride with me on Firely. Is she not a beautiful mare? Come, dry your eyes."

The soothing words gradually calmed the girl until her tears ceased, but her eyes did not lose their look of terror. She allowed herself to be helped up onto Firely and pointed out to her rescuers the direction of her home, but she seemed unable to speak. "My name is Rebecca Clayborne, and you are to call me Rebecca. My friend is Constance Exton. May I call you Elvira?" The girl nodded her head. "Who is that bully?" Rebecca asked finally. It appeared at first that the girl would not answer, but when she spoke at last the flood gates seemed to open wide.

"He is my Uncle Lawton, my guardian. My parents died a year ago in an accident and he came here and lives with me in the manor house, when he is not in London. He is so mean to me! No matter how hard I try to please him, he is never satisfied. Today the kitchen maid cut her hand very badly and Uncle Lawton was not on the estate, and the groom was away with him. So I said I would ride for the doctor. Only there was only Hotspur, the bay, you know, in the stables, and Marlys, of course, but she is old and lame. He sold my lovely gray, saying I should not need such a horse! He does not allow me to ride Hotspur or Lark, the horse he was on, but I had to get the doctor, and so I took him. I knew he would not like it, but I had no choice. At least I found Dr. Mantles before I had the accident. He must be there by now, for he was driving his gig by the road."

"Well, Elvira, I am sure if you explain it all to your Uncle Lawton he will understand," Rebecca said kindly, and Constance, too, smiled reassurance.

"No, he will not," the girl said sadly. "He will whip me as he always does."

The young ladies shared a shocked glance, and Rebecca asked gently, "He has whipped you before?"

"Yes. Not a week goes by when he is at the manor that he does not find some reason to whip me," she said matter-of-factly. "He is a cruel man, and I pray every night that he will return to London. He whips the horses —they have become quite skittish—and the groom, too, for the smallest things."

"Have you no other relations living with you, poor child?" Rebecca asked.

"No, I have no other relations that I know of at all," Elvira replied.

"And what of the staff?" Constance asked, with a troubled frown.

"There is Mrs. Hodges, the housekeeper, but she is rather deaf and was hired by my uncle. There is a cook and kitchen maid and one other maid. Most of the house is in holland covers. There is only the one groom. All of the servants who were here when my parents lived were turned off, even my governess. Uncle Lawton said they were too expensive. He will not keep an estate manager but handles the accounts himself. He says that I should be grateful that he is saving me so much money to inherit one day. I would be grateful if he would go away!" she exclaimed, and then her fear overcame her again and she said urgently, "You must let me down here. If Uncle Lawton thought I had not walked home he would be even angrier."

Rebecca drew in the mare and assisted Elvira to the ground. The girl was trembling again, and Rebecca said impulsively, "Let us come with you. We shall talk to your uncle."

"No, it would only make matters worse. I must face the consequences by myself." She lifted her shaking chin. "Thanks for everything. You have been most kind."

"Listen, Elvira," Rebecca said urgently. "I want you to know that we are your friends, and we want you to come to visit us. You do not seem to have anyone to help you." She explained carefully where their cottage was located, and the girl nodded hopefully, then trudged along the high stone wall, pushed open the iron gate and disappeared from sight.

Rebecca and Constance watched her until she was out of sight, and then turned to each other. "It is the most distressing thing ever I heard of!" Constance exclaimed.

"I know. I cannot believe that she spoke other than the truth, but it is hard to comprehend such a situation. I have heard of servants being whipped and think it a cruel use of power in their masters. When he was young, Meg's Will told us of how the boys at school were birched and it was enough to make you blanch. I could see not the least sign of mischief in Elvira, let alone evil. I hope she will visit us. Perhaps we can lighten her burden, for she is but a child." They were about to ride on when the sound of an angry voice froze them where they were.

From the courtyard beyond the wall they could hear Elvira's Uncle Lawton screaming at her, "How dare you take the bay? How often have I told you that you may not ride him?" There was a resounding slap and a stifled cry.

"If you please, Uncle Lawton, I had to ride for the doctor for the kitchen maid and Marlys is lame. I did not mean to vex you," her voice came soft and unsteady.

"There is no excuse for your behavior. Bring me the whip!" Rebecca and Constance gasped in dismay and Rebecca made to enter the gate, but Constance stayed her.

"Remember what Elvira said, Rebecca," she pleaded. "It will only make matters worse for her."

Her friend stopped and struck her hand against the wall. "I know you are right, but I cannot bear to stand idly by."

"You must. We shall see what we can do for the child, but we must not intervene here." Constance was looking pale.

"Now bend over the trough, miss," the harsh voice roared from the courtyard. After each of the three blows there was a muffled cry and the sound of sobs. Constance put her hands over her ears but was unable to block out the sounds. Rebecca stood white-faced and rigid.

"You are a hard one to teach," grated the panting voice. "Get to your room. There will be no food for you tonight."

There were soft sounds of a hasty departure, and then a roar of ugly laughter, as the man shouted after the departing girl, "You won't be able to sit for a week!" The

192

laugh continued unabated, and Rebecca felt a chill run down her spine.

"I think he must be mad. To whip her like a boy and then laugh about it. Really, Constance, we must do something to help her."

"I know, Rebecca, and we shall think of something. Come, we can discuss this at home. I want to be away from here."

Seventeen

Clayborne was surprised a few days later to receive a letter from his wife. When he saw it lying on the tray in the hall, his heart gave an unexpected leap which he attributed to his fear that something might be wrong, since he was convinced that she did not intend to write him. He picked up the mail calmly, deposited his hat and gloves, and walked off to the library. Setting the other letters on he table, he proceeded to seat himself carefully, forcing himself to smooth out his pantaloons before breaking the seal.

Dear Jason (Rebecca wrote),

I find that I must write you and call upon the help you offered, though I hesitate to do so for it is a matter not to do with me, really. Nevertheless, it is urgent and I beg that you will give us any assistance you are able. Yesterday while riding Constance and I came upon a young girl, I should think about fourteen, who is being mistreated by her guardian. He whips her, Jason, and it is not our imagination for we heard the whole! We have spent the morning gathering what information we could in the village. (I will not try to hide where we are now, for you shall need to know in order to help us.) We are in Chipping Campden in the Cotswolds and a mile west of town lies Campden Manor, which was owned until a year ago by Sir John Carstairs and his wife. Their daughter Elvira is our concern. Her guardian is her mother's brother, Eustace Lawton, and I think from things Elvira said that he not only mistreats her but is also intent on robbing her fortune. He comes to London often and I hope that you can find out something about him there. Please do not think it none of my business, Jason, for I cannot but think of Mary or Meg in such a situation with no one to help her. I await your reply.

Fondly, Rebecca

As he reread the letter, Clayborne felt a twinge of regret, and some fond exasperation for Rebecca's involving herself in the plight of the young girl, but he determined to pursue the matter immediately. He called for his curricle and made stops at his banker's, his solicitor's, and his man of business's before wandering into White's for something to quench his thirst, and perhaps a game of cards. To his surprise he found his Uncle Henry there.

"Sir, I did not expect your return until next month," he exclaimed, shaking the elder man's hand warmly. "Have you had a pleasant trip?"

"Yes, my boy, but my gout has been flaring up and I thought me of the comforts of my own home. I see you well?" he asked, noting the drawn look about his nephew's face.

Clayborne professed to enjoy excellent health. When questioned about his wife he replied, "She is not in town just now, but I received a letter from her today and she seems to be in fine fettle."

Sir Henry frowned thoughtfully and remarked, "You leave your wife alone too much, Jason. She is young and should be enjoying the pursuits of London with you. An admirable young woman, high spirited and of excellent understanding. It surprises me that she is content to stay at Gray Oaks when you are away from home."

Spared the necessity of answering these remarks only by the arrival of several of Sir Henry's cronies, Clayborne greeted them cordially, but was soon lost in abstraction, vaguely contemplating his wine glass. The older men fell into a discussion of Egyptian rituals and customs which ordinarily would have interested Clayborne, but he was concerned with Rebecca's request and annoyed that he had just deliberately avoided telling his uncle that Rebecca was no longer living with him at Gray Oaks or anywhere else. His attention was only claimed by the discussion around him when he heard his uncle saying, "Damned finicky the Egyptians are about virginity. Their young women are intolerably coddled, to my mind. No bareback riding, no strenuous activity which might conceivably break the maidenhead. Excessive caution, I call it. And some of their other rituals on the same subject are absolutely grotesque, I assure you." His cronies were absorbed in this diatribe and did not notice Clayborne's arrested look. They were, however, somewhat startled when Clayborne abruptly took his leave of them, pressing his uncle to take dinner the next evening at Clayborne House.

"Certainly, Jason. I shall look forward to it. Just remembered a pressing engagement, have you?" he asked quizzingly.

"You have put me in mind of something, Uncle Henry," Clayborne grinned ruefully. "Excuse my hasty retreat. I assure you it bears no bad reflection on your singularly interesting discourse on Egyptian customs. I was fascinated."

"As you say," Sir Henry returned dryly, but shook his nephew's hand and watched him stroll purposefully from the room.

Clayborne emerged from the club into the cloudy street and surprised his groom by asking, "You were employed in Mr. Winter's stables when Mrs. Winter was confined, were you not, Thripps?"

"Yes, my lord," Thripps replied.

"Do you recall what doctor they had for her confinement and where his house is situated?"

"Yes, my lord. Sir John Bradley in Cavendish Square," the startled groom replied.

"Good lad. Hop up."

When Cavendish Square was reached, the groom indicated the doctor's house and Clayborne, looking impatient and hesitant at one and the same time, climbed the stairs and used the knocker firmly. The groom, who watched circumspectly as he walked the horses, saw his lordship admitted immediately.

Proffering his card, Clayborne remarked apologetically, "I have no appointment but if Sir John is available I would be most grateful for a few moments of his time."

The butler ushered the distinguished visitor into an elegant drawing room and hastened off, returning shortly to lead Clayborne to the library where Sir John Bradley rose to greet him.

"A pleasure, Lord Clayborne. Will you take a glass of wine?"

"Thank you, I will," Clayborne said, beginning to wonder how he was to broach such a delicate matter. He sat down when his host did and cleared his throat, attempted to speak, but decided instead to take a sip of the wine.

Sir John regarded him with some amusement, and after waiting a moment for Clayborne to speak, asked encouragingly, "Was there some matter on which I might help you, Lord Clayborne?"

"Hum. Yes." Clayborne got no further for a moment, but finally said irrelevantly, "It was something my Uncle Henry said, actually. Sir Henry Davert, you know."

"I am indeed acquainted with Sir Henry," the doctor admitted, his eyebrows quivering with suppressed laughter. "May I ask what it was your uncle said which brought you to me?"

"He said that . . . at least he intimated that a woman could appear . . . uh . . . unvirginal merely from bareback riding or some other type of strenuous activity."

"Did he? And you have come to me to ask if that is true?" Sir John's eyebrows, magnificent in their bushiness, lifted in query.

"Exactly so," Clayborne replied, fascinated by the individual hairs of those eyebrows, which stuck out at a multitude of angles. Rebecca could draw a marvelous cartoon of Sir John, he thought.

The doctor regarded him with wonder. "An easier consultation I seldom enjoy," he murmured, the eyebrows quivering again. "Yes, it is true. There are a number of means by which a maidenhead may be destroyed, other than intimacy. It is rare, you understand, but by no means unknown. Occasionally a female is born without. Again, unusual but possible. Does that answer your question, Lord Clayborne?"

Clayborne was regarding him with a stunned look, slowly shaking his head as if to clear it. "Is this something I should have known? That is, I always understood . . ."

"It is an unusual situation, therefore seldom thought of or discussed. I should think most people are not aware of it. I have myself, however, known authentic cases."

Clayborne gulped the rest of his wine, rose to his feet and shook hands enthusiastically with Sir John. "Most enlightening," he mumbled. "My thanks, sir." He precipitately strolled from the room wrapped in his own thoughts, leaving Sir John to the enjoyment of his long suppressed amusement.

Decidedly unsettled by this interview, Clayborne took himself to Jackson's Boxing Saloon to work off a bit of his vexation. Even if it were possible, it was not necessarily so. In fact, in an effort to stem a rising tide of hope, he told himself firmly that it was not in the least likely, to be sure. Gentlemen Jackson was impressed with his pupil's ferocity, though he felt it incumbent upon him to suggest a trifle more concentration. But when Clayborne left No. 13 Bond Street he knew the first peace of mind he had felt in almost a year.

It was several days before Clayborne received any information from the inquiries on Lawton he had set in motion and he was not at all pleased with the intelligence he gleaned. The Eustace Lawton portrayed by his informants was not attractive—a man of perhaps forty who in London led a dissipated life of drinking, gambling and bits of muslin, yet maintained without estates or visible means of income. He seemed to disappear frequently from London at low ebb, only to return to his dissipation within a month or so, apparently well-heeled once again. Lawton was known for his disagreeable temper and was not received socially in even the most modest circles. What alarmed Clayborne most was a rumor that Lawton had once abducted a young heiress with the intent of forcing her to marry him, though he had not succeeded, the girl's family having discovered them in time. Clayborne could not verify this information, but, in light of the other facts he had obtained, this totally unscrupulous behavior did not seem out of character.

Clayborne's solicitor informed him that it was a very serious matter, and usually unsuccessful, to bring an action against a guardian for mistreatment of a ward. He suggested that Clayborne concentrate on the charge of mishandling estate funds, which could be proved more easily and agreed that the indications clearly warranted further investigation. Determined to get to the heart of the matter himself, Clayborne left London.

Elvira shyly presented herself at the cottage a few days after they had met and the young ladies welcomed her enthusiastically. "We are just in the middle of a cookery lesson," Rebecca informed her, patting her floury hands on a sparkling white apron, "for Constance is determined to learn how to make cakes and stews and such things. Do you know, it is quite fun?"

"When my mama was alive and Mrs. Troobles was in the kitchen she let me help her sometimes. It was one of my favorite things," Elvira confessed.

"Good. Then you can help us. Come along," Constance urged.

Since Rebecca and Constance had spent the previous afternoon under Harpert's supervision beating sweet almonds with loaf sugar and the yolk of an egg, and fashioning rout cakes in numerous fantastic shapes, this afternoon the cakes were baked and then were ready to decorate. They ornamented them with nonpareils, candied peel and icing, spilling more on the whitey-brown paper than perhaps was strictly necessary, but enjoying themselves all the same. Casting aspersions on the mucilage of gum arabic needed to make the nonpareils adhere, Rebecca assured Harpert there was no need to rush out and purchase a brush for spreading it. "We'll do very well with our fingers. They couldn't get any stickier than they already are."

"I was once," Rebecca told Elvira, "at a party where they made the most remarkable structure out of rout cakes and barley sugar. I think it was supposed to be a miniature of the host's castle in Kent but it bore quite a noteworthy likeness to Westminster Abbey, so perhaps the chef had not been out of London. There is an amusing account of such an edible model in *Headlong Hall*, only it is of a mountain with milk punch flowing down miniature rocks. Have you read it, Elvira? If not, I shall lend it to you, for it is vastly diverting."

When the cakes were ready and tea had been made, Harpert served them in the parlor. Rebecca could not help but notice that Elvira seated herself gingerly on the sofa, and a flash of anger went through her. Giving her a warning look, Constance proceeded to discuss the neighborhood with their visitor. Elvira, who had had a governess until the death of her parents, now occasionally received some lessons at the vicarage, but for the most part did not receive any instruction at all. Constance was indignant about this and urged that the girl come to them for some studies, as they were already teaching Harpert and would be glad to include her.

"You are very kind, ma'am, and I should like it of all things. I cannot be sure when I can get away, though, and I should not like to be a nuisance," she said.

"Come when you can. We're often here, since we're trying to refurbish the cottage and its furnishings. We'll teach you when you can be here," Constance assured her.

"My governess said I was quite handy with a needle. Perhaps I can be of some help to you in return."

"We could use some help," Rebecca laughed, "but you must not feel obliged."

It became obvious to Rebecca and Constance as the days went by that their offer meant a great deal to the girl. When questioned as to her friends in the neighborhood, they were surprised to learn that she had few, and none whom she could have to her home, as her uncle had forbidden it, just as he had forbidden her to visit them, saying they were not equal to her in class or fortune and did not make suitable companions.

"And what do I care of their fortunes or rank?" the girl expostulated. "The squire's daughter is of an age with me and we have been friends all our lives. And though

Uncle Lawton can have no objection to her on that score, he says she is a giddy thing and he will not countenance my even talking with her or he will ... Well, he does not allow me to see her either, and I am afraid to speak to her even in the village when we meet lest he should hear of it somehow. No doubt she thinks me very rude by now, for I have taken to avoiding her." She sighed sadly.

"And what does your uncle say of your coming to us?" Rebecca asked grimly.

"He does not precisely know of it," she admitted. "That is, I have merely said that I am off to my lessons, and if he believes that I go to the vicarage, well, let him."

Constance frowned. "I do not like to think of your deceiving him, but perhaps in this case it is for the best. You could get in trouble if he finds out, though."

"Yes, but then I get in trouble for almost anything, so what odds is it?" Elvira asked fatalistically.

"Let us hope he does not learn of it," Rebecca said mildly, and changed the direction of the conversation.

But Eustace Lawton did learn of it a week later, and his descent upon the cottage was immediate and furious. Constance was out at the shops choosing some material for her bedroom and Rebecca was sewing in the parlor. The day was exceedingly hot and she was dressed in a flimsy, low-cut sprigged muslin with the front window open for a breath of air to pass through the room and cool her. There was a loud, imperative hammering on the front door which startled her into pricking herself with the needle and exclaiming vexedly. Harpert opened the door only an inch to assess the caller.

"I am Eustace Lawton and I will see your mistresses immediately," he growled.

"I shall see if they are receiving," she informed him tartly and made to close the door.

"That will not be necessary," he said as he shoved the door wide and pushed past her. "I have seen one of them in the parlor and I intend to see her whether she likes it or not."

Harpert was helpless to stop him, and since Rebecca had heard the whole conversation and was now at the door of the parlor, the maid looked imploringly at her.

"All right, Harpert. I shall see Mr. Lawton," she said coldly, returning to the parlor but not seating herself. Harpert left the door open and did not leave the entry hall, although she was aware that some biscuits were likely to burn.

"Please state your business, Mr. Lawton. I am not in the habit of having gentlemen barge into my house this way."

"Are you not?" he sneered. "I should have imagined you were. Which one are you, Exton or Clayborne?"

"I am Mrs. Clayborne."

"I take leave to doubt you are a married woman," he scoffed.

"Nevertheless, I am. Did you come here to insult me, Mr. Lawton?" she asked frigidly.

"I am here to inform you that my niece will be attending no more 'lessons' here. I can just imagine what she learns from two lightskirts in Chipping Campden."

"Get out of my house, Mr. Lawton, and do not present yourself here again," Rebecca ordered. When he did not move but stood leering at her heaving breasts, she called, "Harpert, see this person out!"

Harpert, wielding a broom she had grasped from inside the kitchen door, approached the visitor menacingly, whereupon he gave a snarled laugh but took himself off.

"Thank you, Harpert. You are not to admit that person again," Rebecca shuddered.

"I should think not, ma'am! Can I bring you a cup of tea? You look dreadful pale," she said solicitously.

"Best make it a glass of wine. I am sorry to have put the burden on you, Harpert, but I could not bear to have that despicable man in the cottage a moment longer. You were very brave and I admire your foresight in arming yourself with the broom. You looked like an avenging Fury." Rebecca smiled tremulously.

"Just you rest a moment, ma'am, and I shall have a glass of wine for you."

When Harpert had bustled into the kitchen, Rebecca shakily sat down on the nearest chair, despite the fact that it had no seat cover on it. For the first time since she had come to the cottage she questioned the wisdom of three women sharing a cottage alone. However, momentarily her anger prevailed, and she realized that they had been doing well enough before meeting Mr. Lawton, and that he alone suddenly made everything appear sordid and distressing. She had not been exposed to anyone of his disgusting nature in her life and she found it hard to know how to handle him. If only Clayborne would do something about him! But she could not be sure that Clayborne had paid any heed to her letter, as she had not heard from him. That lowered her spirits considerably, and they were further lowered when she realized that Elvira had no doubt suffered for her friendship with the two older women. What a tangle!

When Constance returned and was apprised of the situation by Rebecca, she took a very firm stand. "If Clayborne is not looking into the matter, I shall write to my brother. He is no doubt busy, but if I request it of him urgently, I am sure he will come. And Rebecca, you must carefully avoid Lawton. I would not put anything past him."

"Nor I," Rebecca shivered. "Really, he is so intent on bending everything to suit his own demented notions that I cannot but believe he is deranged. To call us lightskirts, Constance! He has not the least claim to being called a gentleman."

"No, and we must remember that he is not, and cannot be expected to behave as one," her friend replied worriedly. "I cannot like being here alone with such a villain in the countryside. And we can no longer do a thing for Elvira. I fear she has paid dearly for our acquaintance already."

"I have just been thinking that myself. Perhaps we had best speak with the vicar and see if he can help us. He seemed a pleasant enough man when he visited, if rather vague. I shall write to Clayborne today and ask if he has instigated any inquiries. If not, we must turn to your brother, I suppose, though I dislike having to involve him."

When Rebecca had written her letter, the two young

women posted it in the village and proceeded to the vicarage where Mr. Andrews lived with his sister and a dozen cats. Miss Maria Andrews was delighted to see the visitors and immediately rang for tea, announcing that her brother would be returning shortly and they should await him with her. Miss Maria was a tall, angular woman of faded mien and indeterminate years. If she was curious about her visitors, there was no sign of it, for she merely began a long, rambling discourse on the various cats who padded about the room, brushing lazily against the young ladies' skirts.

"Now Sophia there has had five litters since she came to us, and I have not been able to part with more than three or four of the kittens. Sox and Sother are two of hers, and the striped one on the writing desk, Somat, is also. They were the naughtiest little kittens, but have become quite well trained now," she proclaimed, as Somat knocked over a vase of roses, and she gently scolded him. Perhaps feeling that the subject had proved infelicitous, she queried the young women on their cottage.

"We are making great progress," Rebecca informed her. "I imagine in a few more weeks you would not recognize it. I hope you and your brother will come for tea when we finish."

"That would be delightful. The cottage has been empty for a short while, and the elderly man who lived there before was in no position to care for it as should have been done. I have lived here many years with my brother, and I am sure Mr. Peter was there when we came. He must have been ninety when he died."

This conversation was interrupted by the arrival of Mr. Andrews, who appeared to remember the visitors from his early call at their cottage, even if their names eluded him. He seated himself comfortably in a chair beside Constance and began to speak of parish matters with them.

"We have come to speak with you on a rather serious matter," Rebecca gently interrupted him after a while.

Miss Andrews immediately excused herself, but Rebecca and Constance assured her that it was not necessary. "We wish to discuss Elvira Carstairs," Rebecca explained to her, "and you may be of assistance."

Miss Andrews again seated herself, and murmured, "The poor child."

Mr. Andrews regarded the two young women curiously. "You have met Elvira?"

"Yes, we met her out riding one day," Constance replied. "She has come to our cottage several times."

"I am surprised her uncle allows it!" Miss Andrews exclaimed.

"When he found out, he forbade it," Rebecca admitted. "We had been giving the child some lessons and, I hope, providing her with some much needed companionship. From what we've seen and heard, we're convinced that her uncle mistreats her."

"Now, now, I know he is a strict man, but surely not unkindly so," the vicar said soothingly.

"You do not consider his whipping her over trivialities to be unkind?" Rebecca asked hotly.

"Purely a child's imagination," the vicar protested condescendingly, "which adults should listen to with the proper incredulity."

"It is no such thing," Constance asserted. "We have heard him whip the girl quite shamelessly. He has denied her any contact with children her age, has rid the manor of all the servants she knew and loved, including her governess, and has sold off her father's stable for the most part. Surely that is not a child's imagination!"

The vicar regarded her sadly. "If what you say is true, nonetheless there is nothing that can be done. Elvira must learn to bear the burden God has seen fit to lay on her shoulders."

"God has not laid it on her shoulders," Rebecca said scornfully. "Her uncle has done so, and certainly there must be something that can be done."

Miss Andrews cast a reproving look at Rebecca and said, "My brother's concern is with the souls of his parishioners, Mrs. Clayborne. When Miss Elvira comes to us infrequently for lessons, as some of the village children do, my brother instructs them in the words of the scriptures, and a very elevating time it is. I would that some of the adults in the village took such heart from his words," she said meaningfully.

"I am sure Mr. Andrews is quite noted for his uplifting services," Constance replied soothingly. "It did in fact occur to Mrs. Clayborne and myself that if he were to visit Campden Manor occasionally and speak with Mr. Lawton, it might ease Elvira's situation somewhat."

Mr. Andrews's face became flushed as he said quietly, "Mr. Lawton has indicated to me that my visits to Campden Manor would not be welcome. I did try going there when first he came, you understand, and he allowed that the child might attend my scripture classes occasionally if she were not required at home."

"And has Elvira attended many?" Constance asked.

"Not above half a dozen in the last year," he admitted.

"But when she came did she not give you some idea of the situation at Campden Manor?" Rebecca pressed.

"What she said was most distressing," Miss Andrews sighed.

"Did you not believe her?" Constance asked coldly.

"She is not a child given to fancy," Mr. Andrews allowed, "but she is young, and her parents' death was a shock to her. I daresay she is unused to being other than indulged, as only children often are," he replied pompously.

"So in fact you are well aware of the situation at Campden Manor and intend to do nothing about it," Rebecca said sadly.

"There is nothing I can do except give her the benefit of my guidance and my faith," the old man pointed out self-righteously.

"She will grow accustomed to her uncle's ways and learn to accommodate him," his sister assured them.

"There *is* no accommodating him," Rebecca retorted. "He uses the flimsiest of pretexts for punishing her severely and allows her no companion with whom she may share her troubles, or even her joys, if she has any. Thank you for your time, Mr. Andrews. We need not trouble you further."

Eighteen

From London to Oxford Clayborne made very good time on his journey to the Cotswolds; he drove his own curricle with his groom up behind. After Oxford, however, he made frequent stops and detours to the towns and villages in the area, using the letters of introduction his solicitor had thoughtfully provided. In Chipping Norton, Long Compton and Shipston he was unable to gain any information, but his inquiries were more rewarding in Broadway and Evesham. There Eustace Lawton was well known and, which Clayborne found not at all surprising, heartily disliked. Clayborne had been referred to a particular solicitor in Broadway, a young man who seemed clever and honest, and to him he confided the whole of the matter concerning Lawton and commissioned him to investigate further. After passing the night at an inn there he at last turned toward Chipping Campden.

Clayborne passed Campden Manor on his way to the village, but he saw no activity there and did not pause. When he arrived at the Lygon Arms he entrusted his curricle and pair to his groom and went in to bespeak a room. He was soon on friendly terms with the landlord who, fortunately for Clayborne's purposes, was a very talkative, confiding fellow.

"Ay, I knows Eustace Lawton, but I misdoubt your honor be a friend of his. More like he be a friend of the devil. Never seed such a mean man in me life. Your lordship would hardly credit the way that man treats a horse! Once he tried to hire a horse here when his was lame, but never would I allow it. Told him meself twasn't a one not spoken for. Nor did he believe it. But what odds is that, I ask you? I couldn't care less for his custom. Took it out on the groom he handed his own horse to, would you believe it? Very nasty fellow. Steer clear of him I would were'n I you," the landlord cautioned.

"I thank you for the warning," Clayborne said. "He sounds a most unsavory character." He had meant to ask Rebecca's direction, but thought better of it. After seeing his valise taken to his room, he strolled out of the inn, sure he could recognize the cottage from his wife's drawing. And although there were similar stone cottages, none was so bedecked with roses as the one for which he searched, and he was not long in finding it. His tap on the door brought Harpert peering out through a small crack.

"Lord Clayborne," she gasped in astonishment, throwing the door wide. "Do come in, your lordship. Mrs. . . . ah, Lady Clayborne is not in at present, but Miss Exton is in the parlor. One moment, I shall announce you," and she dove into a room off to the right, closing the door behind her. She returned immediately to usher him into the parlor.

"Jason," Constance cried, holding out her hands to him. "I was never so glad to see anyone!"

Clayborne clasped her hands firmly, and noted the pallor of her cheeks. "Is something amiss, Constance? Is Rebecca all right?"

"Truly, I don't know, Jason, for I have just arrived home to hear from Harpert that Rebecca has gone to meet Elvira. I cannot like it! Elvira's uncle came to the house some days ago and informed Rebecca that Elvira was not to see us any more. He called us lightskirts, Jason," Constance cried, "and was very insulting to Rebecca!"

The muscle in Clayborne's jaw twitched and his lips tightened. "I have heard nothing but evil of the man. Please have Harpert come here."

Harpert appeared immediately to the summons and stood nervously before Clayborne. "I want you to tell me exactly what happened this morning, Harpert."

"Well, sir, Lady Clayborne was sketching in the

parlor, and Miss Exton was out to the butcher shop when there was a tap on the kitchen door. There was a young lad there, kind of surlylike, and he thrust a note at me and run away. Lady Clayborne has been teaching me to read and I could tell it was for her, so I took it right in. She comes out directly and says, 'Harpert, it is from Miss Elvira. Tell Miss Constance that she says she has to see me and I am to meet her in the old stone quarry north of the village right away.' Then she grabs a bonnet and leaves. She took Firely, of course, though she didn't stop to saddle her," the maid said, wishing to be perfectly precise.

"How long ago was this?" Clayborne asked.

"A matter of perhaps half an hour," Harpert replied.

"Do you know where this stone quarry is?" he asked them.

"Not precisely, Jason, but on our rides I have noticed a sign for Quarry Lane," Constance said, and told him how to reach it. "Take my horse. It will be faster than going to the inn."

Clayborne hesitated momentarily. "You do think she may need help, Constance? I should not like to interfere if it is nothing."

"Oh, Jason, you have not met that hateful man. It may be simply a note from Elvira, but I cannot feel easy in my mind. I fear it is a trick of Lawton's for Harpert can tell you how he spoke to her, and looked at her." She blushed.

"I shall find her," he promised, and left for the stable if not precisely at a run, then the closest thing to it. Constance watched after him, wringing her hands in agitation, while Harpert assured her that his lordship would see matters to rights and offered to bring her her vinaigrette. As there were only sidesaddles in the stable, Constance soon saw Clayborne bareback on her mare, urging the horse in the direction she had given him. Then she turned to Harpert, refused the vinaigrette, and said only, "I pray you are right."

When Rebecca had read the note from Elvira, she was not so unheeding of the possibilities as Constance believed. Before speaking with Harpert she slipped a scissors into her reticule and, feeling a little ridiculous for such cloak and dagger methods, nevertheless slipped the reticule over her wrist. In addition she thrust a wicked-looking, lengthy pin through her bonnet to hold it on in the back, though it tied securely under her chin. She did not wish to desert Elvira if she were in trouble and needed help, but she did not wish to be caught at a disadvantage, either. She briefly cursed Clayborne for not having acted on her letter, knowing that this might be unjust, but not particularly caring at the moment. She did not take the time to saddle Firely, for she had become accustomed to riding bareback again and she found the sidesaddle a nuisance.

Rebecca did not, however, have any clear idea of where the old stone quarry was located, and was forced to stop several village children before she received the information she sought. The young lad who provided it stared at her open-mouthed, noting her lack of a saddle skeptically.

"You'm like to fall off that way," he advised. "The lane to the quarry be very overgrown and rocky."

"Thank you, young man," she laughed, "but have you ever ridden with a sidesaddle?"

He shook his head in bewilderment and she said, "Try it some day. It does not make the most secure seat," and she wheeled the mare and was off. He watched her out of sight admiringly.

When she reached the quarry Rebecca could see no one, but her mare whinnied and another horse answered from not far away. She called softly for Elvira, but there was only silence. Not wishing to dismount, as it might put her in an adverse position, she retained her seat and walked the mare closer to the abandoned pit. There were bushes encroaching on the open scar and the horse's hooves raised clouds of dust which nearly choked her. Suddenly there was a movement to her left and before she could urge the horse away her arms had been grasped and she was pulled roughly down to the ground. Firely danced away from the stranger and stood eyeing him from some distance.

"What is the meaning of this, Mr. Lawton?" Rebecca asked coldly, as she lay in the dust at his booted feet.

"You shall see soon enough," he gloated, retaining his grip on her arm.

"Where is Elvira?"

"Locked in her room at the manor, where she shall stay for the next week on bread and water, you may be sure. The grand lady did not wish to write a note for me," he mocked, "so I was forced to punish her."

Rebecca felt a shiver of fear and loathing shake her and Lawton, seeing it, roared with laughter. "Ah, yes, but I have other plans for you, doxy."

"And you think you shall get away with this?" Rebecca asked, trying to force down the panic and make her mind work. Suddenly the scissors and the pin did not seem such effective weapons against this maniac, his grip on her arm so strong that it had become numb.

"Who is to stop me?" he countered. "Your legendary husband? Your lightskirt companion? Your broom-wielding maid? You shall not dare to say a word of it or it shall go very hard with your precious Elvira," he snarled, flicking the whip in his other hand. "Get up!"

Rebecca stumbled to her feet and tried ineffectually to brush the dust from her gown, the reticule gripped firmly in her hand. She was thoroughly convinced now, if she had not been before, that he was mad. It occurred to her that she might place herself at better advantage if she appeared more in keeping with his demented idea of her.

"Well, you know, I really am married," she said as casually as she could, continuing to work at the dirt on her gown.

"About as much as I," he laughed wildly, enjoying his own joke. "And where might your husband be?"

"I cannot rightly say," she answered demurely.

"That I can believe."

"He is quite a well-known man, very rich and powerful," she asserted lightly.

"No doubt that is why you are not with him," he snarled.

"He sent me away," Rebecca said, managing a becoming blush. Now he must ask her, for if she had not found the information she had sought in Clayborne's books, she had learned a number of very interesting things, especially in an old medical text she had found.

"Very likely," he growled. "No man is likely to send away such a choice bit as you."

"But he did, you know," she said calmly, nodding her head wisely.

"Why?"

"As to that, I do not think I should tell you," she replied evasively.

"Enough of this foolishness. I shall have you now and no more talking."

"It would serve you right," she said, simulating exasperation.

"What do you mean by that?"

"Well, Jason said, you know, that he would not keep me about to give *him* the pox," she replied, imitating Clayborne's accent every bit as well as Mary had.

Lawton abruptly released his hold on her arm and stepped back from her. "I don't believe you!" he screamed, but made no move toward her.

"Do you not? Why else should I come to this God-forsaken place, I ask you? There are balls and parties going on in London right now which I should be attending, and that odious toad has banished me here for such a stupid reason. *You* would not care, would you?" she asked coaxingly, as she smiled at him with the full effect of her dimples and reached out a hand to him.

Lawton leaped from her touch and flung curses at her as he hastily untied his horse, hidden in the bushes. As the hoofbeats died away Rebecca gave in to the rubberiness of her legs and sank shaking to the ground, at last shedding the tears she had been holding back in her fright. Once she began to cry she was unable to stop, her body racked with sob after sob. And then there were strong arms about her and a handkerchief was wiping away her tears. A familiar voice was saying, "I cannot think why we should all have imagined that you would need my help!"

"Oh, J—Jason, I was so afraid. I b—brought a scissors and an enormous p—pin in case it was a trick, but suddenly they s—seemed quite useless. F—forgive me, I c—cannot seem to stop c—crying," she gasped.

"Hush now. Cry as much as you wish," he urged, rocking her in his arms and brushing the black curls from her wet face. The racking sobs continued for a while, followed by long shuddering breaths, and finally little hiccups. "Do you feel a bit more the thing now?" he asked gently.

"Y.—Yes. How do you come to be here, Jason?"

"Constance was much disturbed by Harpert's message from you and she sent me to protect you." He could not help but smile. "Really, Rebecca, I cannot imagine how you could believe that a scissors and a hat pin would be of the least use to you."

"Well, and so they might have been but for his having that wicked whip with him. You did not overhear what I told him, did you?" she asked shyly.

"Oh, yes, I did. Practically every word of it! For a moment there I thought I should have to intervene, but you were such a complete hand it was certainly not necessary. I didn't wish to precipitate matters if I could avoid it, for your friend Elvira's sake. It should only be a matter of a day or so now before I can confront him with enough evidence to force him out of the country. Though if you prefer I shall shoot him for his attempt to . . ." Clayborne was unable to finish his sentence, his eyes flashing with fury.

"No, no. You were perfectly right to do as you did," she said, as she gently extracted herself from his arms and allowed him to help her to her feet. "Constance will be worried. We should go immediately to set her mind at rest."

Clayborne stood looking down at her, making no move. She lifted her enormous blue eyes to his inquiringly, her face streaked with tears and dust and her bonnet crumpled beyond recognition. He longed to crush her to him, to protect her always, but he realized that he had thrown away his right to do so by his lack of trust in her.

His voice was anguished as he took her hand and asked softly, "Can you ever forgive me, Rebecca?"

"There is nothing to forgive, Jason. I should never have taunted you with unkindness, for you have stood by me when I needed you and I am very grateful. Do not distress yourself over this incident. When Mr. Lawton is no longer in the neighborhood, Constance and I shall be quite safe enough, I assure you." She smiled timidly up at him and then whistled to Firely, who immediately trotted up to her. "Would you hand me up, please?" she asked Clayborne. When he hesitated, as he wished to say more, she said gently, "I am fagged to death, Jason, and want nothing more than to lie down for an hour or so."

"Of course you are. I'm sorry." He handed her up onto Firely and retrieved Constance's horse from a ways down the lane. They rode back to the cottage in silence, where Constance rushed out crying, "Oh, Rebecca, are you hurt? You look awful!"

"How unpleasant of you to say so," Rebecca laughed. "I am fine. No harm has come to me, but I should like to wash my face and lie down for a while. Jason will tell you all about it when he returns from stabling the horses." She refused to divulge any further information but went directly to her room, where Harpert appeared immediately with a can of hot water. Constance clucked about her while she washed and changed into a night dress.

As she tucked in the covers, Constance said, "Get some sleep. We'll talk later," and practically before she was out the door Rebecca was sound asleep.

When Constance returned to the parlor she found Clayborne pacing up and down the small room. "What has happened, Jason? Rebecca is done in and did not say a word."

"It was as you feared, Constance. Mr. Lawton was there, not Elvira. I was not in time to hear how he managed to make her write the note, but I can imagine."

"But you were in time to protect her from him?" Constance begged.

Clayborne smiled ruefully. "There was no need for

my help at all, Constance. Rebecca managed to rout him by herself."

"She took a weapon with her?" Constance squeaked.

"Well, as to that she had armed herself with a scissors and a large hat pin, but she did not feel they would be effective, as he was waving a whip about. No, she talked him out of forcing his attentions on her."

"Talked him out of it? Don't be ridiculous, Jason!" she exclaimed in exasperation. "The man is mad. He would pay no attention to her pleadings."

"She did not precisely plead with him," Clayborne admitted, biting his lip to suppress a smile. "She told him that her odious toad of a husband had sent her to the country to avoid contracting the pox from her."

"She never! Oh, Jason, it is too much," Constance crowed with laughter. "I can just hear her."

"Yes, but she was very frightened by the whole, Constance," he said more seriously, "and she'll need to rest. I feel it will be only a matter of a day or so before I have enough evidence to confront Lawton with. I would gladly kill him for this, but Rebecca prefers that he be driven from the country. We'll then be able to have the court appoint a new guardian for Elvira." He studied his hands thoughtfully as Constance regarded him closely.

"I do not believe she has any other relatives, Jason."

"It is a matter which I shall have looked into," he replied calmly.

Because neither of them could voice any hopes that might make it possible for them to consider Elvira's future, they sat silently for a while. Constance pulled herself up from her abstraction and began to tell Clayborne of their stay in Chipping Campden, the decorating they had been doing and the villagers they had met, as well as an amusing account of their cookery lessons and the horseback riding in the neighborhood.

When Clayborne rose he said, "I shall go to the inn now—I'm at the Lygon Arms—but with your permission I shall return later to check on Rebecca. I know you'll take good care of her."

"Of course I will. Plan to stay to dinner, Jason," she urged.

"We shall see if Rebecca is up to it. Do you think Elvira is like to suffer for this last start of her uncle's? Should I try to do something about that?"

Constance considered this for a moment. "It is possible. Perhaps I can persuade the vicar to pay a visit to Campden Manor this afternoon to forestall any retribution. He was reluctant before this episode, but now I think I can persuade him to do something for us, especially if I mention that *you* are taking a personal interest in the matter." She smiled bitterly. "I think Rebecca would prefer that you remain in the background for the moment as far as Mr. Lawton is concerned."

"As you wish. Just send for me if I am needed." He made her a bow and departed. At the inn he engaged a young man who could recognize Mr. Lawton to keep a watch at the cottage for him and inform Clayborne immediately if he should appear in the vicinity. The young man was quite pleased with this lucrative assignment and took himself off speedily to spend a very dull afternoon in the sun at the corner of the lane.

Nineteen

When Constance had peeped in at the door of Rebecca's room and assured herself that her friend was sleeping soundly, she told Harpert that she was going round to the vicarage and would return shortly. "Should Lady Clayborne awaken, you may tell her so, and that Lord Clayborne is at the Lygon Arms should she need him. I'll be only a short while."

Mr. Andrews was writing a treatise on patience as a God-given virtue and did not take kindly to the interruption, but upon Constance's insistence he shortly joined her in the parlor. "I would not have come had the matter not been urgent, Mr. Andrews," she explained. "This morning Mr. Lawton sent a note to Lady Clayborne signed by his niece. It begged her to come to the girl's assistance, but when my friend arrived Mr. Lawton attempted to ... ah ... force himself upon her. Fortunately she was able to extricate herself, and her husband, Lord Clayborne, brought her home. Lord Clayborne has most kindly looked into the matter of Mr. Lawton and his treatment of the girl and the mismanagement of her estate and intends to see that Mr. Lawton does not continue his nefarious activities. I have come to you to beg that you visit Campden Manor as soon as possible to ensure that the girl is not punished unjustly for this latest misadventure of her uncle's. Will you do that for us?" Constance asked calmly.

"You say Lord Clayborne has come to Chipping Campden? Mrs. Clayborne is actually Lady Clayborne? Why did she not say so?" he asked querulously.

219

"She had no wish to cause a stir in the village, Mr. Andrews. Will you go to Campden Manor?"

"You are sure that Lord Clayborne has interested himself in these matters? They certainly have nothing to do with him," he replied dampingly.

"At his wife's request he has indeed involved himself. I myself assured him that I would ask you to go to Campden Manor to visit Elvira. Lord Clayborne would prefer not to go there until he has sufficient proof of Mr. Lawton's crimes to confront him effectively. Will you go to Campden Manor?" Constance asked for the third time, her patience wearing thin.

"Certainly. I shall set out at once. You may tell Lord Clayborne so," he said, beaming benevolently upon her.

"Thank you," she replied rather tartly. "I am sure he will be very obliged. And if you would stop round at the cottage on your return I would be grateful to hear of your mission."

"Of course, of course, my dear. Perhaps Lord Clayborne himself will be there," he suggested.

"Perhaps. I will see you later, then. I must return to Lady Clayborne now, for she is done in by this morning's events." Constance managed to make a hasty exit and returned to the cottage to find that Rebecca had awakened and had insisted on sitting in the parlor.

"How are you feeling now, Rebecca?" Constance asked with concern.

"I am quite well, do not worry over me. Harpert is cosseting me for the two of you. Why did you go to the vicarage?"

"I sent Mr. Andrews to Campden Manor to call on Elvira. I thought it might spare her if Mr. Lawton thought to take out his temper on her."

"Yes, a good idea. I imagine it took some strong words, though," Rebecca laughed, "to move the old goat."

"No, not at all. Only two—Lord Clayborne."

"Magic words indeed. No doubt he will expect a contribution to his church for assisting his lordship. No matter. Jason can easily handle the likes of Mr. Andrews if he wishes to do so." Rebecca sighed and leaned back on the sofa. "Jason told you what happened?"

"Yes, and I had a good laugh," Constance grinned. "I know it must have been a fearful experience, my dear, and I cannot imagine how you kept your wits about you so. I am sure I should have fainted."

"I shudder to think what would have happened had I done so," Rebecca said grimly. "I could not stop crying afterwards, and my legs would not hold me up. Oh, let us be done speaking of it, for it makes me feel shaky still."

"I cannot doubt it. Since we have missed luncheon in all the excitement, shall I have Harpert bring something in here?" Constance arranged for a light meal and chatted about the draperies for her room. With her encouragement, Rebecca took up her needlework while they waited, and soon they were busily engaged in their decorating schemes again.

They had barely finished a light but sustaining repast when Mr. Andrews was announced. Harpert whisked away the tray of empty dishes and was instructed to bring some tea and biscuits for their visitor.

Mr. Andrews cleared his throat and, assured of the young ladies' attention, began to deliver an address on his visit to Campden Manor. "I took the gig out shortly after Miss . . . ah . . . Exton left, as I am not fond of riding, myself. It seems an informal manner of travel, not to say undignified exactly, but not perhaps in keeping with my clerical duties. I should not like to smell of the stables, ha ha. I proceeded to Campden Manor, which is but a mile out of town, as no doubt you know. Once there I inquired for Mr. Lawton but was informed that he had left for Winchcomb an hour or so before my arrival and would not be back until tomorrow or the next day. I was of course quite relieved to hear that, ha ha. I then asked to see Miss Elvira and was informed by the housekeeper, a rather churlish woman I must say, that the girl had been in her room since early morning, indisposed. I did not like the sound of that, as you will understand, and I became very firm with the woman. I instructed her that as I was the vicar it was my duty and responsibility to visit the sick in the neighborhood. She told me that Miss Elvira was to have no visitors, so I asked her on whose authority," he pronounced triumphantly and awaited Rebecca's and Constance's looks of admiring approbation before proceeding.

"That of course stymied her for a moment, but she retorted that the girl's guardian had so instructed her. Now, I have studied reasoning and logic to some extent, and I fancy I was very clever in overcoming this objection. I pointed out to her that as her guardian had left for Winchcomb and was therefore in no position to judge of the girl's continuing indisposition, and as he was not expected to return for a day or two that I, being the spiritual leader of the area, was the logical person to assess the matter. The woman could not answer me there! I told her that I would see the child right away and no more nonsense. She still hesitated, but I maintained my right to see the child, and I fancy it did no harm to point out that I was God's emissary. These country women are rather superstitious. In any case she allowed as how I could follow her and led me up to the first floor where the child's room is located toward the rear. And would you believe it, she drew a ring of keys from her apron pocket and unlocked the door! The child had been locked in, and there was a tray there with a glass of water and a stale piece of bread on it. I was never so shocked!"

Rebecca and Constance managed to stifle their annoyance with Mr. Andrews's self-righteous histrionics and urged him to continue. He was eager to do so. "Miss Elvira was curled up on the bed and when the housekeeper announced that I had come to call, she buried her face in her hands. I sent the housekeeper away and closed the door firmly after her, as you can imagine I had no desire to have her listening in on our conversation. When I spoke to the child, she said I should not have come, for her uncle would be very angry. I told her that her uncle had left for a day or two, and I could hear her sigh of relief. She still would not look at me and so I asked her if I could help her. Then she began to cry and say that she had betrayed Mrs. . . . ah . . . Lady Clayborne and could

222

do nothing about it. I assured her, of course, as Miss ... ah ... Exton had assured me, that Lady Clayborne had managed to ... ah ... avoid any disastrous consequences from the episode. The child raised her head in her joy and I was horrified! Her face was bruised and swollen and her lip was cut, with dried blood on it." He shivered at the memory.

Constance gave a cry of pain and Rebecca's eyes blazed with fury. "The despicable bully!" she uttered and then waited impatiently for Mr. Andrews to continue his lengthy, self-justifying narrative.

"I had no idea, of course, that Mr. Lawton could do such a thing. Had I believed it possible I would have taken some action to see the situation put to rights. I called to the housekeeper for some warm water and bathed the child's face with my own handkerchief. Such a pitiful sight! I assured her that Lord Clayborne was acting on her behalf at his wife's request and that she would not long have to suffer such treatment. She was properly grateful to Lord Clayborne, and to you, of course, Lady Clayborne, and to me for coming to her then. I ordered the housekeeper to bring her a proper meal and to turn over the key to the room to me so that the child could not be locked in again. I assured her that she would have to answer to God for her cruelty, and to me for any further mistreatment of the child. She could only say that Mr. Lawton had given her her orders and that he was the child's guardian. I informed her that all children are in the care of God and that I as his emissary intended to see to it that no further harm came to the child. I assure you she quaked before me," he announced proudly.

"You feel, then, that she will be safe until her uncle returns?" Constance asked softly.

"I am sure of it. As I mentioned before, these country women are superstitious if not always religious. We must, however, arrange for her protection when Mr. Lawton returns. Obviously he does not hesitate to do her harm. I do not believe this is the first time he has struck the child," he observed, as though this were information likely to enlighten his listeners.

Rebecca bit back a scathing retort and managed to thank him for his assistance. "I am sure Lord Clayborne will make some arrangement for Elvira. He has been gathering the necessary evidence to end Mr. Lawton's guardianship of her. Please do not let us keep you from your duties any longer. We sincerely appreciate your kindness."

Constance helpfully rose and escorted Mr. Andrews to the door, while that worthy proclaimed all the while his earnest desire to be of whatever assistance he could. Before Constance returned to her chair, Rebecca had started to pen a most devastating cartoon of the cleric. Constance laughed and said, " 'Tis a marvelous way to vent your spleen. I could scream for his sanctimonious blathering! Oh, Rebecca, the poor child. How she has suffered. I hate to think that we are the cause of some of her pain."

"We must not do so, Constance, for she herself would be the first to assure us that her uncle needs little provocation for his attacks upon her. And we shall see an end to this mistreatment if I have to steal her away myself. Jason does not think it will be long now before he can free her of that beast."

"I hope he's right for I cannot bear to think of it. It is so hard to sit here and do nothing."

"Let us take a ride, then, for it will make us both feel better," Rebecca suggested.

"You cannot feel up to a ride!" her friend protested.

"But I do. There is nothing I long for more," Rebecca replied, laying down her sketchbook.

When they returned an hour later Clayborne was awaiting them in the parlor. He was tempted in his concern to scold his wife for overexerting herself, but he refrained from doing so. He could tell from the twinkle in her eye that she had observed his struggle and he smiled ruefully.

"I'm glad to see you feeling more the thing, Rebecca," he said, as his eye fell on the sketchbook. "The local vicar, I have no doubt."

"Quite right. He accepted Constance's assignment and told us of his adventures in great detail. Constance will tell you of them for I cannot trust myself to do so."

Constance was able, in a few pithy sentences, to enlighten Clayborne on the situation the vicar had found at Campden Manor as well as her own thoughts on that worthy himself. Clayborne's brows drew together in anger and he remarked, "I shall go back to Broadway in the morning to do what I can. At least Lawton is away for a bit, and I shall post someone at the gates of Campden Manor to advise me of his return. I don't expect he will be back right away but we must be prepared. I would have Elvira come to you but that would be dangerous for all of you. She might best find security at the vicar's. Rebecca, if you will write a note to her, I can see it delivered in the morning. Suggest that she go to the vicar's if her uncle returns. I do not think she will be in danger there."

"No, even Eustace Lawton would hesitate to do her harm there, but he would have the authority to drag her home."

"Yes, but by that time I can be summoned. You must trust me in this," he said calmly, bending the penetrating brown eyes on her.

"Of course I do," she said, meeting his gaze steadily. "I always have."

Clayborne, painfully aware that it was true, wished to speak of his shame in not having believed in her, but Constance's presence forestalled him. The conversation turned away from Elvira to a discussion of London and whom he had met there.

"Uncle Henry sent his fond regards. He is home from Egypt due to the gout, but he seems in plump currant now. Lady Stonebridge asked to be remembered to you, also. On the other hand, your parents, being the only ones who know that you are not with me, were provoked with the two of us. You may expect a scathing letter from your mother any day, no doubt."

"I am sure that Mama is only concerned with the scandal. She is so looking forward to presenting Mary in the spring, and she will look on this as a setback," Rebecca replied.

"She does. And when the news spreads to London, as it eventually shall, of course, I have no doubt she will drag your papa off to Farthington Hall without delay."

"Where Mary will inform her that she couldn't care less for a London season, as she has already expressed to me in a letter I received a few days ago. In fact, she begged to come and stay with us here."

"From past experience I should look for her on your doorstep any day," Clayborne said with a grin.

"You do not really believe that, do you?" Constance asked, aghast.

"Well, she did run away from my aunt in Bath to join us in London," Rebecca admitted, "but she does not know where we are, as the letter came through Mr. Darcy."

"I doubt that would stop her," Clayborne commented dryly.

"No, perhaps not," Rebecca mused, "for Mary is very resourceful. However, if Mama is soon at Farthington Hall, she shall put a stop to any such plans."

Clayborne stayed to dinner and the young women provided some music afterwards, but it had been an exhausting day and Clayborne soon excused himself, taking Rebecca's letter for Elvira with him. Constance made sure that Rebecca was settled for the night before she adjourned to her own room, where she lay awake for some time, considering the events of the day and trying to push from her mind the thought that tomorrow they would have been in the cottage for a month.

Twenty

Rebecca was startled the next morning to find Constance dressed in her prettiest outfit, a rose-colored morning dress trimmed with white loops. Of course, Rebecca herself had discarded the older gown Harpert had laid out for her and had chosen instead to don a pale green walking dress whose high collar framed her face. It had been included in her trousseau but had not yet been worn. The same young lad was seated at the corner of the lane when they went out to the shops, but they were sure it was an arrangement of Clayborne's and they could only be grateful for his care of them.

After purchasing some lengths of ribbon and thread, as well as meat and vegetables from Harpert's list, the young ladies strolled home down the sunny lane past other stone cottages, the flowers fragrant in the summer morning. Constance was the first to spot the carriage before their door and a blush of pleasure suffused her face. Rebecca took one look at the carriage she had ridden in for several days and then looked at Constance, saying with a sigh, "I have been blind indeed, for I thought he was interested in Mary. Why did you say nothing, Constance?"

"There is nothing decided as yet," she replied, blushing more fiercely.

"Well, come, it is time there was. I shall stay only to greet him and then leave you alone," Rebecca said, grinning gleefully at her friend. "And your mama does not even know him!"

When Rebecca had greeted Mott enthusiastically

and seen him seated near Constance, she excused herself on an imaginary errand. He did not reseat himself after rising for her exit, but instead wandered about the room for a few moments, admiring the improvements they had made. Constance sat with her hands folded in her lap while her eyes followed him.

"I have been to see your brother," Mott finally announced abruptly.

"How is Charles?"

"He is well and sent his fondest regards to you. I have a letter from him somewhere, but I cannot remember precisely where I put it."

"I am sure it will turn up. His wife and children are well?"

"Oh, yes, all are fine. Did I forget to say so?" he asked distractedly.

"I was sure you would remember eventually," Constance teased him.

"You are laughing at me." He grinned. "I don't know why this should be so difficult. I asked your brother for his leave to pay my addresses to you." He stopped expectantly.

"And what did Charles say?" Constance prompted.

"Oh, well, as to that, he said you were your own mistress and should make up your own mind on the matter. But he did give us his blessing, should you decide to have me. I know I may not be everything you look for in a husband, and I have lived secluded for a very long time. There is little George, too. As you know, he is a handful and forever where you do not precisely wish him to be."

"I am very fond of George," Constance admitted, her eyes laughing up at him.

"Constance, you are *trying* to make this harder for me," Mott accused. "Will you do me the honor of becoming my wife, for I love you dearly."

"Now that was quite an admirable declaration," Constance mused. "You know, I am very tempted . . . Yes, I shall accept you."

Mott pulled her into his arms and kissed her soundly. "And are you a little fond of me, too?" he asked, eyeing her exasperatedly.

"Yes, Gregory, I love you," she replied, and returned his kiss as ardently as he could have hoped.

When they finally seated themselves on the sofa, holding hands and smiling idiotically at each other, Mott asked, "Can we be married soon? Now that I have found you I am anxious to take you home with me as soon as may be."

"And I wish to go with you, but there are any number of things to consider. I shall have to bring you up to date on our ... ah ... activities this last month." It took some time to do so, and Mott watched her with fascination as she unfolded the lengthy tale of Elvira and her wicked uncle.

"Clayborne is here?" he asked, when she had finished.

"He is gone to Broadway this morning, but I expect he shall be back soon. So you see, Gregory, there are several matters to be settled before I may be wed. I do not like to leave Rebecca here alone, either, but I know she would be very put out with me if I were to delay the wedding on her account. She is the most generous of friends."

"She cannot reach an understanding with Clayborne? You know, he is an excellent fellow, and she is an admirable woman. They are so perfectly suited that I cannot feel their separation is at all right."

"I know," Constance sighed. "I cannot understand it, for I feel sure they are fond of each other. But she will not speak of it, and I do not wish to interfere."

"I know. I tried to speak with Clayborne and he intimated that they were both at fault, but he would brook no meddling. Like to snapped my nose off when I pursued the matter."

"Well, they shall have to work it out for themselves. Let us tell Rebecca our news!"

Clayborne found his trip to Broadway well worthwhile. The young man assisting him in his inquiries had immediately contacted the former estate manager for

Campden Manor and had obtained enough information from him to present a case to the local magistrate, but Clayborne instructed him to delay this until he had had a chance to speak with Mr. Lawton himself. As he approached Campden Manor late in the afternoon, Clayborne felt fortunate indeed to meet with his groom riding swiftly to fetch him, for Mr. Lawton had just returned. The groom was thanked, and, much to his chagrin, informed that he might return to the inn. He rode off muttering, "Keeps all the sport for hisself, he does."

Without hesitation Clayborne drove his curricle straight through the gates and up to the manor house. He handed the reins to the startled groom who sauntered forth from the stable, and ascended to the front door. He was greeted, though that might be an exaggeration, by the churlish housekeeper, who assured him that Mr. Lawton would be unable to see him. He assured her in turn that Mr. Lawton could and would see him, for he had no intention of leaving until he had spoken with the man.

"Wait here," she grumbled and shut the door, leaving him standing on the doorstep. Already in disgrace with her employer, who had returned to find Elvira was no longer locked in her room and was in fact not in the house at all, she shuffled off to Lawton's study. He had threatened to dismiss the housekeeper should she displease him again and she had no doubt that this latest arrival would displease him exceedingly.

"There be a London swell at the door insisting on seeing you, sir. Says he'll not leave 'til he's done so. I told him, I did, that you wasn't receiving, but him not likely to listen to the likes of me!"

"Send him away. I'll see no one," Lawton grunted.

"I'll tell him, but I doubt it will do any good," she replied darkly, and left to convey the message to Clayborne.

It did no good at all, of course, for Clayborne was not used to be left kicking his heels, and he merely set the housekeeper aside and entered the hall. While she stood loudly declaiming his manners, Clayborne patiently opened each door off the hall to find his quarry. Lawton would have had to be deaf not to have heard the commotion, and he angrily slammed out of the study and stood confronting his visitor.

"What is the meaning of this intrusion?" he screamed. "Get out of my house!"

"Not until I have had a word with you, in private," Clayborne said coldly.

"Well, you shan't, so get out," Lawton cried, his face suffused with an angry red.

"Perhaps it would interest you to know that my name is Clayborne," his visitor suggested grimly.

Lawton backed away from him saying, "So what of it? I have nothing to say to you."

"But I have a great deal to say to you," Clayborne replied softly, advancing toward the man, who edged his way into the study. Clayborne followed him and shut the door in the astonished housekeeper's face. "You tried to force your attentions on my wife."

"I did no such thing! The jade encouraged me," he smirked, but not for long, as Clayborne put to use the skills he had been acquiring at Jackson's Boxing Saloon. Lawton picked himself up from the floor and advanced menacingly on his adversary. He had very little form, but his strength was considerable. Clayborne dodged the low blow aimed at him, and planted a hit to the jaw which sank Lawton to the floor again. "I think you should apologize for your rudeness," Clayborne commented, watching the other man pick himself up again.

If the truth be known, it gave Clayborne considerable pleasure that Lawton was not yet ready to apologize. Although Elvira's uncle had engaged in many brawls with men unequal to his powerful right, the man had not met the likes of his opponent before. Clayborne calmly evaded the punishing right and the kick aimed at his groin and knocked Lawton down three more times before the latter was willing to make a grudging apology. Since it was unlikely that he had ever apologized in his adult life, it was not surprising that the apology was not everything expected by Clayborne. Once again Lawton found himself on the floor, this time with a bloody nose, which he protested had been broken.

"Perhaps it would be easier if I were to frame a

suitable apology for you to repeat," Clayborne suggested quietly. "I think I might be willing to accept your saying, 'My apologies to you and Lady Clayborne for my disgusting and cowardly behavior and for my disparaging references to that good lady.' "

Lawton's puffing right eye and bleeding nose notwithstanding, he had a difficult time repeating the sentence Clayborne proposed, and he had to be prompted several times before he completed the task. "Now we shall turn to other matters," Clayborne said composedly, as he seated himself comfortably and watched his host drop dejectedly into another chair.

"My wife wrote me some days ago that she was concerned about your mistreatment of your ward," Clayborne began conversationally. "She also intimated that you were most likely misappropriating your ward's estate." He noted that Lawton paled considerably but maintained a belligerent expression. "I took the liberty of looking into these matters and have found that my wife was correct on both heads."

"Much you could do about it even were it true," Lawton sneered.

"True, there is a good deal I can do about it," Clayborne mockingly agreed. "I came here today to settle the first matter with you, as you will understand, privately. I have not met your niece as yet, but I am assured by my wife that she is a proud girl and would not enjoy the scandal that a public trial of her uncle would create. However, as she is a minor she can have no say in the matter. Nevertheless, I am here to inform you that if you yourself wish to avoid imprisonment, you had best flee the country today, for tomorrow the necessary information will be laid with the local magistrate, who cannot fail to act on it. That is all I have to say. Good-day," Clayborne said and strode from the room, leaving Lawton open-mouthed and looking sick in his chair.

Lawton screamed after his departing guest, "You are lying! You cannot prove a thing!" But he knew that Clayborne was not bluffing. Greedy as he was, he had not been clever enough to cover his tracks. His only hope had ever been to tame his niece to the point where she would never question his management of her estate, and marry her to a man of his choice before she came of age. But Lawton had been unable to break Elvira's spirit so far and now there was nothing left for him to do but take Clayborne's advice. His body ached as he lifted himself out of the chair to prepare for the journey.

When Elvira had heard hoofbeats approaching the manor she had slipped down the back stairs and out the door, waiting in the shrubbery until her uncle was in the house. Avoiding the stable, she walked the mile to the vicarage, where she was kindly invited to take tea with Miss Andrews. The vicar was from home at the time, but returned shortly to find her there.

"My uncle has returned," she explained, "and Lady Clayborne had written me a note suggesting that I come here if he did."

"Of course, my child. I imagine it will be some time before Mr. Lawton learns of your whereabouts," he said nervously.

Elvira regarded him pityingly, her face still puffed, and said, "I am sure if he comes here he shall only want to take me home."

"True, true. And I am a man of the cloth," he consoled himself. He drifted off into a discussion of his treatise, which could not be expected to be received enthusiastically by the girl and even seemed to bore his sister. This was interrupted by the entry of the maid announcing Lord Clayborne. "Show him in directly," ordered the smiling cleric.

Although Clayborne expressed his pleasure at meeting the vicar and his sister, and his appreciation of their assistance, his attention was drawn toward Elvira. He took her hand gently in his and said kindly, "I have been with your uncle. I believe he will flee the country this very day, for tomorrow we shall place sufficient evidence with the magistrate to unseat him as your guardian. I hope I have done the right thing; Lady Clayborne desired it so for your sake. She thought you would not wish to see him imprisoned in spite of his treatment of you and your estate."

"You are very kind, Lord Clayborne, and it is exactly as I could wish. My only desire is never to see Uncle Lawton again in my life," she whispered fervently.

"Should you like me to take you to Lady Clayborne now? I am sure there is no more danger to any of you."

"If you please," she replied, confidently placing her hand on his arm.

Regretfully the vicar bade his aristocratic visitor farewell and watched them depart in his lordship's curricle. With a gusty sigh he asked for another cup of tea, picking up his discourse as if there had been no interruption.

Twenty-One

"Oh, Lady Clayborne, I have never been so happy," Elvira sobbed. "Lord Clayborne says my uncle will have to leave the country."

Rebecca hugged the girl while her husband dug a handkerchief from his pocket. "Is that true, Jason? Whatever did you do to him?"

"Was Elvira away from the manor when he returned?" Constance wanted to know.

Gregory Mott, never having met the girl, and finding her surrounded by her two friends, chose to shake hands with Clayborne. "Good to see you again, Jason."

"I had no idea you would be here."

"Congratulations are in order. Constance has agreed to marry me."

After this announcement there was only a confused babble.

"Oh, Miss Exton, that *is* wonderful!"

"Gregory, I don't believe you've met Elvira Carstairs. This is my fiancé, Gregory Mott, Elvira."

"How do you do, sir."

"Constance, when did this happen? You said nothing to me yesterday."

"Well, I knew nothing of it yesterday. It has come as the greatest, and most delightful, surprise."

"Mr. Mott has a son, has he not? I think Lady Clayborne mentioned that one day when I was here."

"Yes, he has a four-year-old named George, who has just gotten a pony of his own."

In the midst of the chaos, Harpert poked her head out of the kitchen to ascertain that there were likely to be yet two more people for dinner, and disappeared with a resigned expression to see what she could manage.

When the explanations and congratulations had finally been sorted out, Clayborne managed to get Rebecca aside from the others for a few moments. With some satisfaction he delivered Lawton's apology and assured her that Lawton had uttered every word of it. She eyed him suspiciously and asked, "And you are sure that he is in fit condition to make a journey today?"

"Hardly, but I assure you he will make it all the same," he replied grimly. "Rebecca, I'm very happy for Constance and Gregory, but I cannot believe you will wish to stay here alone and I don't think they wish to delay their wedding for long."

"No, he has already approached her brother and received his blessing. I wonder where they will be married."

"They could be married at Gray Oaks if you would come home," he said softly.

Rebecca did not answer but sat thinking, staring at her hands. "What is to become of Elvira?" she asked at length.

"The solicitor in Broadway questioned the old estate manager about possible relatives. He believes there are some distant relations in Shropshire, but it will take some time to seek them out and ascertain if they would be proper guardians for the girl. I should not like to see another mistake made on that head."

"Nor I. She deserves to have someone who will care for her. What will happen in the meantime?"

"I suppose the magistrate will appoint a temporary protector for her. I am afraid he would not allow you to have her on your own, Rebecca, if that is what you are thinking of. But I am sure he would entrust her to the both of us if I were to ask. I think Elvira would be happy at Gray Oaks for a few months, and we would be able to see the new situation she is getting into and satisfy ourselves as to its suitability."

"What would I do with the cottage?" Rebecca asked numbly.

"We could have the renovations completed and sublet it for the term of your lease. I would see to that."

Rebecca continued to contemplate her hands sadly. Of course, Constance and Gregory could be married anywhere, but wherever they were married it would leave Rebecca without the companion she needed in her isolation. Perhaps, too, Elvira could be placed with a protector in the neighborhood, but not the vicar and his sister, God forbid. Constance would love to have Elvira with her, too, but in marrying Gregory there was already little George to be thought of. Elvira deserved to be with someone who wanted her and had time to help her erase this last horrible year. And the cottage. Rebecca had come to love it and consider it her refuge. If she returned to Gray Oaks she would be faced again with the daily pain of being with Clayborne and yet apart from him. And yet she really had no choice at all. She had made Elvira her responsibility, turning the lives of half a dozen people upside down to right the child's life, and she had no intention of walking away from her now. When the girl had a kind family to go to, well perhaps then Rebecca could think about her own life again.

Without raising her eyes Rebecca said softly, "I shall come back to Gray Oaks with you, Jason. You are kind to have me back and to offer Elvira a home for a while."

Clayborne was aware of the pressures which persuaded Rebecca to accept his offer; he had silently watched the struggle on her face before she spoke. But there was no help for it, the situation knew of no other logical solution. He ached for her sadness but he was grateful that he would have her back on any terms, if even for a while. "Thank you, my dear," was all he said.

Dinner was announced by a slightly flustered Harpert, who was rewarded with a beaming smile from Constance and a wink of approval from Rebecca. Over the meal, which was remarkably good under the circumstances, Rebecca said quite matter-of-factly, "I plan to return to Gray Oaks, and I hope that you and Gregory will honor us by being married there." Her eyes twinkled when she said aside to Constance, "It will make it so easy for your mama to come to the wedding!"

Delighted that Rebecca should be returning home, they agreed with hardly a murmur of protest.

"And, Elvira, if it should suit you, tomorrow Jason shall speak to the magistrate about your coming with us until a permanent guardian can be found for you. Your old estate manager remembers some distant relations in Shropshire, but that will have to be investigated. Jason feels confident that the magistrate would allow you to come with us for a while. Would that please you?"

"Of all things! I cannot thank you enough," the girl cried.

"Well, and you need not. You will like Gray Oaks, I think, for there is a lovely house, and a stable to make your eyes open, and a topiary that is a legend in Jason's family," Rebecca laughed. "And I shall invite my sister Mary to stay with us if Jason agrees, for I have received another letter from her today which I have barely had time to read, but it convinces me that she is not happy at Farthington Hall just now." She grinned impishly at Clayborne and said, "My parents have returned there."

"I understand," he said wryly. "Yes, I think it an excellent idea that Mary come, and Gregory shall bring George to stay with us after the wedding so that he and Constance may have a honeymoon."

Constance blushed with pleasure and Gregory smiled his appreciation of this comprehension of the situation. Clayborne felt that the larger the party at Gray Oaks, the easier Rebecca would be. It was not the time to tell her of his own feelings. She had no choice but to return to his home, and until she was free to decide what *she* wanted to do, he would not burden her further. So the matter was settled.

Within a week Clayborne left Chipping Campden with Rebecca, Constance, Elvira and Harpert, while Mott returned to Yorkshire to bring George to Gray Oaks. A letter was dispatched to Rebecca's parents placating them with the news that she was returning to her husband's home and inviting Mary to join them immediately. Since the wedding was planned for a month hence, preparations began in earnest and Constance's brother was enlisted to urge the extreme suitability of the marriage on his mother, who was reluctant to believe that Constance could have found an eligible match by herself after all her mother's years of effort.

Mary arrived in the Farthington Hall carriage with her abigail, "For," as she explained, "I told Mama I would not come if Turnip was to come with me. And Mama was so grateful to be rid of her unfeeling daughter that she gave in within a day!"

"I cannot thank you enough, Mary, for I don't think I could have tolerated Turnip just now," Rebecca admitted frankly. "I want you to meet Elvira, who is staying with us, and little George will be here soon with his father. You'll not be able to get any sense out of Constance, for she has her head in the clouds."

"Pay no attention to her, Mary dear. I'm sure I have been the soul of practicality, making lists I promptly lose and purchasing items I do not need. But I am told everything will come about in the end," Constance confided.

"I'm so pleased for you, Constance. Mott is the nicest of gentlemen, except for Clayborne, of course." Mary's enthusiasm was so sincere that Rebecca, who had worried that her sister's heart might have been touched by the widower, felt immeasurably relieved.

"Your room is ready for you, Mary, but Elvira is in the stables and wished to meet you as soon as you arrived, so I shall send for her. She's a girl Constance and I met in the Cotswolds and she'll be staying with Jason and me for several months."

"No, don't send for her. I shall go to the stables right now, for I wish to see Firely first thing and I'll meet her there."

Fortunately, the two young ladies enjoyed each other's company from the start, which was not cause for surprise since they shared such an enthusiastic interest in horses. By the time they returned to the house, they were chatting like old friends, which delighted Rebecca and Constance, since they knew only too well that the preparations for the wedding would absorb much of their time for the next few weeks.

The local dressmaker insisted that the numerous fittings she required of Constance were absolutely essential and the bride acquiesced, until Mott arrived with George. Fortunately, since Constance spent most of her time with him, the majority of the work was far enough under way to demand less of her attention to it. The ribbons and trimmings did not necessitate fittings, and if Mrs. Potter did not receive prompt answers to her inquiries on whether the white crape apron should be narrower at the top, and whether the black jet beads should be in a pattern on the rouleau, she was indulgent of Constance's distraction. One could not expect the full attention of a bride.

Clayborne did not expect any attention at all from his wife. Although Mary and Elvira took charge of little George, including him in their expeditions and rides, Rebecca found the time to read to him from books Clayborne had had as a child, tolerantly agreeing to read the story of a medieval barony several times, as it had caught George's fancy. Clayborne stood in the boy's doorway, where he had come to bid his nephew goodnight, and listened to Rebecca read, her head bent over the book and her arm encircling the lad's shoulders. And he ached to have her in his arms, to set all right again. When she glanced up and saw him, she smiled. "We are nearly finished, Jason."

They left the room together but he had no opportunity to speak with her, as she had promised Constance that she would come directly to see the gowns which had been delivered that day. On the way she chatted of the decorations, food, flowers and rooms to be prepared for the guests staying at Gray Oaks for the wedding. In addition to these tasks, he knew she spent an hour or so a day with Elvira, reading with her or showing her needlework stitches. She also walked or rode with Mary daily and was willing to listen to Constance's plans or Mott's concerns at any time. Clayborne seldom had any time alone with her and, what worried him more, she seldom had any time to herself.

Pausing before her friend's door, she said, "I have planned an excursion for the girls to see the Norman Cathedral in Chichester tomorrow, Jason. We may go on to Bosham or Fishborne. Do you think George would like that? I don't know how I came to forget mentioning it to him."

"I do. You have too many things on your mind, Rebecca. Couldn't Mrs. Lambert handle more of the details?"

"I enjoy it, Jason, and she is doing more than enough already." Poor Mrs. Lambert, Rebecca thought. Although she must have been extremely curious about my return, she did not indicate it by word or deed, and her iron rule over the other indoor servants has kept their interest within bounds. "Do you think George would like to go with us?"

"Yes, I imagine he would, but, Rebecca . . ."

Constance thrust her head out the door. "I thought I heard you here, my dear. Have you time to see my gowns?"

"Yes, it's why I've come. Thank you, Jason. I shall ask George in the morning."

A few days before the arrival of the first guests for the wedding, and the day after Rebecca had entertained some neighbors to a musical evening, Clayborne found her in the small parlor gazing longingly out the window, a list with most of the items crossed off in front of her on the secretaire. She smiled up at him, trying to hide her weariness, and said, "I think the preparations for the wedding are well in hand."

"I am more concerned with you than with the wedding. You've been working too hard. I didn't bring you back to Gray Oaks to be a slave but to enjoy yourself. You may have a choice," he said firmly, taking her hand and bringing her to her feet. "You may go to your room and rest, without a single list, mind you, or you may come for a drive with me in the curricle. Which is it to be?"

"I would love to go for a drive. It's such a beautiful day," she sighed. "But I have things still to do."

"Not for the next hour, you don't. Now get your bonnet and I'll expect you at the front door in fifteen minutes."

"Such a tyrant!" she laughed. "I shall be ready."

Clayborne drove her through the sunny country lanes and along the coast road. At first Rebecca talked of their guests and the wedding but she gradually relaxed into a companionable silence, enjoying the play of the light on the water.

"Could we walk on the beach?" she asked suddenly.

"Of course. We can do anything you wish."

He tied the horses in the shade of some hawthorn trees and handed Rebecca down over the stones to the beach. Rushing like a child to the water, she sat down on the pebbles and, without the least embarrassment, pulled off her stockings and slippers. Her skirts held high with her hands, she waded into the water, squealing with delight as it washed about her legs. Clayborne was tempted to join her, but instead sat on the beach and watched her delight. Her bonnet hung back on her shoulders and the sun gleamed on her black locks as she wandered along, picking up stones with one hand and clutching her skirts in the other, though they inevitably dipped into the water. After a while she joined Clayborne to sit on the beach while she let the sun dry her feet. They did not speak, but listened to the lapping of the water and the cries of the birds and watched the glinting of the sun on the water. It was a long time before Rebecca reluctantly reached for her stockings, saying, "I hate to leave. It's so peaceful here."

"We shall come again then," Clayborne replied, setting the bonnet back on her head and tying the ribbon securely.

Rebecca chuckled and when Clayborne looked questioningly at her, said, "I could not help remembering how you kept pushing Lady Hillston's hood back on her head at Vauxhall."

It occurred to him that perhaps this snippet of his

past should irritate him, but he could not help laughing. "Wretch! I would dearly have loved to see you and Mary in your disguises. Was I odious to you afterwards? You must have thought that very strange, coming from a man who had spent the evening with another woman."

"No," she whispered, "I . . . understood."

Because he wanted to kiss her then, and feared to do so, he touched her lips gently with his finger. He could tell her now, tell her that he had come to believe her. Beg her to forgive his lack of trust. Because if she could not, it would make her stay at Gray Oaks a misery, and she could not leave until the wedding was over and Elvira settled. Though it would suit him to unburden his heart, it would not be fair to her. She must be in a position to say no, and leave.

Rebecca raised her eyes to meet his. Why did he not kiss her? She could see that he wanted to, that he was rigidly controlling the impulse. He had been so very gentle with her since her return, never a reproachful glance, not a sharp word. No longer drawn into himself, he had been more like the Jason she remembered from their engagement. Still, when unaware of her observation, she had noticed his sad countenance. How she wished she could erase his troubles, and, oh, how she needed his love! Rebecca had very nearly worked up the nerve to stand on tiptoe and kiss his cheek when he turned away to retrieve her reticule from the pebbles. With a sigh she took his arm for the climb up the bank to the curricle. "Some day soon I must show you my cartoons."

"I have hoped you would. Shall you show me the ones of myself?" he taunted her.

"How do you know there are any of you?" she asked, but added, "You shall see them all."

They drove back at a leisurely pace, discussing the guests who were expected soon. Mrs. Exton was likely to prove a troublesome member of the party, but Constance's brother Charles and his wife were well-disposed to the match and were very pleasant people into the bargain. There were various other relations on both sides attending, but neither Clayborne nor Rebecca knew them and most would not stay above a night or two.

"Just remember, Rebecca, that Mrs. Lambert will be only too willing to see to everything necessary for the house guests. Don't tire yourself. Constance will be disappointed if you don't enjoy the wedding, you know," Clayborne said as he handed her down from the curricle.

"You're right, of course. I'm glad you took me out this afternoon, for I enjoyed myself and feel more rested. Thank you, Jason."

"It was my pleasure. We shall do it again soon if you like."

"After the wedding, if you please," she laughed. "I shall not work my fingers to the bone, but there are still matters to be seen to and the wedding is less than a week away now."

When Rebecca returned to the small parlor she was greeted enthusiastically by Mary and Elvira, desiring to know if they could use some materials they had found in the attic, and borrow her sewing basket. "What are the two of you up to?" Rebecca asked quizzingly.

"It's a secret," Mary explained. "A surprise we will have ready in a few days. Really, it's for George and I promise you it will keep us all out of mischief for some days."

"I find that singularly difficult to believe," her sister retorted, "but you may have the material and the sewing basket. You will not do anything too dreadful, I trust."

"It's just for sport," Elvira said, "and I think you will be quite pleased with it."

"Run along, then, and if I can help just let me know," Rebecca waved them off.

Whatever the project was, it did seem to keep them occupied, for they were gone for the better part of the next few days, either in the stables or in the girls' rooms. The guests had begun arriving and arrangements were completed for the wedding, but Elvira, Mary and George were rarely to be found. Mrs. Exton grudgingly admitted that Mott was unexceptionable, but declared she did not envy her daughter the care of a four-year-old such as George. Charles Exton reminded her that he had often been told of his own extreme youth by his mother and thought he could not have been much less of a handful.

244

"Much worse, you were," she declaimed proudly and assured Constance, with no heed to the contradiction, that little George was an angel compared with her brother at that age.

As matron of honor, Rebecca took part in the beautiful wedding with mixed emotions. The ceremony was impressively solemn, though the vague Mr. Rivers did lose his place twice, and Mott was remarkably nervous. Clayborne as groomsman and George as ring-bearer supported the groom to the best of their differing abilities, but the couple were as relieved as they were joyous to be pronounced man and wife. Rebecca's heart went out to them, but she was unhappily reminded of her own wedding a year ago and the expectations she had had. Just so had she and Jason stood before a cleric and heard the time-honored phrases read, thinking that they were beginning a new and rewarding phase of their lives. Surrounded by approving family and well-wishing friends, the venture had seemed propitious. Rebecca thrust aside her despairing thoughts and smiled at the couple as they walked hand in hand down the aisle. No such cloud would darken their horizons, she felt sure.

The wedding breakfast at Gray Oaks was opulent in the extreme and alive with the color and smell of the late summer flowers Rebecca had caused to adorn every conceivable niche of the house. Every door stood open for the summer breezes to play through the rooms, ruffling the bride's golden hair and ivory lace wedding gown, and cooling the groom's flushed cheeks.

Rebecca went with Constance to help dress her in her traveling clothes. "How can I thank you for everything, Rebecca?" Constance asked, her eyes shining with happiness. "It was the most beautiful wedding ever."

Pleased with the success of the day, Rebecca only smiled and said, "I've loved every minute of it. Now you are to have a delightful trip and do not be concerned for George. We'll be happy to keep him as long as we may. Mary and Elvira are up to something with him, but I have not as yet discovered what it may be. You shall hear all about it on your return, no doubt!"

After enduring her mother's tears and hasty reminders, and hugging Mary and Elvira and George, Constance placed a kiss on Clayborne's cheek and assured him that he could not have been more generous. Mott helped her into the traveling carriage, everyone waved vigorously, and the carriage departed. There was a letdown after all this activity, but soon the house guests began to arrange for their own leave-takings. Carriages were called for and the bustle began again. Charles Exton and his wife were accompanying his mother to Brighton, and despite her expressed desire to remain for another day to recover from the shock of it all, she found herself leaving Gray Oaks only a few hours after her daughter.

Twenty-Two

Mary and Elvira were impatient to change from their wedding finery into their riding clothes and did not wait for the last departures. They had debated springing their surprise on the assembled wedding party but had agreed that Rebecca just might not approve of that, good-natured as she was. Intent on astonishing Clayborne and Rebecca with their clever idea just before dinner, when everyone had had a chance to recover from the festivities, they hurried off to make the final preparations.

George was not long in following them to the stables, where the three of them began putting the final touches on their project. Fascinated by the stories of medieval life and jousting, he had asked Mary to fashion a blunt-ended lance for him to carry on old Bessie, who was once again at Gray Oaks. Mary had enlisted Elvira's assistance and they had gotten carried away in a spate of authenticity. Not only two lances but two masks as helmets, and two shields, were fashioned. They had practiced with these in secret and were delighted with the results, but George had seen a picture of a horse in trappings of white with red standing lions on them and he was not content until Mary promised to duplicate this costume for Bessie.

Poor Bessie was very patient with all the fittings which this took, and even allowed a sort of mask with enormous eye holes to be placed over her head. Numerous little bells were attached to her harness and she seemed pleased to jingle as she trotted along. Mary abso-

247

lutely refused to make more than one of these costumes, but she allowed as how Elvira's mount should have bells also. Now all was in readiness for their debut for Clayborne and Rebecca, but they decided to have a practice joust in the far meadow so that they might stage the match perfectly. Sort of a dress rehearsal, Elvira giggled. Mary had decided to coordinate this event rather than participate in it, so she gave the direction for the two protagonists to face each other and come forward. George's lance was a bit heavy for him to manage, but he valiantly aimed it at Elvira's shield. The ensuing chaos ended in whoops of laughter and the decision to stage the event immediately for their proper audience, as George did not wish to tire himself out.

Rebecca sadly wandered about the house after the last guests had departed. She would miss Constance sorely, even with Mary and Elvira, to say nothing of George, still about the house. She had celebrated the first anniversary of her own wedding just two weeks previously, and, though Clayborne had given her a charming locket and a delightful Rowlandson print he had found at Mistress Murphy's cartoon shop in St. James' Street, and promised a surprise which would not be ready for a few weeks, she had felt so depressed that her thanks had seemed even to herself to lack enthusiasm. Clayborne, however, had sought to ignore this and had been genuinely pleased with the drawings Rebecca had given him of Gray Oaks. There had been one of him near the house, one of Mary, Elvira and George out riding and one of Constance and Mott in the topiary.

"The set is incomplete, my dear," he teased. "There should have been one of you in the small parlor with a list in your hand."

"I did try to draw myself," she replied seriously, "but I could not feel that it was successful."

"I should like to see it, all the same," he urged, and she had gone to her room to fetch it for him. It had given him a start to see the drawing she brought, which depicted her sitting in her room gazing wistfully out the window. "May I keep it?" he had asked, not looking at her.

"Yes, if you like. But I shall try to draw a better one for you." He had made no comment but tucked the fourth drawing into the folder with the others and excused himself.

Now that Constance had left it occurred to Rebecca that she might draw some scenes from the wedding as a present to her and Gregory. She took her drawing paper to the small parlor and quickly sketched three or four scenes, some serious from the church and some amusing from the wedding breakfast, with Mrs. Exton predominant in tears in one and George doing a somersault in another. She was just putting them carefully away when Clayborne entered.

"Oh, Jason, come and see the sketches I have done of the wedding," she offered. "In fact, you shall see all of my sketches now if you like, as I have been meaning to show them to you."

Rebecca handed him all the sketches except those of himself, reserving them for last. Clayborne was fascinated, and frequently commented on the ability his wife had for catching a character with a few carefully chosen lines. When he came to the one of Lady Hillston, he smiled wryly and remarked, "Oh, yes, I remember this one."

"Mary was quite taken with it. She told me, you know, that she had intended to spirit it off to a print shop, but then she felt better after Lady Hillston's horse bolted with her, so she didn't." When Clayborne looked aghast at this she laughed and explained, "It was Lady Hillston's comment about your playing nursemaid to Mary that annoyed her."

"Of course. Thank God she didn't. Though, on the other hand, I should have loved to have seen Alexis's face when she saw it!"

He continued to go through the sketches, murmuring, "That is wonderful of Uncle Henry" or "Ah, yes, the dinner party," as he went along. When he was finished he set them aside and looked at her quizzingly. "I do not think that is quite all."

"No, for I have kept back the sketches of you. You must understand, Jason, that sometimes I draw in anger, that it makes me feel better to set pen to paper. You may see them if you will keep that in mind."

"I promise," he said calmly, but he did not feel very calm when he saw some of the drawings. There were those that were drawn with incredible tenderness, to be sure, but more where he was pictured as a very disagreeable man. He forced himself to look at them and see himself through her eyes, and he was shocked because he knew that she had not unduly exaggerated. "My poor dear. I hope these were drawn a while back," he said, indicating the harsher ones.

"Yes, some months ago. You have been very kind to me of late."

Clayborne drew his hand over his eyes and handed the cartoons back to his wife. He wanted to speak to her now, but he did not know quite what to say, and he did not want her to think that it was just the cartoons that had prompted him. "Would you like to go for a drive?" he asked abruptly.

Rebecca smiled at him, afraid he was embarrassed by the emotion betrayed in the cartoons. "I would rather ride with you, for I have promised Constance to exercise her mare while she's gone."

"I'll have the horses saddled."

They rode down a lane not far from the house, Constance's mare rather skittish from lack of exercise, for the wedding had occupied not only the household, but the stable staff as well, with the extra horses and carriages of the guests. They were rounding a bend in the path when it happened.

George had halted his pony to retrieve his lance and swung back up so that the party could proceed. In high spirits now, as they approached the house, they urged their mounts gaily forward. The jingling of bells and the startling sight of the pony in bright trappings and hooded head, as well as little George masked and armed with shield and lance thrust forward, was too much for Constance's mare. The terrified horse shied wildly, rearing abruptly and throwing Rebecca, who had not been concentrating on her riding, but on the need to reassure Clayborne. She fell to the ground, her head striking a rock, and lay still. Clayborne was at her side in an instant, while the jousting party sat stunned on their mounts. Mary's face went white, and she stiffly dismounted to kneel beside her sister. "Oh, dear God, no," she whispered. "We meant no harm, Rebecca."

Clayborne's face was ashen but he said gently to Mary, "She is alive. We must send for the doctor immediately. Will you see to that while I carry her home? Are you all right?"

Mary blinked back the tears that had started to fall and choked as she said, "I can get the doctor. Rebecca has pointed out his house to me."

"Good girl. Elvira, take George to the stable and send someone for the horses. Can you manage?"

"Yes, Lord Clayborne. George, give me the lance and shield and we will go faster." George did as he was bid, but he was crying soundlessly. "The doctor will help your aunt, you shall see," she comforted him, not knowing whether to believe it or not. Mary had already ridden away, and Clayborne's and Constance's horses had wandered off, so the two children started on their way, the sound of jingling bells mocking their passage.

Clayborne lifted his unconscious wife in his arms and walked off down the lane, the sickness in him growing until he feared that he could not contain it. For a while he did not realize that he was speaking, that his thoughts were being voiced automatically. "Please don't die, Rebecca. I can let you go anywhere, but I cannot bear a life where you are not somewhere, laughing and riding and drawing. Only live and I will not press you to stay with me. I have not deserved you. I wanted only to make you happy when we married, and I ruined everything because I didn't trust you."

There were grooms coming now, sent by Elvira, and he merely motioned them down the path to the horses. Soon he carried Rebecca into the house and up to her bedroom, with an anxious Mrs. Lambert dogging his footsteps. Harpert hovered over her mistress, feeling about her head when Clayborne explained what had happened. She found a cut and swelling at the back and asked for hot water and towels. "Have you sent for the doctor?" she asked tersely.

"Yes, Mary has ridden for him," Clayborne said, seating himself beside the bed and taking his wife's hand in his. He watched as the maid carefully washed around the cut.

"It don't look so bad, but head injuries is the very devil," Harpert grunted. She proceeded to tuck the covers in around her fully clothed mistress and sat down on the other side of the bed. "I can keep a watch on her, your lordship."

"I wish to stay," he replied. When Mrs. Lambert bustled off to look out for the doctor, Clayborne and Harpert sat unspeaking in the bedroom. It was all of a half hour later when Dr. Baker arrived. He had already been apprised of the nature of the accident by Mary, and went directly to the bed and probed the wound, checked Rebecca's pulse and eyes, and felt for any broken bones.

"Concussed, most likely. Pulse is weak, but then it would be. Might be hours before she is sensible, but she could come around any time. Hard to tell with a blow to the head. Can cause serious damage, of course. Must wish for the best. I'll come by in the morning. If there seems a change for the worse, send for me, though there would be little I could do, I fear. Keep her warm and quiet." And he was gone.

Harpert grunted again and offered to sit with her mistress, but Clayborne preferred to be alone with her, sending Harpert to reassure the young people. The maid, unoffended, said she would send him up some dinner on a tray, and when the food came he managed to eat a little of it before setting the tray aside. As dusk set in he was still sitting there quietly stroking Rebecca's hair and holding her hand. Harpert looked in to see if anything was needed and to tell him Mary wanted to know when her sister was conscious. Clayborne agreed and urged her to rest, for she might be needed later. The maid nodded and left.

When the moon had risen and Clayborne had lit a

252

candle there was a faint stirring on the bed. Rebecca's eyes opened slowly and there was a vacant look about them which caused Clayborne a moment of panic, before they focused on him and she smiled faintly. "I should have been paying more attention. Careless of me. What were they up to?"

"I think," he said wryly, "that they had planned to give us a jousting exhibition."

"And I have spoiled their fun. Mary will be very annoyed."

"Mary has been most concerned about you, as we all have."

"Well, my head hurts and my stomach feels funny, but I doubt there is anything to worry about."

"Shall I send for some food for you, or a drink?"

"No, I could not face that just yet."

"Rebecca, do you feel well enough for me to talk to you a bit? I know this is not the time but I have been waiting for the right time and it never comes. I cannot bear to wait any longer."

"Of course, Jason. But you must not speak out of pity for me, you know, for I shall be all right. I'm sorry to give you such a scare."

"Pity? It is an emotion I cannot even conceive of in connection with you. Perhaps I should have told you," Clayborne said slowly, "that I was in love with you when I married you."

Rebecca's startled eyes searched his face and knew that he spoke the truth.

"I did not wish to tell you because I knew you didn't love me and I was afraid of frightening you away. I was so used to thinking myself possessed of an endless passion for Lady Hillston that I didn't recognize it myself for some time." He paused and sighed, rubbing his forehead as if to clear his thoughts. "When I thought, on our wedding night, that you had deceived me, I was truly shattered. I thought that I had again chosen to love someone who was not what I had believed her to be. No, perhaps chosen is not the right word. Never mind. You know that I went back to Lady Hillston in my hurt and rage. I did not do it to cause you pain. I did it as some sort of punishment to myself, I suppose. By then I was well aware of Lady Hillston's real worth."

He stopped talking for a while, trying to best phrase his next words. Rebecca did not speak, but she kept her eyes on his, her countenance unreadable.

"I tried to tell myself a hundred times, a thousand times, that you were just such another. At first your attitude enraged me, and I was sure I could hate you as easily as I had loved you. But it was not so. I could not bear to be near you then; but when Meg came and I was home again, I knew that I would always love you. You must not think I let you go so easily to the Cotswolds because I wanted to rid myself of you. I let you go because I loved you and could not bear to see what I was doing to you."

"Yes. It was then I knew that you loved me. I had not known before," Rebecca said quietly.

"You knew then? But why did you go if you knew?" he asked in anguish.

"Because you believed that I had deceived you. There will never be any way I can prove that I did not," she said sadly.

"I am a proud, stubborn man, Rebecca. As long as I thought there was no other possible explanation I refused to believe you. I have learned that there *are* other explanations, and I do believe you now. No, don't say anything. I realize my lack of faith in you has destroyed our chance for happiness together. You have trusted me through all of my rages and slights, and I am ashamed of myself. If you will accept it, I shall deed Gray Oaks to you; it is not entailed. You may live here always as your own home. I shall live elsewhere and be content that you are happy. Oh, and the setter is old enough to leave his mother now."

"The setter?" Rebecca asked, confused.

"Your anniversary present. He was too young then, but you can have him tomorrow. I thought of him because, well, because of the dog you gave to Thomas Burns."

"Now how could you possibly know that I gave Rags to Thomas?"

"I know you. It was the only explanation. I have felt terribly jealous of Thomas," he admitted wretchedly.

"Well, you need not have. I was infatuated with Thomas, even though I knew he was to marry. It was silly of me and it did not last long, but there was a singular lack of men around Farthington Hall," she grinned, "and I was flattered by his admiration of me. Giving him the dog was a sort of farewell gesture. I shall be pleased to have a setter of my own. But you know, Jason, I shall not want to live here at Gray Oaks alone."

"Perhaps Mary could live with you. Or another of your friends," he suggested helpfully.

"No, I don't think that would be satisfactory. I am a married woman. I did tell you once what I expected out of marriage, did I not?"

"I remember the occasion well," he admitted with a lopsided grin.

"And you still do not think you could accommodate me?" she asked wistfully.

"I am certain I could, wretch."

"It is the strangest thing, you know, for I feel sure you could, too. And should you still expect me to observe the proprieties and offer you obedience?" she taunted.

"No more than would put a strain on you, I feel sure."

"Then the matter is settled?" Rebecca asked.

"Not quite. I think you still have something to tell me, little one."

"You must ever have your way," she sighed.

"But I need something to ease the pain of being called an insufferable toad," he retorted.

"I love you, Jason. I seem to have loved you for a long time," she admitted shyly.

"Do you suppose it would hurt your head if I . . ."

When Mary peeped in at the door and saw her sister passionately kissing his lordship, she withdrew, giggling, but they were oblivious to the interruption. Mary was delighted that her sister was recovered and that the young people would be able to stage their jousting exhibition very soon after all.